H'10

W9-CBZ-241

GATHERING STORM

GATHERING STORM
1837–1868
*Book Two in the Saga
of Tall Bird and John Crane*

BILL GULICK

A DOUBLE D WESTERN
Doubleday
NEW YORK LONDON TORONTO SYDNEY

All of the characters in this book
are fictitious, and any resemblance
to actual persons, living or dead,
is purely coincidental.

A Double D Western
Published by Bantam Doubleday Dell Publishing Group, Inc. 666 Fifth Avenue, New
York, New York 10103

A Double D Western and the portrayal of the letters DD are
trademarks of Doubleday, a division of Bantam Doubleday Dell Publishing Group, Inc.

Library of Congress Cataloging-in-Publication Data

Gulick, Bill, 1916–
The saga of Tall Bird and John Crane.

(A Double D Western)
Contents: bk. 1. Distant trails, 1805–1836—bk. 2.
Gathering storm, 1837–1868—bk. 3. Lost Wallowa, 1869–1879.
1. Nez Percé Indians—Fiction. I. Title.
PS3557.U43S24   1988   813'.54   87-34337
ISBN 0-385-24164-X (v. 1)
ISBN 0-385-24165-8 (v. 2)
ISBN 0-385-24166-6 (v. 3)

PART ONE

Wagon Wheels to Oregon
1837–1843

1

Hearing that his half brother, John Crane, had come to the Green River rendezvous, Tall Bird went to William Craig; because of Craig's long association with the *Nimipu,* Tall Bird trusted him more than any other *Suyapo.* He asked Craig to point out the man without revealing Tall Bird's relationship to him. Because it was common knowledge among the Nez Perces that a number of persons about Tall Bird's age had been sired by members of the Lewis and Clark party, William Craig had long been aware of the relationship.

"Sure, I'll show him to you," Craig said genially. "But if I was you I wouldn't go near the booger till he sobers up. When he's on a toot the first week of rendezvous, John ain't very civilized."

Watching the long-haired, shaggy, unshaven white man swagger drunkenly about the camp for the next few days and nights, Tall Bird was glad he had not disclosed himself. So far as he could observe, his half brother was a lecher, a loud mouthed braggart, and a fool.

Tall Bird noted that, after a week of heavy drinking and debauchery, John Crane did begin to act more sensibly, sobering up, shaving, getting his hair trimmed, and donning decent-looking clothes. Still, Tall Bird did not approach him, deciding to wait until just before the breakup of rendezvous, so that if he were rebuffed or insulted he would not have to endure his half brother's presence for long.

But when he did seek the man out the day before leaving with his family and the party of white missionaries, he found John Crane so drunk and disheveled that it would have been impossible to communicate with him, even if he had wanted to. So, with loathing and disgust, Tall Bird left the man lying in his own vomit and filth in the shade of his brush lean-to, vowing never to attempt to talk to him again.

Soon after meeting the two missionary couples, Tall Bird had sensed that friction existed between them. Friendly and outgoing, Marcus and Narcissa Whitman liked the Indians and the mountain men, relished the excitement of rendezvous, and were inclined to overlook the rowdiness of this brief annual carnival as a relatively harmless expression of high spirits.

On the other hand, Henry and Eliza Spalding were horrified and repelled by the excesses of the trappers; they kept to themselves, and showed by their stern faces and dour looks that they disapproved of everything that was happening around them. While Narcissa Whitman was radiantly healthy and full of energy and high spirits, Eliza Spalding could not tolerate a diet of buffalo, antelope, elk, and dried salmon; languishing for days ill in her tent, she spent a great deal of her time writing in her diary, reading her Bible, and praying. Even so, she persisted in her quest of a working knowledge of the Nez Perce language, spending several hours each afternoon talking to the Indian women whom she insisted Tall Bird bring to her.

Between the Cayuses and the Nez Perces, an intense competition developed as to which tribe would play host to the white missionaries. Always an aggressive, quarrelsome tribe despite their relatively small numbers, the Cayuses insisted that the first mission be established in their homeland, the Walla Walla Valley.

Even more insistent was the Lapwai chief, *Tack-en-su-a-tis,* who declared that the mission must be established in his part of the country. It had been the Nez Perces and Flatheads who organized and carried out the journey in search of the Book of Heaven, he said, so it was only simple justice that the white religious teachers build their first mission in the heart of Nez Perce and Flathead land. Furthermore, had he not proved his loyalty to the Americans by fighting with them against the Gros Ventres at Pierre's Hole, suffering the grievous wound which had given him his name?

"Indeed, this is true, Rotten Belly," Tall Bird said dryly. "But the *Tai-tam-nats* are men of peace, not of war. They do not approve of killing."

"Just as you do not?"

"I obey my *Wy-a-kin,* as a man must."

When rendezvous broke up, the small band of Cayuses and the large party of Nez Perces accompanying the white missionaries toward Fort Hall argued so vociferously over where the first mission should be located that the usually cheerful Narcissa Whitman became alarmed.

"The Nez Perce women say we are going to live with them," she wrote, "and the Cayuse say we are going to live with them. The contradiction is so sharp they nearly come to blows."

So far as the Indians were concerned, the dispute was settled amicably enough after a few days on the trail, when the Reverend Spalding pompously announced, with Dr. Whitman nodding silent agreement, "We have reached an important decision. Two missions will be established—one among the Cayuses, with the Whitmans in charge; the other among the Nez Perces, with myself and my wife in charge."

While the joy on the faces of the listening Indians of both tribes was unrestrained, Tall Bird noted that the expression on Narcissa Whitman's face was one of quiet relief. Though she seemed to genuinely like Eliza Spalding and sympathize with her physical frailties, it was obvious she had no use for her dour, unbending husband. Nor did Marcus Whitman treat Spalding with anything more than cold politeness. In fact, the two men were increasingly at odds over the light Dearborn wagon which the Reverend Spalding had insisted on bringing along, but whose management he was leaving more and more to Dr. Whitman.

As the summer days turned hot, dusty, and dry, the terrain became rougher and more difficult to negotiate. When Spalding suggested that the baggage be transferred to packhorses and the wagon left behind, Whitman became so exasperated he could not contain his anger.

"Leave it, you say? If I had known you were going to give up so easily, Henry, I would not have sold *my* wagon—which was heavier and better suited to rough trails—in St. Louis, and put our baggage in *your* wagon—which is too lightly built for this kind of country."

"You had seen the country, Doctor," Spalding said testily, "while I had not. You should have known the difficulties of taking a wagon across it. In fact, it is my firm belief that Mr. McKay is right when he says that taking a wagon through to Oregon is impossible."

"Thomas McKay is a Hudson's Bay Company man, with good reasons for discouraging our taking a wagon through. But I say it can be done. With a bit of perseverance, some shovel and ax work, and a lot of sweat and muscle power, we'll take the wagon through. Damned if we won't!"

"Profanity ill becomes your calling, Doctor."

"Then pray for me, Reverend. But while you're praying, I'd be obliged if you'd put a shoulder to the wheel."

Despite Narcissa's concern that her husband's strenuous efforts to take the wagon through by sheer brute force would injure his health, he refused to give up, no matter how many times the wagon mired down at stream crossings, upset on sidling slopes, or careened down steep pitches with frightening speed. To him, taking a wagon through to Oregon was a symbolic act, Tall Bird realized, which would demonstrate dramatically that the continent could be spanned by a wheeled vehicle.

"The Bible, the wheel, and the plow," Tall Bird heard him say to his wife one evening, after an especially exhausting day. "Where they go, civilization follows."

Though she sympathized with his goal, Narcissa secretly rejoiced when the wagon took a particularly bad fall on a steep slope near Fort Hall and shattered its front axle on a rock. Because no hardwood from which to fashion a replacement was available, she was sure the vehicle that had become such an obsession and burden to her husband would now be abandoned, with the baggage it carried transferred to packhorses. But she underestimated her husband's stubbornness.

"I'll cut it down to a two-wheeled cart," he declared. "I'd be obliged, Mr. McKay, if you'd loan me a saw."

But at Fort Boise the ungainly, battered, weathered cart was abandoned, for the long journey west had become a race against time. Giving the forlorn-looking, empty cart a last yearning glance, Dr. Whitman shook his head wearily.

"I've not given up yet," he told Tall Bird. "Next summer, after we've built the missions and gotten ourselves settled, I'm coming back to Fort Boise for the cart. Mark my word, I will take wheels through to the Columbia."

2

Reaching Fort Vancouver in mid-September, the men of the missionary party enjoyed Dr. John McLoughlin's hospitality for a week before heading back upriver to select sites and start building shelters. Though McLoughlin questioned the wisdom of establishing separate missions, and urged them to leave the two women at Fort Vancouver until next spring, neither Marcus Whitman nor Henry Spalding would change his mind.

"We told the Cayuses and the Nez Perces we would establish separate missions," Spalding said dogmatically. "That is what we intend to do."

"Our wives want to be with us," Whitman said. "In four or five weeks, we'll have some sort of shelter thrown up and will come for them."

At Fort Walla Walla, *Tack-en-su-a-tis,* Tall Bird, and a large band of Nez Perces were waiting for the missionaries, as were a number of Cayuses. Whitman and Spalding wasted no time selecting sites.

The spot chosen by Dr. Whitman in Cayuse country was on a flat, open, grassy plain between a clear-flowing creek and the Walla Walla River, with the two streams joining a short distance to the west. Because of the tall, grainlike grass growing in marshy areas along the stream, the Cayuses had called the flat *Waiilatpu*—"Place of the Rye Grass." Located twenty-two miles east of Fort Walla Walla, it was midway between the bone-dry, sagebrush-covered, sandy desert country flanking the Columbia River and the lush, tree-covered, much moister western slope of the Blue Mountains.

"Here we'll have the best of two worlds," Whitman told Tall Bird. "The sunshine, good soil, and mildness of the low country, and the timber, dependable water supply, and cooling night breezes of the high country. The site is ideal for a productive, self-sustaining mission."

Assisted by William H. Gray—an opinionated and contentious but highly skilled craftsman who had been employed by the American Board to help the missionaries—Whitman drew up plans for a house, a gristmill, fenced fields in which to keep the cattle he had brought along, and a large area to be plowed and planted with vegetables and grain. Meanwhile, the impatient *Tack-en-su-a-tis* and the Lapwai Nez Perces urged the Reverend Spalding to ride on with them and select the site for the mission he would build in their country.

Lapwai meant "Place of the Butterflies," Tall Bird explained as he rode with and interpreted for the missionary. By white man's measurement, it was 120 miles from the Cayuse mission site to the place where this band of Nez Perces wanted him to settle.

"But our country is big and has many beautiful valleys," Tall Bird said. "You should not choose a site until you have seen it all."

"Are the other leaders of your tribe as eager to hear God's word as *Tack-en-su-a-tis*?"

"Lawyer, of the Kamiah band, whose father cared for the Lewis and Clark horses, is most anxious to welcome religious teachers. *Ta-moot-sin,* of the Alpowa band, has heard God-talk from Spokane Garry, and is eager to join the church. *Tu-eka-kas,* head chief of my own Wallowa band and my cousin, has said that wherever the *Tai-tam-nat* establishes his mission in Nez Perce country, he will go there to live and listen until he has become a Christian."

"That is gratifying to hear. But since *Tack-en-su-a-tis* has made such a great effort to welcome me, I feel a site in his country must be given first consideration."

Because of the hot and rainless summer, the steep, barren brown hills of the Clearwater Valley offered a bleak visual prospect in early October as the party rode eastward. Tall Bird could see that Spalding was depressed by the look of the country.

"It's so mountainous and broken," he complained to Tall Bird. "There's no good soil or flat areas for crops and pasturage. We could never subsist our people in this kind of country, let alone a large band of Indians. Is it all like this?"

Before Tall Bird could answer, *Tack-en-su-a-tis,* who had guessed what Spalding was feeling, dropped back and rode beside them. Signing for Tall Bird to interpret truly, he spoke to the minister.

"We are now near the place where there is good land, if anywhere in the Nez Perce country. Perhaps it will not answer, but if it does I am happy. This is all my country, and where you settle, I shall settle. And you need not think you will work by yourself. Only let us know what you want done, and it will be done."

Ten miles above the juncture of the Clearwater with the Snake, *Tack-en-su-a-tis* and the band of Nez Perces turned south up the valley of Lapwai Creek. Here Spalding's spirits lifted visibly, for this valley contained good soil, was over half a mile wide, and supported a growth of small trees. Two and a half miles up the creek, the missionary halted and nodded.

"This will do fine. This site meets all my requirements."

"I am full of joy," *Tack-en-su-a-tis* said fervently. "Now tell me what you want us to do."

Selecting a building site at the foot of Thunder Mountain near a good spring, the Reverend Spalding told the Nez Perces, on October 12, 1836, that he intended to leave at once for Fort Vancouver. There he would pick up Mrs. Spalding and Mrs. Whitman, along with a large quantity of supplies and tools that the American Board was obtaining from the stores of the Hudson's Bay Company.

"Can your people meet me with plenty of horses in five weeks at Fort Walla Walla?"

"We can."

"Uncomfortable though it may be, Mrs. Spalding and I can endure living in a tent until our house is finished. When we come back, we will set one up near the site."

"A tepee will be warmer and drier. We will have one waiting for you."

Whatever Henry Spalding's faults as a person may have been, lack of energy was not one of them. Six days after leaving Lapwai, on October 18, he arrived at Fort Vancouver and began assembling the baggage and supplies to be taken upriver. Heading up the Columbia on November 3, he and his party reached Fort Walla Walla ten days later. There they were met by 125 Nez Perces, with a large herd of spare horses. The efficiency of the Nez Perces amazed Spalding.

"They took entire direction of everything," he later wrote, "pitched and struck our tent, saddled our horses, and gladly would have put victuals to our mouths, had we wished it, so eager were they to do all they could to make us comfortable. I was astonished at the ease with which they handled and packed our heavy bags and cases, the latter sixteen inches square, thirty inches long, and weighing usually 125 pounds. Our effects loaded twenty horses."

It was clear to Tall Bird that the missionaries had come to stay. In addition to the five thousand pounds of farming tools, provisions, clothing, books, and building materials the horses were carrying, Spalding took five cows, one bull, and two calves out of the herd that had been driven west from the States.

At first, relationships between the Spaldings and the Nez Perces at Lapwai were good. *Hin-mah-tute-ke-kaikt,* the *tewat,* accepted the missionaries cordially enough, joined the church, and was given the Christian name James. *Ta-moot-sin,* who moved his lodge from the Alpowa country to Lapwai, and *Tu-eka-kas,* who moved from the winter home of the Wallowa band at the mouth of the Grande Ronde to the vicinity of the mission, were Christianized and given the names Timothy and Joseph. Piqued by the way the three Indians had ingratiated themselves with his prize, *Tack-en-su-a-tis* refused to join the church or accept a Christian name for the time being; while Lawyer, of the Kamiah band, shrewd politician that he was, decided that he, too, would stay out of the church until he saw which direction it was taking his people.

Working together, Spalding and Gray designed a house eighteen feet wide by forty-two feet long that could be used both as living quarters and as a meeting place. With considerable help from the Indians, they completed the principal work on the structure in three and a half weeks. Logs for the building, which had been cut some distance upriver and then floated down the Clearwater, were carried on the shoulders of the Indians more than two miles from the river to the site. Boards were whipsawed for the floor. The roof was made of timbers covered with a layer of grass and then a layer of clay—a not very satisfactory covering, for when it rained, mud oozed through cracks between the timbers and into the rooms below.

Skilled though William Gray was as a carpenter, he was bitter and discontent with the role he was playing at the missions. Fanatically religious, he wanted to serve God as a minister, doctor, or both, he told Tall Bird, though he was not qualified for either profession.

"If they'd just let me go back East next summer, I'd spend the winter studying medicine and reading the Bible. Come spring, I'd be as qualified to doctor as Whitman and as fit to preach as Spalding. Which ain't very fit. He's a bastard, you know."

"You mean, he had no father?" Tall Bird asked.

"Oh, he had one all right, like every bastard does," Gray said with a shrill laugh. "Trouble was, nobody except his mother knew who he was— and she never told. In fact, she thought so little of Spalding she gave him away to another woman when he was only fourteen months old, and never saw him again."

"How did he become a minister?"

"Plain bullheadedness and guts. At twenty-one, he could barely read and write. But he kept going to school till he finished Franklin Academy and Western Reserve College at the age of thirty. His wife, Eliza, who is a lot better educated than he is, ran a boardinghouse to help him through college. He don't like Narcissa Whitman because years ago he asked her to marry him and she turned him down."

Despite his contempt for Spalding's background, Gray was eager to enlist his aid in setting in motion a plan which would give Gray the mission of his own that he so deeply desired.

"What you Indians need are milk cows, beef cattle, and white teachers. You've got thousands of horses. If I could persuade your chiefs and Whitman and Spalding to let me have a few dozen good horses, I'd take them to fur rendezvous next summer, go to St. Louis with a brigade, trade the horses for cattle in the settlements, spend the winter in the East studying and recruiting people and funds, then the next year I'd come back and set up a mission of my own. Among the Flatheads, maybe. Or in the Spokane country. What do you think of the idea?"

"Such important matters can be decided only by chiefs," Tall Bird said cautiously. "But I am sure that the cattle and the teachers would be welcomed."

Though Tall Bird had returned to the winter village at the mouth of the Grande Ronde by then, he heard that William Gray and the Reverend Henry Spalding went in March 1837 to the Spokane country, where Spalding preached a sermon to the Indians, with Chief Garry interpreting. Afterward, they worked out a deal by which Spokane, Nez Perce, and Flathead leaders supplied Gray with a number of horses to be taken East next summer and traded for cattle. If the American Board approved his request, he would return in the summer of 1838 with the cattle, substantial reinforcements for the two missionaries already in the field, and authorization to inaugurate a new mission of his own. Accompanying him would be half a dozen Nez Perce and Flathead Indians.

Exactly what happened during the eastbound trip would forever remain in the realm of speculation, so far as the Nez Perces and mountain men friendly to them were concerned. Reaching rendezvous grounds several weeks before the caravan from St. Louis was due to arrive, Gray abandoned his plan to cross the plains under the protection of the returning fur brigade, impatiently deciding to proceed without it.

"It was a damn fool thing to do," William Craig later told Tall Bird grimly. "Jim Bridger advised him agin it, saying the Sioux would be bound to attack such a small party, kill the Injuns in it, and steal the horses. But he was bound and determined to go."

Near Ash Hollow, in Sioux country, Bridger's prediction came true. The Indians who were with Gray were killed and the horses stolen, Gray himself barely managing to escape with his life. Despite his later self-justification of his behavior, the verdict among Indians and mountain men was that he had cravenly deserted his Indian friends in a tight spot, trading their horses and lives to the Sioux for his own.

Though the American Board was displeased with Gray's unauthorized trip east, and horrified by his account of the killing of his Indian friends, they did come up with the funds and personnel to supply a substantial reinforcement to the missions in the Oregon Country.

Because he wanted to build a gristmill and needed Gray's assistance as a carpenter and millwright, Spalding reluctantly accepted him at Lapwai upon his return in late summer 1838. But after hearing what had happened on the way east, Spalding was deeply concerned about the reaction of the Nez Perces to the killings.

"It is said," he wrote, "they will demand my head or all my property."

No violence was done him by the Indians, but he was obliged to give cows to the chiefs who had lost horses. From that time on, Tall Bird knew, *Tack-en-su-a-tis,* who had lost a relative, and the white mountain men living near Lapwai, who had taken Indian wives, had little use for missionaries . . .

Through his cousin *Tu-eka-kas*, who now preferred to be called by his Christian name, Joseph, Tall Bird kept informed of events at Lapwai. The peace chief of the Wallowa band now lived there during the cold months of the year, though each summer he and his family still migrated to the high country in the Land of the Winding Waters, which he loved deeply. Affairs at the mission were going well, Joseph said, as the Spaldings endeavored to enlighten the Nez Perces in the white man's ways.

For a time the relationship between Spalding and Joseph was that of blood brothers. On one occasion after Joseph had returned to his village in the Wallowa Valley, he became seriously ill. Summoning Tall Bird, he said in a very weak voice, "Ride to Lapwai and tell Brother Spalding I am sick. Tell him only his healing magic can save me."

Between the Wallowa Valley and the Lapwai Mission lay one hundred miles of the roughest terrain. Using a relay of horses, Tall Bird, who was in the peak of physical shape, made the ride in a flat twenty hours. After telling Spalding the seriousness of Joseph's condition, he saw the missionary mounted on a strong Nez Perce horse, told him the arrangements that had been made for a relay of horses on the return trip, but was himself so exhausted that the Reverend Spalding soon outdistanced him on the ride back to Wallowa. Later, the missionary recorded the grueling trip and its result in his diary, the entry dated August 26, 1840:

About 4 P.M. I jump onto one of the horses the Indians rode up and start to see my dear brother Joseph. Find the horse very hard. Reach the river [the Snake] and cross, dark. My guides are soon far behind and asleep. Stop 11:30 P.M.

August 27th. Start early, eat a bit of dry buffalo, my horse is too weak to ride easy. Suffer much from riding. Reach the spruce plain about 5 P.M. Am in great pain. Find two young men with a spare horse waiting. Find it extremely easy. Ride fifteen miles and arrive about sundown. Find Joseph weak with high fever, pulse ninety, no passage for several days. I give dose of calomel and jalap and bleed.

August 28th. Give Joseph another dose of calomel and jalap. Soon copious passage. Pulse at eve down to seventy. Thank the Lord for his goodness.

August 31st. Joseph speaks again of giving me a horse. I refuse again and tell him I came not for horses but because I loved him. Finding Joseph grieved, I consented. The horse is large, stout, and tame.

During their summer sojourn in the Wallowa country in 1840, both Tall Bird and his cousin Joseph became fathers again. Because the girl baby born to Flower Gatherer was such a happy infant, gurgling and crooning every waking hour, she was given the name "Singing Bird." Because of his religious conversion, Joseph went to the Reverend Henry Spalding and made a special request.

"Since you have given me the Christian name Joseph, may I pass it on to my newborn son? To avoid confusion, from now on I will be called 'Old Joseph,' while he will be called 'Young Joseph.' Can this be done?"

"Yes, my brother in Christ. So long as you raise him as a Christian, you may call him by the name I have given you."

"He will be taught the ways of God, just as you have taught them to me," Old Joseph said humbly. "He will grow up to be a great chief, who will lead his people in the paths of peace . . ."

Beaver was done. No two ways about that, the fur trade was finished by the summer of 1840, so far as big companies and mountain men holding rendezvous in the high country of the West were concerned. Good times for free trappers were gone. In the world of fashion now, beaver was out, silk in. In the commercial contest between a handsome, hardworking, fur-bearing animal and an ugly, wriggly, inch-long spinner of gossamer filament, the lowly silkworm had won.

Following the final gathering of the clan at the American Fur Company rendezvous on Green River—to which John Crane, Joe Meek, Robert Newell, and William Craig brought plenty of plews but received so little for them they could hardly afford a decent spree—the four friends said farewell to a way of life they would live no more. Somewhat grandiloquently, Doc Newell summed up their feelings.

"Hear me, men, we're done with this life in the mountains—done with wading in beaver dams, freezing or starving—done with Indian trading and Indian fighting. The fur trade is dead in the Rocky Mountains, and it is no place for us now, if ever it was. We are young yet and have life before us. We cannot waste it here."

So what to do next?

"What I'm of a mind to do," Joe Meek said, "is head for the Willamette Valley, where I hear tell the quarrels twixt Americans and Britishers are gettin' right lively. On the way, I'm gonna stop by the Whitman Mission and see if Mrs. Whitman won't take Helen Mar off my hands."

Fur trade legend had it that Joe Meek had read only one book in his life —a romantic novel, *Scottish Chiefs,* loaned to him one winter by a trapper friend. He had been so entranced by its heroine, a lovely, ethereal girl named Helen Mar, that when his Shoshone woman, Mountain Lamb, had born him a daughter, he had a name all ready for her. But with Mountain Lamb fled, lost, or mislaid, he'd been unable to take proper care of the little girl. Now five years old, the dirty, vermin-infested, sullen child didn't look like much of a heroine, but Joe Meek was hoping the mission would take her in.

"What I'm of a mind to do," William Craig said, "is go back to Lapwai and see how my wife and kids are makin' out. Hear tell them missionaries have been givin' my wife's father a bad time. But I can fix that."

"Me, I got a chore I don't relish much, though it will pay some money," Doc Newell said. "Man named Harvey Clark brung three wagons and half a dozen people who claim to be missionaries to rendezvous. Says he'll pay me two bucks a day if I'll guide 'em to the Willamette. Whyn't you fellows come along?"

Why not? John Crane mused. A man had to live someplace, and going west suited him a damn sight better than going east. The hurt caused four years ago by the outrageous stunt his father and Susan had pulled by marrying each other, dying, and turning his and Susan's natural son, Luke, over to the Board of Directors of the bank for them to raise, with John himself not allowed a dime of his father's estate or a word in how the kid was to be brought up—that hurt had eased with the passage of time, though it was still there. Rather than cut himself off completely from his own flesh and blood by threatening a lawsuit he'd likely have no chance to win, he'd written a letter, civil in tone, to the Bower & Crane Mercantile Bank attorney, Samuel Wellington:

> I'm sorry as I can be for what I've done, though I know being sorry won't fix things. You just go ahead and do what's best for Luke and don't be concerned about me trying to interfere. I'm keeping busy and doing all right financially, so I don't need money. Can't say when I'll be getting back to St. Louis—but someday I will. Meantime, I'd be obliged if you'd write me now and then, letting me know how Luke is doing in school and all. When he learns how to read and write, I'd sure like to have a letter from him, too. He looks like a bright little boy . . .

Apparently relieved and pleased by his reaction, Samuel Wellington had written twice a year since then, reporting on the child's health, growth, and schooling. Going on eight years old now, Luke himself had written two brief, surprisingly well-phrased notes, beginning each with the salutation "Dear Father . . ." and then relating such important bits of news as: "I have a dog. He is smooth-haired, black and white, and will go fetch a ball when I throw it. I call him 'Spot.' I am going to have a pony when I am older . . ."

Talking it over with his mountain men friends, which he'd done after the initial shock eased, John admitted a person didn't miss having family ties until all his family was gone. Sure, he'd lied when he wrote Samuel Wellington that he was busy and doing all right financially. The truth was, he was broke and had no prospects. But he didn't dare turn the attorney hostile and alienate his son by admitting how bad off he was. When the boy got older, maybe he'd begin to understand what had happened, and forgive his father. When he turned twenty-one and came into control of his inheritance, maybe he'd feel kindly toward his father and give him his rightful share of the estate, which John might be needing badly by then. Anyway, there was good reason to keep the door open.

Since John Crane, Joe Meek, and William Craig were heading west anyway, they tagged along with Robert Newell, the three wagons, and the Harvey Clark party. So far as John Crane was concerned, it was a toss-up which was the sorriest—this greenhorn bunch of religious pilgrims or the thin, bony, splayfooted horses that had dragged the falling-apart farm wagons out from Independence without any of them having the least notion what they were doing.

At Fort Hall, a weary, disgruntled Harvey Clark let employees of the Hudson's Bay Company—which had bought the post from Nathaniel Wyeth for next to nothing four years ago—persuade him to abandon the wagons, trade the worn-out draft horses for half that many fresh packhorses, cut their baggage down to absolute necessities, and forsake trying to travel any farther west in wheeled vehicles.

"It's impossible to take wagons through to the Columbia, they say," Clark told Newell. "I'm sure they know what they're talking about."

"Well, I'm sure you promised to pay me two dollars a day for guiding you," Newell said laconically. "I'd be obliged for the money."

"The bargain we made was we would pay you to guide our wagon train through to the Willamette Valley," Clark said. "Since we're abandoning the wagons and going on by packtrain, and will be traveling with Hudson's Bay Company people, we won't be needing your services."

"You saying you ain't gonna pay me?"

"We're short on cash, Mr. Newell. We'd counted on obtaining funds from our friends in the Willamette Valley—after we got there. But since you won't be traveling with us—"

"I won't get paid," Newell grunted. "For a parson, you're a mighty dishonest cuss. S'pose I tried to take my wages out of your hide?"

"Please, Mr. Newell, there's no need to resort to violence. Though we have little money, we do have the three wagons. Could you accept them as payment for your services?"

Well, it "beat no payment at all," Doc Newell told his three mountain men friends. Let that be a lesson to him. Herding pilgrims to Oregon should be done on a cash-on-the-barrelhead basis.

Being in no particular hurry, the four ex-trappers loafed around Fort Hall for several days after the Harvey Clark party left. For lack of anything else to do, they tinkered with the wagons, tightening wheel rims, greasing the running gear, and making the beds watertight for stream crossings. When Doc Newell tried to sell them to the Hudson's Bay Company, the clerk laughed at him.

"What would we do with them? This isn't wagon country."

Thinking maybe he could find a buyer for the wagons at Fort Boise, Doc Newell told his friends he reckoned he'd take them that far, if they'd give him a hand with the driving. Having nothing better to do, they trained their tough, strong, Nez Perce saddle horses to pull as teams, and set out across the hot, dusty, sagebrush-covered desert. When they reached Fort Boise a couple of weeks later, the trader in charge of the post, François Payette, made three mistakes.

First, he invited Robert Newell to be his guest in quarters within the fort, while John Crane, Joe Meek, and William Craig were left to camp outside its walls. Second, he sent out a company servant with fillets of sturgeon for the three ex-trappers, who, feeling insulted, rejected them with pungent comments. Third, he told the four mountain men that taking wagons across the Blue Mountains was impossible; his considered advice was to leave them behind.

" 'Considered advice,' he says!" Doc Newell snorted indignantly. "What right does a Britisher in this part of the country have giving us 'considered advice' when it comes to traveling? I told him what he could do with it!"

"That all you told him, Doc?" Joe Meek asked.

"Not by a damn sight! I told him you were bullheaded, I was level-headed, John Crane was stubborn-headed, and Bill Craig was redheaded. Being Americans, ain't a one of us will take a dare. Those wagons will cross the Blues, I told him, if we have to carry them on our backs! Are you with me, men?"

They were . . .

Floated across the Snake; tugged and pushed up brushy, rocky Burnt River Canyon; skidded, jolted, and careened across the dividing ridge to the Powder; driven across the lovely, fertile valley of the upper Grande Ronde; then again tugged and pushed, sweated and bullied, cajoled and cursed up steep grades and through thick trees that must be felled to make a road, until the 3,700-foot height to be called Deadman's Pass was crested; and then down through still bigger timber on the slopes of Emigrant Hill until the westward-flowing Umatilla was reached—the wagons moved.

Somewhere along the way they lost their beds, but when they pulled to a stop in the yard of the Whitman Mission their wheels and running gear were intact. For the first time it could be said that wheeled vehicles had crossed the continent to the Columbia River watershed.

Others soon would follow . . .

5

Before heading east to Lapwai from the Whitman Mission, William Craig invited Doc Newell, Joe Meek, and John Crane to pay him a visit when they got tired of the eternal drizzling rain in the Willamette Valley.

"Hell, Bill," Joe Meek teased, "since Isabel talked you into letting that preacher marry you in a regular Christian ceremony, bein' around you ain't no fun. You've given up chasing women. Next thing, you'll give up drinking, playing cards, and racing horses. Why, likely when you git back to Lapwai, you'll join Henry Spalding's church and organize a choir for him."

"That'll be the day!" Craig snapped, his temper flaring. "Sure, I let Reverend Walker marry Isabel and me, when he came out to rendezvous on the Popo Agie with William Gray a couple of summers ago. Why not, when she's been my wife by Nez Perce custom for ten years? But that don't mean I've got any use for preachers."

"Hear tell Spalding and your wife's father have been squabbling," Doc Newell said. "Old James claims that Spalding is making dogs and slaves of the Nez Perces. You know anything about that?"

"No, but I aim to find out," Craig said grimly. "If it's true, we'll put a stop to it."

Because his grandfather had been a Presbyterian minister and his father a strong advocate of establishing missions among the Indians, John Crane was curious as to what the Whitmans had accomplished during the four years they had spent in Cayuse country. Physically, Waiilatpu was a substantial settlement now, with buildings, fenced fields enclosing domesticated cattle, sheep, and hogs, extensive acreage of vegetables, melons, and grains, a network of canals by which the crops could be irrigated, a large pond, and a gristmill for grinding wheat and corn into flour.

Spiritually, the Whitmans had not fared so well, as far as converting the Cayuse Indians was concerned, for, although "cousins" to the Nez Perces, they were not nearly as friendly and cooperative. In fact, after talking to some of the mission people, Joe Meek said the Cayuses struck him as a mean, ornery breed.

"Seem to think they ought to be paid rent for their land. Can't get a lick of work out of the men, though the women will hoe weeds for a peck of potatoes or a few pounds of flour. Ain't none of 'em joined the church yet and the kids ain't interested in school."

Remembering how beautiful, radiant, and healthy Narcissa Whitman had been at rendezvous four years ago, John Crane was shocked at her appearance now. "Why, she looks like she's aged twenty years," he told Doc Newell. "Do you suppose she's been sick?"

"Worn out, probably, by all the work she has to do. And the little girl drowning knocked the spirit out of her, they say."

The way John Crane had heard the story, the first white baby to be born west of the Rocky Mountains, Alice Clarissa Whitman, had come into the world March 14, 1837. During the brief span of life allotted her, she was a bright, happy, healthy child, a treasure to her parents and a delight to the Indian women, who called her a *Cayuse Te-Mi,* "Cayuse Girl." But on June 23, 1839, she went down to the bank of the nearby Walla Walla River, apparently intending to fill two cups with water, fell in, and drowned. It was doubtful that Narcissa Whitman, now thirty-two years old, would ever have another child.

In his well-meaning, blundering way, Joe Meek hoped to give her a start on a new family by turning his own daughter over to her.

"I know she don't look like much, Mrs. Whitman," he said humbly. "But she's bright as a button and minds purty good, if you're firm with her. And she sure does need a good home."

"All right, you can leave her here for a while," Narcissa said reluctantly. "Come, child. We'll give you a bath, cut your hair, and put you into some decent clothes."

"I'm obliged, ma'am, truly I am. Her name is Helen Mar. You see, I read a book once . . ."

Eying the stripped-down, battered wagons the mountain men had parked in the mission yard, Dr. Marcus Whitman told them of his own attempt to bring a wagon through four years ago and of his inability to find the time to go to Fort Boise and bring what was left of it on across the Blues. Had they encountered any difficulties bringing their wagons across?

"None that a little muscle power and a lot of swearing couldn't handle," Meek said. "Course, praying probably would work just as well."

"When word gets back to the States that wagons have crossed the country, the future of Oregon will be assured," Whitman said thoughtfully. "It will become American, rather than British. The nature of this mission will change."

Finding Whitman disturbed over a recent killing in the Cayuse camp, where for no apparent reason one Indian had shot another down in cold blood, with no effort made to stop him and no punishment meted out to the murderer, John Crane agreed to investigate and find out what had happened. He was not surprised to learn that the act had been one of blood vengeance taken by the father of an ill son, who had died after being treated by a Cayuse *tewat.*

"It's their way, Doc, and not to be changed."

"But this is paganism!" Whitman exclaimed. "As Christians, we must teach them it is wrong!"

"If I were you, Doc, I'd work on making them Christians instead of doctoring them. Leave that to the *tewats.* Like Joe Meek says, the Cayuses are an ornery breed . . ."

Time comes to settle down. A couple of years on the wrong side of thirty now, with trapping done, no family ties to speak of, no trade, not much education, and no skills other than those he'd picked up traveling in wilderness country, fighting Indians, and living off the land for eight years, John Crane guessed the advice given him by Joe Meek and Doc Newell was about as good as any, so far as his prospects for the future were concerned.

"Find yourself a widow with a growed-up family and a good farm. Make sure she can cook and won't nag. Marry her and keep her happy in bed. You'll be set for life."

When he did find a widow and marry her, life hadn't become a bed of roses overnight. Four years older than he, the woman, whose name was Felicia Warren, had come west with her husband Roger and their three daughters, Faith, Hope, and Charity, with the Jason Lee party in 1834. Originally a lay worker in the Methodist Church, Roger Warren had given up on Christianizing the Indians of the Willamette Valley as quickly as the Reverend Lee had, taking squatter's rights to a square mile of land and developing a productive farm. Drowned while attempting to cross a flood-swollen stream in the spring of 1840, he had left behind daughter Faith, eighteen; Hope, seventeen; and Charity, fifteen, in addition to his widow, Felicia—all stunned by the sudden loss of the man around the house.

Being well spoken of by Joe Meek, Robert Newell, and other friends in the area, John Crane was readily accepted by the widow and her three pretty daughters—destined not to last long as unmarried maidens in this girl-scarce country—and soon found himself head of a ready-made household containing four women determined to domesticate him with no fuss and bother.

As all parties concerned soon learned, there was fuss and there was bother, for the one talent John Crane lacked was the talent for settling down.

Oh, he tried. But the dawn-to-dark drudgery of day after day, week after week, month after month plowing, planting, cultivating, and harvesting lost what little charm and novelty it held for him; he'd stuck to the routine pretty faithfully through the first year, only to learn when the second spring rolled around that a whole square mile of farmland was lying there demanding that he do it again.

The oldest girl, Faith, had gotten married by then. Luckily, she'd taken as a husband a tall, husky young neighbor boy who loved to farm, was good at it, but owned no land of his own. Unselfishly, John approved the idea of turning a quarter section of the farm over to them, where they built themselves a cabin, and wasted no time starting a family of their own. When this arrangement worked out so well, Felicia agreed with his suggestion that the second quarter section be turned over to Hope and her husband, when they married the next year, with the third quarter going to Charity and her man when they got hitched the year after that.

"Way I see it, we'll have the young folks as neighbors," John said, "where we can help them and they can help us, as parents and children should. We'll still have a quarter of our own to farm, which is about all we can handle."

Though at times Felicia did drop broad hints that running a few dozen cattle and twenty or so horses on 160 acres of prime Willamette Valley farmland wasn't "handling" it in the most productive way, she didn't really nag him about it; since the death of husband Roger she had placidly come to accept whatever the Good Lord in His infinite mercy chose to give her. With three daughters well married, living nearby, and wasting no time starting families, she wasn't going to be lonely as she grew older, that was certain; and while John might spend more time hunting, fishing, and roaming around the country with his ex–mountain men friends than he did farming, he was pleasant enough company when he did stay home, didn't get very drunk very often, and had no meanness in him.

As for John himself, he was reasonably content, though when Joe Meek or Doc Newell stopped by and suggested he go down-valley with them to Oregon City or Fort Vancouver to see what kind of squabbles the Americans, Britishers, French-Canadians, Indians, and various mixtures thereof were getting involved in, he was ready to go on a moment's notice.

Being the agitator that he was, Joe Meek was always trying to stir up some kind of excitement, while Doc Newell, who loved politics, was always trying to get some sort of government organized so that he could get himself elected to office. Locally, people were a strange mixture of loyalties. On the Oregon side of the Columbia across from Fort Vancouver, retired Hudson's Bay Company employees, American missionaries, ex–mountain men, and an ever-increasing number of American merchants and farmers had settled. So far as most of them were concerned, the Company was all the government they needed or wanted. But the Americans were creating farms, building sawmills, gristmills, and towns; they wanted titles more solid than squatter's rights to the properties they were accumulating.

When an ex-trapper named Ewing Young died in 1841, matters came to a head, for he had left neither will nor heir. Disposition of his holdings in land and cattle was a problem to be solved by a probate court, his neighbors felt.

"But we've got no court," someone protested.

"Hell, let's organize one!" Joe Meek shouted. "I'll be bailiff or sheriff or whatever a court requires!"

"Hold on a minute!" Doc Newell protested. "Before we can have a court, we got to have a government. Here's what we should do . . ."

What they should do, the community agreed, was start thinking in terms of establishing a local government. After prolonged argument as to *how* local the government should be, they expanded their concept, took in all the vaguely defined area called Oregon, and set up a meeting to be attended by all interested parties at Champoeg in early May 1843. Three factions would be in attendance: those favoring a provisional government inclined toward the United States; those desiring a government inclined toward Great Britain; and those favoring an independent government that would remain neutral.

But before that meeting could take place, a self-proclaimed executive with a uniquely different solution of his own rode up to John Crane's house one afternoon, requesting his services as an interpreter in the Cayuse and Nez Perce country upriver, where the Indians were about to be given a code of laws that would bring them under the rule of church and state once and for all.

Like the Old Testament prophet in the wilderness, his name was Elijah . . .

6

Dr. Elijah White had come out to the Oregon Country as a medical missionary and had lived in the Willamette Valley from 1838 to 1840, John knew. White was a politically ambitious man. Returning to the East, he had wangled an appointment from the federal government as Indian Agent for all of Oregon, even though the region still was under the Joint Occupancy Treaty in existence between the United States and Great Britain. Stopping at Waiilatpu September 14, 1842, White delivered a packet of letters. The one he gave Marcus Whitman from the American Board contained bad news. Because of the dissension of the past few years among the missionaries, as expressed in their many complaining letters sent East:

The Spaldings were being recalled . . .

Waiilatpu must be closed and sold . . .

The Whitmans must move to the Spokane country . . .

According to Elijah White, the seeds of dissension among the missionaries had been sown long before, and had been nurtured by adversity, frustration, jealousy, unrequited love, conceit, and a zeal that at times lapsed into madness. This was the bitter harvest.

"Must have been quite a shock to the Whitmans and Spaldings," John Crane said. "What did they do?"

"When I left Waiilatpu six weeks ago, Dr. Whitman was planning to call a meeting of all the missionaries upriver. I later heard that in the meeting a joint letter was written and signed by the concerned parties explaining the past controversies and pointing out that they all had been solved. Dr. Whitman then set out overland for Boston in an attempt to persuade the American Board to change its mind."

"When did he leave?"

"October third, I was told."

"Traveling alone?"

"No. A man named Asa Lovejoy went with him. I met Lovejoy when I stopped at the mission. He's an attorney, I believe, from Massachusetts. Apparently this seemed to him a good opportunity to go home."

"What a fool thing to do!" John exclaimed. "Leaving Waiilatpu in early October won't put 'em across the Rockies 'fore winter comes. From what I've heard, the Sioux and Pawnees are on the warpath all across the high plains country east of the Divide. If Whitman and his friend don't freeze or starve to death, the Injuns are likely to kill them."

"I know. But Dr. Whitman is a very determined man, with his life's work at stake. He'll get through or die trying. Meanwhile, it's my duty to impose a semblance of law and order among the Indians upriver . . ."

What he planned to do, Elijah White explained, was put together a party of Hudson's Bay Company people and American settlers which would go to Lapwai and Waiilatpu and discuss law and order problems with the Indians. Thomas McKay, Cornelius Rogers, Baptiste Dorion, and six citizen volunteer soldiers already had agreed to go, he said, which would give the party an appearance of authority.

"I need you as an interpreter to the Nez Perces at Lapwai. I hope you will go."

"Hell, Doc, Bill Craig lives just a couple of miles from the Lapwai Mission. He speaks Nez Perce a sight better than I do. Why don't you get him to interpret for you?"

"Because he's part of the problem," White said grimly. "You won't believe what a nuisance he and his mountain men friends have made of themselves to the Reverend Spalding. Drinking, carousing, playing cards, hell-raising at all hours. Why, one night they even torn down Spalding's rail fence and used it as fuel for a bonfire to keep themselves warm. When Spalding went out and tried to stop them, they grabbed him and threw him onto the fire. If he hadn't been wearing a heavy buffalo hide coat, he would have been burned severely."

"The boys must have been having quite a party," John muttered. "Did Spalding save his fence?"

"Eventually, yes. They kept pushing him into the fire and he kept getting up and pulling out the fence rails. Craig finally said he thought they'd had enough fun for one night, and the party broke up."

"Probably the boys were just teasing Spalding. They ain't really mean—except when they drink a lot."

"But they do drink a lot. And they put the Lapwai Nez Perces up to all kinds of meanness. Like siccing dogs on Spalding's sheep and hogs. Chopping tails and ears off his cattle. Egging on boys to strip stark naked, paint their bodies hideously, and then run through the schoolroom where Mrs. Spalding is conducting a class. This has to stop—and the only way to stop it is to select a chief who will be given authority over the whole tribe, and who will enforce a code of laws agreed to by all of the Indians."

"Sounds like a mighty tall order, Doc," John said, shaking his head. "But if you're willing to tackle it, I'm game to go upriver with you. Maybe between us we can calm Bill Craig and his friends down a bit."

Because of shame, guilt, or pure contrariness, William Craig and his boisterous mountain men friends did not attend the law and order meetings between the Elijah White party and the Nez Perce leaders at Lapwai, which continued for several days. Neither did Old James, *Tack-en-su-a-tis,* or any of the Indian dissidents who had grown so antagonistic to the presence of the missionaries.

Even with most of the important leaders not present, Dr. Elijah White managed to achieve his purpose of selecting a head chief to rule over the entire Nez Perce nation. Called Ellis by the whites, he was the thirty-two-year-old son of a venerable ninety-year-old Nez Perce named Bloody Chief, who at the beginning of the conference proudly recalled the Lewis and Clark party many years ago.

"Clark pointed to this day," he said in Nez Perce, with John Crane interpreting, "to you, and to this occasion. We have long waited in expectation; sent three of our sons to Red River to prepare for it; two of them sleep with their fathers; the other is here, and can be ears, mouth, and pen for us."

While John suspected that the old man might be confused in his memory of which Nez Perces had gone where in search of religious instruction, it was clear that Ellis had obtained schooling somewhere, for he could speak, read, and write English. Solely because he could communicate effectively and would agree to whatever was proposed, Dr. White decided that he was the ideal person for the office. After declaring the "election" of Ellis as head chief unanimous, Dr. White then read the set of eleven laws he was proposing be adopted, and again declared the laws "unanimously adopted." These were:

LAWS OF THE NEZ PERCES

1. Whoever wilfully takes life shall be hung.

2. Whoever burns a dwelling house shall be hung.

3. Whoever burns an outbuilding shall be imprisoned six months, receive fifty lashes, and pay all damages.

4. Whoever carelessly burns a house, or any property, shall pay all damages.

5. If anyone enter a dwelling without permission of the occupant, the chiefs shall punish him as they think proper. Public rooms are excepted.

6. If anyone steal, he shall pay back twofold; and if it be the value of a beaver skin, or less, he shall receive twenty-five lashes, and if the value is over a beaver skin he shall pay back twofold and receive fifty lashes.

7. If anyone take a horse and ride it without permission, or take any

article and use it without liberty, he shall pay for the use of it and receive from twenty to fifty lashes, as the chiefs shall direct.

8. If anyone enter a field, and injure the crops, or throw down the fence so that cattle or horses go in and do damage, he shall pay all damages, and receive twenty-five lashes for every offense.

9. Those only may keep dogs who travel or live among the game; if a dog kill a lamb, calf, or any domestic animal, the owner shall pay the damages and kill the dog.

10. If an Indian raise a gun or other weapon against a white man, it shall be reported to the chiefs, and they shall punish him. If a white person do the same to an Indian, it shall be reported to Dr. White, and he shall redress it.

11. If an Indian break these laws, he shall be punished by his chiefs; if a white man break them, he shall be reported to the agent and be punished at his instance.

Observing that Elijah White and Henry Spalding frequently conferred with each other while the talks with the Nez Perces were going on, John imagined that the "laws" had been inspired by the missionary's clashes with the dissidents. The afternoon the talks ended, John rode two miles up the valley to William Craig's place, where he took supper and shared news with his longtime friend.

"Got yourself a wife and three daughters, I hear," Craig said. "How's it feel livin' with four women?"

"Oh, not too bad. Felicia don't chew on me much. And the girls are all married now, with husbands and homes of their own. Lucky for me, their men are good farmers—which I damn sure ain't."

"Hear Doc White give the Nez Perces a code of laws."

"Yeah. The Ten Commandments—plus one. But I doubt they'll be enforced."

"Not by Ellis, they won't. He don't pack the power."

"You and Old James still fighting with Spalding?"

"Not fighting," Craig said, shaking his head. "We just don't see eye to eye with him on some things, that's all. His wife is a fine woman and we all respect her, but he's as bullheaded as can be and just won't give the Nez Perces no leeway at all, when it comes to the way they live and worship. Course some of the Injuns can be purty bullheaded too. Like last spring when they got mad and busted his dam so he couldn't run his gristmill. By the time he got the dam fixed, Lapwai Creek was running so low he didn't have enough water to turn his mill wheel. This same bunch of Indians took their grain to him and demanded he grind it for them. When he said he couldn't, they got mad again and tried to burn down the mill."

"Well, you may not be plagued with him much longer. He's been dismissed by the American Board back in Boston."

"So I heard. But I also heard Doc Whitman took off across country last fall, hoping he could talk the Board into changing its mind. How do you suppose he made out?"

"Well, he sure didn't let no grass grow under his feet," John said. "Word we got was him and Lovejoy made it to Fort Hall in ten days. That's five hundred miles, good traveling in the best of weather. There was snow in the high country by then. The Sioux and Pawnees were on the warpath on the plains. The Hudson's Bay Company chief trader, Peter Grant, told Whitman they'd be committing suicide if they went ahead. Said they'd better go back to Waiilatpu and wait until next spring. But Whitman wouldn't listen. Snow wouldn't stop them, he said. Far as the Sioux and Pawnees were concerned, they'd detour around them by going south to Taos and the Spanish settlements, then back up the Santa Fe Trail."

"Lord-a-mighty! That's an extra thousand miles, not to mention some of the worst mountains in the Rockies."

"Well, that's what they done. Whether or not they made it, we won't know till next summer."

"Heard tell Mrs. Whitman got a bad scare a while back."

"Yeah. A horny Cayuse buck tried to break into her bedroom one night. Some of the mission people scared him away before he could do her any harm. But to be on the safe side, she and the other white women at Waiilatpu took the children and moved down to the Methodist mission at The Dalles. Reckon they'll stay there till Doc Whitman gets back—if he gets back."

Craig grimaced. "Seem to be getting more missions out here than we need. Course, for my money, *one* mission is too many. Why don't the Bible toters leave us alone and let us live the way we want to live?"

"Like Injuns, you mean?"

"Why not? There are worse people. A sight worse."

"Well, that's according to which breed of Injuns you're talking about, Bill. Your Nez Perces are fine. But the ones we got down our way ain't much better than animals."

"Down your way, I hear, there's talk of settin' up a government— British, American, or neutral. How does your stick float on that?"

"It kind of swirls around, Bill. Way I judge it, there's a small bunch of people favor British government, another small bunch favor American government, and a big bunch favor no government at all."

"Once government talk starts, John, it ain't gonna end till a choice is made. Which looks best to you?"

"If the British win, we'll all pay tribute to the Hudson's Bay Company and the common man won't be allowed to own much of anything. If the Americans win, every white male will be given a square mile of land and the right to do as he pleases. Under British rule, we'll have law and order and little freedom. Under American rule, we'll have squabbles galore and all kinds of freedom. But whichever way it goes, Bill, one thing is certain."

"What's that?"

"The Indians are going to lose their rights and their country. No two ways about it. Down in our part of Oregon, the Indians are so diseased and degenerate, they've lost the will to fight. They'll give up without a struggle."

Looking troubled, Bill Craig shook his head. "What you say may be true for your part of Oregon, John. Not for mine. The Indians hereabouts are a different breed. Push them too far, they'll fight. I see bad times ahead . . ."

7

At Champoeg, May 2, 1843, after a number of impassioned speeches by pro and con advocates, a vote was taken on what form of provisional government should be set up. By one skinny vote, the delegates went American—52 to 50. In poor health, worried about her absent husband, and under the care of a doctor at Fort Vancouver, Narcissa Whitman did not regard the vote as particularly momentous. But by the time a legislative report was adopted, a three-man executive committee appointed in lieu of a governor, and Joe Meek designated marshal and tax collector a month later, a piece of news brought by a fast-traveling expressman employed by the Hudson's Bay Company restored her to buoyant health.

Marcus Whitman had made it through.

Details of his journey across the continent as related by the expressman were incredible. From Fort Hall, Whitman and Lovejoy had headed southeast into the most rugged part of the Rocky Mountains with three horses, a mule, and light packs of food and blankets. Also with them was the dog, Trapper, which had been a pet of the lost child, Alice Clarissa.

Minus the mule and the dog, which had been killed and eaten, the two men reached Taos in mid-December. Both were suffering from exhaustion, frostbite, and starvation. After resting two weeks they moved on to Bent's Fort, where Whitman impatiently left Lovejoy behind in his haste to join a party headed for St. Louis.

Still wearing his disreputable, smelly buffalo hide coat that had kept him from freezing in the high country, Whitman reached Washington, D.C., in early March 1843. Congress had just adjourned. After a brief stay there he went to New York City, where a cabman, taking him for a hick from the sticks, fleeced him out of two dollars of his almost exhausted funds. He had a session with Horace Greeley, who admired him for his courage and principles but thought anybody fool enough to go to Oregon was out of his mind.

Broke and shaggy, he reached Boston in early May and presented himself to Secretary David Greene of the American Board for Foreign Missions. Green was so shocked by Whitman's appearance and smell that he hastily gave him some money and told him to get a bath and some decent clothes.

Clearly the Board did not approve of Whitman's fantastic journey. But the drama of what he had done—widely broadcast in newspapers across the country—overpowered the committee's conservatism. After due consideration, it granted his two most important requests:

Waiilatpu would be continued . . .

Spalding would be retained "on trial . . ."

A month later, more recent news of her husband's doings reached Narcissa Whitman. He was coming home.

With his twelve-year-old nephew, Perrin, he reached Westport May 31, 1843. During previous years, annual migrations to the Far West had been small, consisting mostly of reinforcements for the missions: 14 people in 1839, the Clark party of 3 wagons and 6 people in 1840, 54 people in 1841, 112 in 1842. But this year there was astonishing evidence that a movement unparalleled in the nation's history was under way.

One hundred and twenty wagons, over a thousand men, women, and children, and five thousand oxen, horses, and cattle were preparing to move west, the surprised Dr. Whitman found. To the leaders of the migration, his name and feats were well known, and his appearance at this time and place was regarded as the greatest of good fortune. Eager questions peppered him from every quarter.

Was he returning to his mission station? Could wagons get through to the Columbia? Would he travel with them and give them the benefit of his medical services and advice?

To all questions, he answered yes.

Like air currents vagrantly stirring on the edges of a gigantic weather front, the winds of change had begun with the journey of the Flatheads and Nez Perces to St. Louis in 1831. Until that time there appeared to be nothing of value in the Pacific Northwest but beaver. Wyeth and Bonneville went west to established commercial ventures, failed, and left the region. Fur companies of two great nations fought bitterly for thirty years over the peltries of the area, then gave up the struggle because of a change in fashion brought on by the lowly silkworm. But the missionaries, drawn west by a more altruistic purpose, not only came and stayed but proved two vital facts to the restless, land-hungry masses living in the East: There was a vast amount of fertile land in Oregon, free for the taking; and wagons could cross the continent, carrying women, children, household goods, and farming equipment.

Time to get rolling.

"Ain't no doubt about it now," John Crane murmured when he heard the news. "Oregon will be American. Only question to be settled is where the line will be drawn between us and the British . . ."

PART TWO

Bitter Harvest
1844–1850

1

Going on his *Wy-a-kin* quest at the age of twelve in the spring of 1844, the youngest son of Tall Bird and Flower Gatherer, *Peo-peo Kuz-kuz*—"Young Bird"—had climbed afoot and alone into the high Wallowas, as his father had done. Because he had always been an active, aggressive child who loved to compete in footraces, horse races, hunting games, and war games in which his quickness of muscle and eye usually assured him of winning, the manhood name acquired during the ordeal, *Peo-peo Amtiz*—"Swift Bird"—suited him perfectly.

With more Nez Perce than white blood, he was darker than his father, a few inches shorter, and stouter of build, like his great-uncle Red Elk, whom he idolized as the grandfather he had never seen. Aware of how the world of the Nez Perces was being changed by the presence of the missionaries, Tall Bird and Flower Gatherer agreed that he should be enrolled in the school at Lapwai during the fall and winter terms so that he could learn to read and write and acquire a knowledge of the white man's religion.

"We will not move to Lapwai ourselves," Tall Bird told his wife, "for that would offend Old James and Rotten Belly, who claim it as their territory. We will send him to live with William and Isabel Craig, whose own children are attending the mission school even though Craig and Spalding have quarreled."

Though as quick-witted as he was swift of eye, hand, and foot, Swift Bird proved to be an indifferent student. Blame for that lay chiefly on the fact that he and the five Craig children all owned horses. While the animals ridden by the three girls, Adeline, Annie, and Martha, were too old and sedate to respond to race challenges made by other school-bound youngsters, the younger, livelier mounts ridden by Swift Bird, Joe, and Will Craig were the most spirited they could straddle. If not dared to race by other Nez Perce children on the way to school, they would dare and race each other. When that happened, the chances that the boys would attend school that day were two out of two—slim and none.

After trying for two consecutive fall and winter terms to keep Swift Bird in the Lapwai Mission school, his father and mother gave up and let him live as he wanted to live—as a free Indian. A born rider, he was completely without fear, racing his horse up and down steep mountain trails with breathtaking daring, taking chances over rough, treacherous terrain that seemed suicidal, yet maintaining such perfect control of his mount that he never suffered a serious fall.

As a teller of grandfather tales, Red Elk, who was sixty-five years old, dim-sighted, and rheumatic now, had often related the amusing story of how his sister, Moon Wind, had trapped the naked *Moki Hih-hih*—"White Crane"—when she found him bathing in her pool; how their son, *Peo-peo Kuhet*—"Tall Bird"—had been born of that union, grown to manhood, and made the journey east in search of the Book of Heaven, which eventually resulted in the coming of the white *Tai-tam-nats* to the Cayuses and the Nez Perces. But that particular grandfather tale did not especially interest Swift Bird. In love with action as he was, he much preferred tales of the epic journey the three young Nez Perces had made to the land of the *Hidatsa,* where they traded horses for six rifles; how the great War Chief Broken Arm had wreaked terrible vengeance on the treacherous Shoshones; and how Red Elk himself had slain three Blackfeet and counted coup on two more many years ago in the buffalo country.

"I would like to go to the buffalo country and fight the Blackfeet," Swift Bird said. "But my father's *Wy-a-kin* forbids him to kill, so he will not take me. Will you?"

"My eyes are too old and my joints too full of pain for me to fight Blackfeet anymore," Red Elk said sadly. "But be patient, my son. At fourteen, you are too young to become a warrior. Two years from now, at sixteen, you may do what you please."

Accepting that, Swift Bird made the annual trek with his family from the winter village at the mouth of the Grande Ronde to the high, beautiful valley, river, lake, and chain of mountains called Wallowa. Normally, few white men visited the Nez Perces here, nor did the Wallowa band seek contact with whites other than on infrequent trips to the Whitman Mission or Fort Walla Walla, where they went to trade for vegetables, flour, cookingware, beads, or tools. But since the Great Migration of 1843, when 120 wagons, 1,000 people, and 5,000 oxen, horses, mules, and cows had passed through the upper valley of the Grande Ronde, which was only a day's ride southwest of the Wallowa country, large numbers of American emigrants following the Oregon Trail passed through the area each summer. Shrewd bargainers that they were, the Wallowa Nez Perces found it profitable to meet the trail-weary emigrants and engage in mutually advantageous trades.

Oxen, horses, or mules to pull their wagons were the emigrants' primary need, for the grueling trek from Fort Hall across the Snake River Desert in late summer was a killer, so far as draft animals were concerned. Owning thousands of horses and controlling large areas of nutritious bunchgrass range, the Wallowa Nez Perces met the late-coming migration of fifteen hundred Americans in the upper Grande Ronde Valley in 1844 and found the desperate travelers willing to trade on any terms. At first contemptuous of the smaller Indian horses, which they called "Cayuses" because so many of them were to be found near the Whitman Mission, the emigrants soon came to respect their toughness and strength.

"Can't say as I'd want to hitch one to a plow, but if a team of 'em will get me through to the Willamette Valley, I'll sure as hell use it. Lame, starving oxen ain't worth nothin' to me."

To the Wallowa Nez Perces, oxen, draft horses, and mules normally would have been worth little, either. But they soon learned that when these thin, jaded animals acquired from one year's migration had been fattened and made healthy by a season's grazing on nutritious grass, they could be traded back to next year's emigrants on a two- or three-for-one basis.

The second necessity to the travelers was food. Back in fur-trapping days, large parties could live off the land, for the men were hunters who knew where game was found and how to get it. But wagon trains were confined to low-country trails from whose vicinity, as summer wore on, buffalo, deer, antelope, and elk had moved out to seek better feed in high, cooler mountain basins. Lacking the time and skill to find and kill meat for their hungry families, the household heads often found themselves so desperate for food that they would pay outrageous prices for a few pounds of dried meat, cured ham, or bacon.

By the summer of 1844, Tall Bird knew, the Whitman Mission, where most of the Willamette-bound wagon trains stopped for several days before making the final push to their journey's end, had become a way station for American emigrants rather than a religious school for the Cayuse, Umatilla, and Walla Walla Indians—which had been its original purpose. He knew that an increasingly large number of Americans now were living at Waiilatpu, many of them ill adults and children dropped off there by wagon trains unable to care for them.

Narcissa Whitman's family of motherless children had grown from one to twelve, he heard, for despite the load of work she bore, she could not turn down a child in need of care and love. Learning that Joe Meek had persuaded her to take in his half-blood Shoshone daughter, Helen Mar, Jim Bridger, who'd gotten employment guiding a wagon train to the Willamette, had dropped off his half-blood Ute daughter, Mary Ann, and gotten her accepted. Somewhere Narcissa had found a dirty, starving, badly abused four-year-old child reputed to be half Portuguese and half Cree, whose parents were unknown. Finding that none of the white emigrants would accept this twice-cursed child, she took it in, cleaned it up, fed it, cared for it, and gave it the name of a long-ago church school friend, David Malin.

When a Hudson's Bay Company employee at Fort Walla Walla asked if she would take in and school his two motherless half-blood sons, John Manson, thirteen, and Stephen Manson, eleven, she wearily said, yes, she would take them, too.

"Somewhere, we've got to draw the line and say no," Marcus Whitman told her firmly. "We can't take care of all the world's needy children."

She admitted that they could not. But in late summer 1844, William Shaw, captain of a Willamette-bound train that had had extraordinarily bad luck, appeared at the mission in the company of Dr. Theophilas Degen, with a story so sad that it touched her heart. Starting out with the party from western Missouri had been Henry and Naomi Sager. Traveling with them were their six children: John, age fourteen; Francis, eleven; Catherine, nine; Elizabeth Marie, seven; Matilda Jane, five; and Hannah Louise, three. Naomi Sager was expecting her seventh child sometime during the latter part of May.

After joining the large band of fifteen hundred people headed for Oregon, the Sager family became part of a contingent led by Captain William Shaw. In southeastern Nebraska during a rainstorm the evening of May 30, Naomi Sager gave birth to a baby, which was named Henrietta. It had been a difficult birth in the cold dampness of a leaky tent, and for three days thereafter Mrs. Sager was too ill to be moved. When the train did set out, she lay listlessly in the bed of the springless wagon, with little strength.

Eight weeks later, as the wagon train neared Fort Laramie, she was still unwell when the shocking news was brought to her that nine-year-old Catherine, while trying to climb aboard a moving vehicle, had slipped and fallen and a wagon wheel had run over her left leg, breaking it badly. Setting and splinting the fracture as best he could, Henry Sager sent for the kindly old German bachelor Dr. Degen, who was in another section of the train. The leg had been set as expertly as he himself could have set it, the doctor said. From that time on, he stayed with the Sager family and cared for the injured girl and her mother.

Captain Shaw's section of the wagon train crossed South Pass on August 23, 1844. Shortly thereafter, Henry Sager came down with camp fever. He was put to bed with his still-sick wife, and a young man was hired to drive the wagon. Before he died three days later, he elicited a promise from Captain Shaw that when the wagon train reached the Whitman Mission his sick wife and their children would be taken there and given the proper care.

At Fort Hall, Mrs. Sager's condition worsened and she became delirious. In the middle of the Snake River Desert west of there, she died on September 11, just sixteen days after the death of her husband.

Now the Whitmans were being asked to care for the seven orphans. Called in from his work in the fields to meet them, Marcus Whitman was incredulous.

"Seven!" he exclaimed to his wife. "You say there are seven of them?"

"Yes, dear, seven. The two boys are fourteen and eleven. The four girls are nine, seven, five, and three. The baby is just four months old."

"We could take in the two boys, I suppose. Or the four girls. Couldn't some family in the wagon train take in either the boys or the girls?"

"They don't want to be split up. They want to stay together."

"Then I suppose we'll have to take all the children. But overworked as you are, you can't possibly handle a four-month-old baby."

"I want her, Marcus! I want her most of all! In God's name, please let me have her!"

"If it's to be all or none, then, in God's name, we'll take them all! But no more, hear me? No more . . ."

2

At both Lapwai and Waiilatpu, serious trouble was being stirred up by outside agitators, Tall Bird knew. Because Old Joseph was a man of peace, he had determinedly kept the Wallowa Nez Perces aloof from it, for of all the bands his was the most independent. Unlike Timothy, chief of the Alpowa band, who still went to Lapwai and Kamiah to worship in church and attend outdoor revival meetings conducted for the Christian Nez Perces by the Reverend Spalding, Joseph did not take part in any formalized religious services. Through relatives at Lapwai, Kamiah, and Waiilatpu, he knew that Eastern-educated Indians, like the part-Delaware Tom Hill, and the part-Iroquois Joe Lewis, were spreading their poisons among the dissidents with hate-filled speeches whose message was:

"Kill the whites or they will destroy you—just as they destroyed our people in the East!"

In Cayuse country, Joseph had a half brother named Five Crows who had become so interested in the white man's religion that he had moved to Lapwai with Joseph and Timothy and had become a convert shortly after they had. Told by Old James and *Tack-en-su-a-tis* that he was not welcome, he had returned to his village near Waiilatpu. He was still a Christian, he said, but more and more of late he was puzzled over the religious differences between the faith he had accepted and that professed by the Black Robes, whose priests recently had come into the country and now were vigorously trying to proselyte the Indians.

"Because they are King George men and supported by the Hudson's Bay Company, I am not surprised that they dislike Americans," he told Old Joseph when the Wallowa chief visited him in his village on the Umatilla River, half a day's ride southeast of Waiilatpu. "But this land does not belong to the King George men now. It belongs to the Americans, for a year ago the boundary was set far to the north of where we live. Have you not heard this, brother?"

"Yes, I have heard it. Under the new treaty, the Hudson's Bay Company must close all its trading posts south of the boundary and sell out to the Americans. But it takes time to agree on a fair price."

"Under the agreement made with Dr. Elijah White when we accepted his Code of Laws, I was made head chief of the Cayuse, Umatilla, and

Walla Walla tribes, just as Ellis was made head chief of the Nez Perces. This I have told the Black Robes, who wish to establish a Catholic mission on the Umatilla. But they say they are not bound by the laws of government; they are bound only by the laws of God. Is their God different from the God of the Americans?"

"From what I have learned, brother, God to white men is whatever they say He is, with each *Tai-tam-nat* saying different things. That is why I have chosen to withdraw from the white man's church and worship God in my own way."

Still puzzled, Five Crows shook his head. "The Black Robes say that if the American missionaries truly were holy men, they would not take wives, as the Black Robes do not. If the Americans truly were holy men, they say, they would supply the Indians with food and pay rent for the lands they occupy. Most important of all, they would cure illness among the Indians instead of causing it, as they now do."

"Is it the Black Robes who say these things?" Chief Joseph asked with a frown. "Or is this poison being spread by those evil men Joe Lewis and Tom Hill?"

"This I cannot be sure of. By the time such sayings reach me, I have no way of knowing the long and crooked tongue trail by which they have traveled. But I am troubled in mind . . ."

3

After a two-day trading session between the emigrant train he was guiding and a band of Nez Perces in the upper Grande Ronde Valley, John Crane was troubled, too, though for a different reason. Since the Great Migration of '43, he'd taken up guiding as a business, heading east in early fall, wintering at Fort Bridger or Fort Laramie, then going on to Independence or Liberty, Missouri, where the Oregon-bound trains made up, in time to get a job. Paying four dollars a day, guiding a wagon train wasn't as physically demanding or dangerous as trapping beaver had been, but it did require a goodly supply of patience, judgment, and tolerance.

While the people in each train were different, they were also alike. In a train of say fifty wagons, there'd always be an expert who'd read and memorized all the published guidebooks and couldn't refrain from telling the paid guide how to do his job. There'd be an Indian hater so spooky you'd have to watch him like a hawk, else he'd take a potshot at the first tame Injun he saw, causing all kinds of trouble. There'd be a greenhorn who fancied himself a mighty hunter but would get the shakes so bad when he did sight game he couldn't hit a buffalo with buckshot at two paces.

In one train he'd guided, there'd even been an old man whose sole possessions were a bulldog, a cane, and a single blanket, and who'd figured on sponging his way west by depending on families in the train to feed him and give him shelter when he needed it. He'd made it as far as Fort Laramie, where he'd been kicked out of the train by unanimous vote of the governing council.

This year's train had experienced no more than the usual difficulties east of Fort Hall. West of there, a larger than average number of draft animals had fallen by the wayside or been weakened to uselessness because of the intense heat and the scarcity of grass. So in the upper Grande Ronde Valley, the appearance of the usual band of Wallowa Nez Perces—with fresh oxen, horses, and mules to trade—was welcomed by the emigrants, though they did grumble over what they regarded as an exorbitant three-worn-out-animals-for-one-fresh-one price.

"S'posin' I tell 'em to go to hell?" demanded Adam Peters, a belligerent Kentucky hill-country man who claimed relationship to Daniel Boone.

"S'posin' I set the price and tell 'em if they don't like it they can lump it? What will happen?"

"They won't trade."

"There's only twenty of them. We got 'em outnumbered ten to one. In my part of the country, Injuns won't fight unless the odds are at least that much in *their* favor."

"Happens we ain't in your part of the country now, Adam. The Nez Perces won't be pushed around. Long as I'm guiding the train, you'll trade fair or not at all."

"Damn Injun lover!" Adam Peters muttered. "Once us real Americans take over Oregon, we'll put the red bastards in their place."

Likely they would, so far as the Willamette Valley was concerned, John mused wearily, for white American settlers there increasingly outnumbered the local Indians, whose ranks had been decimated by diseases to which they had no natural immunity; and the fish, the game, and the land upon which the natives had lived from time immemorial was being taken over without their consent.

What troubled John Crane particularly now was he'd reached the age where a man yearns for family ties. Sure, Felicia was a fine woman, and her daughters, their husbands, and the young-uns they were whelping were good people. But they weren't blood kin. To them, he would always be an ex–mountain man who'd married their mother in a fair trade that'd given her a man around the house—well, a *sometime* man around the house—in exchange for a roof over his head, three meals a day, and a comfortable bed, when he chose to use it.

The only blood kin he had in the world, so far as he knew, was the son he'd fathered and deserted before his birth back in St. Louis fourteen years ago, and a half brother sired by his old man and birthed by a Nez Perce woman eighteen months before he himself had been born. Let's see, it had been back in '34—thirteen years ago—when Captain Bonneville told him that the Nez Perce son his father had thought dead still lived and thrived in the Wallowa country. He'd meant to look him up, but first one fool thing, then another, had prevented it.

Queer thing was, from what he'd been told, Tall Bird—which was the name his half brother went by in Nez Perce country—knew about *him* and had looked *him* up during rendezvous on Green River the summer of '36. Bill Craig had told him about it a couple of years afterward; told him how he'd warned Tall Bird to give John a week to finish his first toot, which Tall Bird had done. But then, unfortunately, he'd come back to see John again a couple of days after John had gotten word of all the family deaths from the plague back in St. Louis, his disinheritance, and the taking over of Luke's life by the goddamn bank. From what Bill Craig said, Tall Bird had been so disgusted with what he'd seen of his half brother then, he had vowed never to come near him again.

But times changed. So did a man. Close on the heels of the Champoeg vote that inclined the Provisional Government toward the United States, the Great Migration of '43 assured beyond all possible doubt that Oregon would be American. In 1844, the United States officially notified Great Britain that it wished to end the Joint Occupancy Treaty; in 1845, this was done; and in 1846 the northern boundary of the Oregon Country was set at the 49th Parallel. All that remained to be done now were a few tidying-up details such as appraising and paying for assets owned by the Hudson's Bay Company, and formally organizing Oregon Territory.

Having come west in 1832, John Crane could truthfully say that he had been one of the men who had made the country. He hadn't intended to make it into what it had become, God knows; still and all, he had done it —and it gave him a feeling of respectability. Even a feeling of pride. So after guiding wagon trains to Oregon in '44, '45, and '46, he decided in the spring of '47 to do something he'd been wanting to do for a long while.

He decided to go to St. Louis and see his son, Luke, for the first time.

Ever since the boy had been eight years old, they'd kept in touch by exchanging letters every few months. Still living with the attorney Samuel Wellington, Luke was fourteen years old now. He was doing well in school. He was strong of body and sharp of mind. Enrolled in a private academy that stressed rigid military discipline, he excelled at riding, fencing, pistol, and rifle shooting. He received top marks in history and had an amazingly comprehensive grasp of the expansionary movement now sweeping the country, and of the quarrels with Mexico over Texas, which surely would lead to war if Mexico didn't back down.

Early in March, John Crane wrote Luke a letter saying he was in Liberty, Missouri, was coming downriver to St. Louis on business in a couple of weeks, and would like to see his son and Samuel Wellington, if convenient with them. Because of his association with men like Bonneville and Wyeth during fur trade days and his present reputation as one of the most experienced Oregon Trail guides in the business, both the boy and his attorney-guardian respected him. By return mail, Luke wrote that he would be "very pleased" to see his father. Enclosed in the same envelope was a polite note from Samuel Wellington saying that if John could arrange to be his houseguest "for a week while in St. Louis," he would be most welcome.

Count on a lawyer to imply the terms and state the duration of the visit, John mused sardonically. Well, that was fine with him. What he wanted both his son and his guardian to see was that he was a capable man in a respectable profession, asking favors from no one. Thirty-nine years old now, lean and fit from outdoor living and years in the saddle, his blond hair long but neatly trimmed, no longer a heavy drinker, he knew that he was an impressive-looking man. Wanting to dress like what he was, a professional guide, he chose to wear a combination of white and Indian clothes—a broad-brimmed hat; a fringed, beaded, white buckskin jacket crafted by one of the best tailors in the country (a Crow woman who'd just lost her husband out Popo Agie way, who'd told him she'd trade him the jacket for one of the Nez Perce horses in his string and then sleep with him to seal the bargain); and black woolen trousers tucked into the highest-quality saddle boots to be found in Oregon City, those made by a German immigrant whose family had been bootmakers for three generations.

Playing his role with care and pride, he knew that he made a favorable impression on his son and on Samuel Wellington during the week he spent as houseguest of the attorney. Never having greeted a son before, let alone one that was fourteen years old, he decided it would be better to err on the side of restraint than on the side of emotion. So instead of opening his arms and embracing the boy as he wanted to do, he just smiled and extended his hand. Luke took it, smiling too, though his face was pale and his lower tip trembling.

Lord, what a handsome boy he is! Tall like his father, grandfather, and great-grandfather. Large, wide-spaced eyes that in some light look green like his mother's and in other light look blue like mine. Under it's healthy tan, the skin of his face is milk-white, as Susan's was. But the distinctive feature of his appearance is the one that struck me so sharply when I received the miniature Mother sent to rendezvous eleven years ago—the red, lustrous, curly hair.

On a woman, it would be described as her "crowning glory." On Luke, it must be so described too. *Bet he's been teased no end about it,* John mused; *but the fact that he's still wearing it long and showing off its curliness means he likes it that way, and by God, anybody that teases him about it is going to get his ass whipped.*

Though he had met Samuel Wellington before going west, John had not known him well. A man in his late sixties, the attorney was thin and frail-looking, stooped, white-haired, and polite in manner and speech. He exuded the impression that in matters affecting his ward's welfare he would not intentionally be unkind to his father. But he would intentionally be unbending.

As the two men sat sipping brandies and smoking after-supper cigars one evening, Samuel Wellington came as close to apologizing for the control he was exercising over Luke's life as he ever would.

"Your father was not an unjust man, John. He did not like doing what he did, but he felt he must protect your son's welfare."

"Reckon I've come to realize that."

"If he had lived, I'm sure you and he would have reconciled. To the end, he hoped for that."

"It's water long over the dam, Mr. Wellington, but a couple of days after I got his first letter, I made up my mind to come home. I planned to marry Susan, make up with Pa, and settle down."

"I'm pleased to hear that."

"But two weeks later, his second letter came, saying Mother and Grandfather had died and he'd married Susan to make sure Luke was protected. The same express brought your letter, saying he and Susan had died and that you and the bank would be Luke's guardian. I felt like I'd been poleaxed."

"I can well imagine."

"Tell me: How much does Luke know about all this?"

"Only that Susan was his mother and you his father, and that you had gone west before he was born. He does not know that you and Susan were not married and that your father married Susan after your mother died."

"Will he ever be told?"

"I would prefer that he not be—"

"So would I."

"However, because of certain technicalities in the laws of inheritance, he must be told when he reaches the age of twenty-one, which is when he will acquire full control of his assets, which should be considerable."

"Gonna be quite a shock to him, ain't it?"

"Undoubtedly, it will be. But not nearly as great a shock as it would be if it were disclosed to him by accident or by a person determined to injure him. What I have done, John, is put the details in writing in the kindest and most sympathetic way I could to all parties concerned. I love the boy as if he were my own son. He trusts me. Even if I am not alive to explain matters to him, I am sure he will understand and not condemn you."

"Let's hope so. He's a fine boy and I want him to think well of me. What does he plan to do with his life?"

"If the Bower & Crane Mercantile Bank does well—as it should—he will be a wealthy man, with no need to worry about making a living. But he does have a career in mind. Since he's just received a piece of good news regarding that career, which he's dying to tell you, I won't spoil his pleasure by revealing it myself. With your grandfather a minister and your father a very religious man, the career Luke has chosen may surprise you. But I'll let him tell you about it tomorrow morning . . ."

One of the greatest pleasures of his visit was the daily ride shared with Luke on the fine-blooded horses in the Samuel Wellington stable. While

John's style of riding was casually Western, letting the horse do what it wanted to do, he always kept it under control. Luke's style was disciplined, precise, and Eastern, with the horse always aware of the fact that it was being managed. But the end result of each style was a perfect ride.

Pulling up to let their horses blow, after a two-mile gallop, Luke smiled at his father. "You certainly ride well, sir."

"I've had a lot of practice, son. You're some Injun on a horse yourself."

"Do the Indians out West really ride well?"

"Like they were born on a horse. Which some of 'em practically are. Why, I've seen Nez Perce mothers stick a couple of weeks-old babies in *tekashes,* hang 'em on the saddle horn of a packhorse, and let it take care of 'em. It does, too. Never seen a babe get hurt on the trail."

"What is a *tekash?*"

"A cradleboard made out of soft skins with a stiff back so it will support the baby and keep it safe from harm. Some of 'em are real purty, with beaded flower designs. Practical, too, with a pee tube hanging down to drain the bladder. Lots of ways, Nez Perce women take care of their babies much easier than white women do."

"According to what I've read, the Nez Perces are the best of Western Indians. Would you agree?"

"I sure would. And so would your grandfather, if he were here. Pity you never knew him."

"Are you guiding a wagon train to Oregon again this year?"

"Yeah. It's making up now at Independence, waiting for the grass. If this warm weather holds, we'll be pulling out in a couple of weeks. Like to come along?"

"I wish I could, Father. But I've got to stay in school and keep up my marks. If I do, Senator Benton has promised to get me an appointment to the National Military Academy at West Point when I'm eighteen."

John stared at his son. "Well, I'll be damned! You're going to be a soldier! Who do you think we'll fight in the next war?"

"Oh, Father, West Point trains officers to do a great deal more than fight in a war. For instance, the Academy has an excellent Corp of Engineers, which builds forts, coastal artillery emplacements, bridges, and wagon roads all over the country. To me it offers a fascinating lifetime career."

Gazing at his handsome son, John sensed a maturity in him far beyond his years. Apparently it was a family trait to choose a career at an early age that would fulfill the desire to serve God or country, while at the same time letting one lead an interesting life. His grandfather, the Reverend Peter Crane, had left Boston and pioneered as a Presbyterian minister in the raw frontier village of St. Louis. His father had been a member of the Lewis and Clark party. John himself had run away from home and responsibility, only to eventually mature as a pioneer developer of Oregon Territory. Growing up as Luke was, in a time of national expansion, reading history books full of great deeds done by military men, knowing leaders like Senator Thomas Hart Benton, who grandiloquently made such statements as "Westward lies our destiny and our future—the Orient . . . ," it was only natural that Luke should choose the career he had.

"More power to you, son," John said fervently, extending his hand and shaking Luke's. "Maybe one of these days you'll be building forts and military roads out in our part of the country."

"I hope so, Father. Truly, I do . . ."

Looking back on it now, as the trading session with the Wallowa Nez Perce ended and the emigrant train prepared to move on, John Crane reckoned that the week he had spent with his son in St. Louis had been the most satisfying week of his life. Sure, the fact that Luke would learn the unpleasant circumstances of his birth and his father's craven behavior was deeply disturbing. But that was seven years in the future. A lot could happen between now and then. Meantime, he meant to make a point of looking up his other blood relative, his half brother Tall Bird, whose Indian name, as he recalled it, was *Peo-peo Kuhet*. William Craig would know where to find him, probably. As soon as he'd herded this batch of emigrants to the Willamette, he'd come back upriver and pay Craig a visit. Maybe he'd be lucky again . . .

4

During the years John Crane had guided wagon trains to Oregon, for every one person killed by Indians, snakebite, or accident, twenty-five people had died in epidemics of disease. Cholera, camp fever, whooping cough —if a person came down with such an ailment on the trail, there was nothing to do except let the disease run its course and pray it didn't hit your family.

This year's train had been lucky in having no epidemics of illness before reaching Fort Boise. There, several youngsters belonging to the wagon train apparently picked up a bug from children whose parents were employees of the Hudson's Bay Company. As ailments went, it was not a violent one, its symptoms being fever, sweating, a rapid pulse, and, after a few days, a rash of pustules breaking out on the face and chest. When the train reached Waiilatpu, the children in a dozen families were sick with the disease. At John Crane's request, Dr. Marcus Whitman examined the ill children, then made a diagnosis which relieved the minds of the worried parents.

"Black measles. Not a serious disease, so far as being life-threatening is concerned. The important thing is to keep the children clean, air their bedding and clothes, and bathe the pustules in mildly acidic water to make sure they don't get infected. With a few days' rest, light diet, and plenty of fluids, the children should recover with no complications."

"We're obliged, Doc," John said. "Suppose they caught it at Fort Boise?"

"Possibly. I've seen none of it here before, though it's common enough back East."

"Last time I talked to you, the Cayuses were giving you trouble. Any improvement?"

"No, I'm sorry to say," Whitman said wearily. "If anything, they're worse. Every wagon train that passes through drops off ill or indigent people that have to be cared for. Right now, we have over sixty people with white blood in their veins living at Waiilatpu. The Cayuses resent the fact that I spend more time looking after white people than I do ministering to their needs. But what else can I do?"

"Guess it is a problem."

"For the past couple of years, a French-Canadian named Joe Lewis, who claims to be half Iroquois, has been hanging around the Cayuse camp, telling them we should pay rent for using their land. He says my medicine chest is full of poison I plan to use to kill them so that American emigrants can take over their country. Some of them believe him."

"Can't you run the booger off?"

"I've tried. But he keeps coming back. Then that fool William Gray pulled a stunt that made the Cayuses positive I plan to poison them. Some of their young people were stealing melons out of our garden patch, so to teach them a lesson, Gray doctored a melon with laxative salts; the youngsters stole and ate it, and got sick as poisoned pups. Lewis told their parents it was my doing."

"Seem to recall having the same trick pulled on me, back in my melon-stealing days. But I can see how it would make you trouble with the Cayuses."

"Oh, Joe Lewis manages to put the blame on me for anything bad that happens. One afternoon I reprimanded a middle-aged Indian man for his rude behavior to my wife. In doing so, I tapped him lightly on the shoulder as I told him not to insult her again. That evening, while he was eating, a piece of meat got stuck in his throat, he choked on it, and died. Lewis said I'd put a curse on him."

"In my trapping days, we'd have taken care of Joe Lewis quick enough," John said grimly. "But being a Christian and a doctor, I know you can't."

"The worst of my problems right now," Whitman said, "is that the Catholics have moved in and are competing for Indian souls as if it were some kind of game. They've established a mission on the Umatilla, just twenty-five miles from here, near the village of Five Crows. Though he's been a good Presbyterian, they're trying to get him to recant and join their faith."

"I ain't a very good Christian myself, Doc, but I do know Indians. Competing for their souls by playing one religion against another is mighty dangerous. If you ain't careful, somebody's gonna get hurt."

"I know, I know!" Whitman said wearily. "I've told that to Father Brouillet and his brothers time and again. But they're Jesuits, John. As the saying goes: 'You can always tell a Jesuit—but you can't tell him much . . .' "

The wagon train stayed at the Whitman Mission three days. Following the doctor's instructions, parents of the ill children aired their bedding, washed their clothes, and bathed their pustules in mildly acidic water. By the time the train was ready to pull out, all the children were on their way to recovery. If any of the parents showed their gratitude to Dr. Whitman by paying him a fee, making him a present, or even thanking him verbally, John Crane was not aware of it. But in no uncertain terms, Gerwyn Jackson's wife, Amanda, let John know her low opinion of what she called "a den of thieves."

"Know what them mission people charged me for two measly pecks of potatoes and a dozen turnips? Fifty cents, that's what! Why, back home in Illinois, a dab of vegetables like that wouldn't cost a body more'n fifteen cents."

"We're two thousand miles from Illinois, Mrs. Jackson," John said dryly. "Way I hear it, the mission don't get much financial help from the church people back East. It pretty much has to support itself."

"Well, I got as much charity in my nature as the next person. But if the mission is here to do good and Christianize the Indians, wouldn't you think the first lesson they'd teach the heathen would be not to steal?"

"Seems reasonable, I'd say."

"Well, the red rascals sure stole from me. Two blankets, a dress, a pair of trousers, and a shirt—right out from under my nose night before last."

"They took this stuff out of your wagon?"

"Course not! If they'd come near our wagon, my man Gerwyn would have peppered their greasy hides with buckshot. They stole the blankets and clothes from off the rail fence where I'd hung 'em to air out for a day and a night before washing 'em. When I went to get 'em yesterday morning, they were gone."

"Mrs. Jackson, I've told you people time and again never to leave things out after dark, when Indians are around. That's just inviting them to steal."

"Stealing is stealing, Mr. Crane, whether it's day or night. If Dr. Whitman was any kind of a man, he'd go to that Indian village and get me back my things. Either that or pay me what they're worth."

"He's got bigger troubles to worry about," John said sharply. "So have I. Tell your husband we're rolling out in half an hour . . ."

Hayat Tako—"Root Woman"—the plump, middle-aged Cayuse matron who had found the blankets and clothes draped over the top rail of the fence, was not a greedy person. Because she had a number of nephews, nieces, and grandchildren who needed warm apparel to protect their bodies from the increasingly cold autumn nights, she distributed the two blankets, the dress, the pair of trousers, and the shirt to five individuals who lived in five separate tepees.

In a few weeks' time, an epidemic of black measles was raging through the Cayuse village like prairie fire. Unlike the disease that had mildly affected the white children of the wagon train, this illness in a band of Indians never before exposed to it proved to be a killer so deadly that, by the time it had run its course, half of the Cayuse tribe, which numbered four hundred, died—most of them children.

Bringing his ten-year-old daughter, Eliza, down from Lapwai to enroll her in the mission school, the Reverend Henry Spalding arrived at Waiilatpu Monday afternoon, November 22, 1847. He was appalled by what he saw. Because so many of the children were ill, the mission school had been closed.

"All the doctor's family have been sick," Spalding wrote his wife:

Mrs. Osborn and three children are yet dangerously sick; one of their children died during the week. The doctor's hands are more than full among the Indians; three and sometimes five die a day. Dear sister Whitman seems ready to sink under the immense weight of labor and care. But like an angel of mercy, she continues to administer with her ever-ready hand to the wants of all. Late and early, night and day, she is by the bed of the sick, the dying, and the afflicted.

On Thursday, November 25, Spalding and Andrew Rodgers, a young bachelor teacher at the mission, rode to Fort Walla Walla, where they accepted the invitation of Chief *Peo-peo Mox-mox*—"Yellow Bird"—to spend the night in his lodge. Long friendly to both the King George men and the American missionaries, *Peo-peo Mox-mox* had prospered by trading horses and cattle to the citizens of both nations. But the recent arrival of Catholic priests troubled him.

"I gave them permission to establish a mission in my country, as did my brother, Five Crows," he told Spalding. "But I do not like their talk. How can they say it is more holy for them not to have wives than it is for you and Dr. Whitman to be married? Why do they wear robes while you wear trousers? Why do they drink wine while you do not? Why do they say that because of these differences their religion is better than yours?"

Always eager to engage in theological argument, the Reverend Spalding was about to give the chief a well-reasoned reply when a curious interruption occurred. Stooping low to enter the lodge, then scrambling to his feet with a look of agitation on his face, a Nez Perce brave Spalding had never seen blurted excitedly, *"Tinuguin Tai-tam-nat Whitman?"*

Scowling his disapproval, *Peo-peo Mox-mox* gave a grunt reprimanding the Nez Perce for his bad manners, then made the question sign to Spalding: "Is this true?"

"Of course it's not true!" Spalding said testily. "We left the doctor alive and well this morning."

Without apology or further word, the Nez Perce turned, stooped, and scuttled out of the lodge. Andrew Rodgers, who played the violin, sang well, was an excellent teacher, but had little knowledge of local Indian tongues, gave Spalding a puzzled look.

"What did he say?"

"He asked, 'Is Dr. Whitman killed?' "

"Why on earth would he think that?"

"I don't know. Perhaps he's heard a rumor."

Threats of death against Whitman and himself were nothing new, Spalding admitted. Still, the urgency of the question and the blunt manner in which it had been asked troubled him, for it seemed to indicate that a definite course of action had been decided upon by the dissident Indians.

On Friday, Spalding and Rodgers dined at Fort Walla Walla with Bishop Blanchet, his fellow clergymen Fathers Brouillet and LeClaire, and Hudson's Bay Company Agent William McBean. Whatever his prejudices against the Catholics might have been, Spalding was not averse to selling them supplies for their new mission.

"They asked and I cheerfully agreed to furnish them all needed supplies from my station," he wrote.

Even more cheerfully, he engaged in a heated debate with the Catholic missionaries, in which he disputed their views regarding the theory of transubstantiation, which claimed that the wine and bread used in the Mass ceremony were changed into the actual blood and body of Christ.

"We had an animated discussion on changing the biscuit into God," he wrote, as he gleefully declared himself victor in the argument. "I showed them plainly that they must be deceivers or cannibals."

Returning to Waiilatpu with Andrew Rodgers Saturday morning, November 27, Spalding found Dr. Whitman grimly trying to cope with a new facet of the epidemic—the strange phenomenon that when black measles caught by an Indian from a white person was passed from an Indian back to another white, it became a much more virulent disease. For example, the wife of Josiah Osborn (whom Whitman had hired as a millwright a few months ago), had become ill two weeks ago, then three days later gave birth to a baby that lived only a few hours. Shortly thereafter, her three-year-old daughter, Salvijane Osborn, became sick and, despite everything Dr. Whitman could do, died.

"My wife told Mrs. Osborn it was God's will that the child be taken," Whitman said to Spalding. "With so many Indian children dying, perhaps this death of a white child would show the Cayuses that they were not alone in their suffering. She asked Mrs. Osborn's permission to let a Cayuse father named Green Cap, who had lost three of his own children, see the dead child."

"It may help to keep us all here," Narcissa told Mrs. Osborn. "Otherwise we may have to leave soon."

When Mrs. Osborn consented, Green Cap was ushered into the sickroom by Dr. Whitman. For a long time the Indian stood staring down at the dead child's face, which was mottled with pustules from the disease. Suddenly he threw back his head and laughed with a high, cackling scream, chilling Mrs. Osborn, Narcissa, and the dead child's nine-year-old sister, Nancy, who was cowering in a corner of the room. Still laughing like a madman, the Indian rushed out of the room and ran toward the Cayuse village.

"Perhaps he was mad," Whitman said, as he related the macabre story to Spalding. "Just as all of us will be if this goes on much longer."

"Are you still doctoring the Cayuses?"

"No. They've lost what little faith they ever had in my skills. The *tewats* do their doctoring now. You know what that means."

"I certainly do. Chants, mumblings, and black magic. Sweat baths followed by immersion in an ice-cold stream."

"Exactly. Which only hastens death." Wearily, Marcus Whitman closed his eyes, massaged the back of his neck to ease his fatigue and tension, then gave Spalding a tired smile. "I'm still respected as a doctor in the Umatilla village. Five Crows and Young Chief have asked me to come there and treat their sick. I'm going tonight. Will you ride with me?"

"I'd be glad to."

During the six-hour ride southeast to the Umatilla village through the cold, rainy darkness, Spalding and Whitman exchanged somber reflections on their experiences of the last eleven years. Of the two missions, there was no question that Lapwai was far more successful than Waiilatpu. Realizing that, whether they liked it or not, civilization had come to stay in Nez Perce country, William Craig and his ex–mountain men friends no longer were hostile to Spalding, bringing grain to his mill to be ground into flour, working for him when he needed skilled labor, even sending their half-blood children to the mission school. Though William Craig earlier had urged his father-in-law, *Hin-mah-tute-ke-kaikt,* to make Spalding pay rent or be evicted from the land he occupied, when Craig himself had been given the opportunity to legally dispossess the missionary, he had not done so.

"As the story came back to me, Craig went down to Oregon City to claim a square mile of land, as he was entitled to do under the Donation Act," Spalding told Whitman. "Since the American Board hasn't bothered to file a claim on the mission grounds, he could have taken title simply by swearing that the land was unoccupied. But he refused to do so. Instead, he filed on a piece of land a few miles up the valley."

"You're fortunate, Henry, in having located your mission in the heart of Nez Perce country instead of on the Oregon Trail. You have only a handful of ex–mountain men to deal with. I have emigrants by the thousands— many of them unable to understand that my means for taking care of their needs are limited."

"Is it true you're considering abandoning Waiilatpu and moving down-river to The Dalles?"

"I've told the Cayuses time and again that if they want me to close the mission and leave, I will. But I've put too much into the buildings and land to abandon them without being paid a fair price. I've offered to sell out to the Catholics. But so far they've vacillated, saying they must clear the purchase with Rome."

"Which, translated into plain English," Spalding said cynically, "means they aren't going to pay for property they think they'll eventually get for nothing. Catholics are as cheap as they are bigoted, Doctor."

"Well, something has to change. My wife is so overworked and under such a constant strain, I fear for her health. She can't take much more."

Though Spalding did not voice the thought, he could not help but reflect on how greatly Narcissa's health and his wife's well-being had changed during the past eleven years. Since the death of her only child, Narcissa had lost her cheerfulness and good spirits, putting on weight, working stoically and without joy, doing what had to be done but taking no plea-sure in it. In contrast, his own wife now was happy and fulfilled, in her quiet, unassuming way. Before leaving the East, she had suffered the terri-ble emotional loss of a stillborn child. She had been ill much of the time during the journey west; and after her arrival at Lapwai she had experi-enced a miscarriage with bleeding so severe she nearly died.

Yet during the past eleven years, she had borne four children, who were well and thriving now: Eliza, ten; Henry, eight; Martha, two; and the baby, Amelia, whose first birthday would be celebrated in just a week. Though Narcissa Whitman treated the Cayuse mothers and children with a cold aloofness, preferring to give her love and care to the white mothers and children now living at the mission, Eliza Spalding had given such special care and attention to the Nez Perce children and their mothers that the Indian women and children had come to love her.

"At times I've wondered if it's wise to let our children associate with the Nez Perce youngsters on such familiar terms," Spalding told Whitman. "But my wife says that far more good than harm comes from it. For instance, our daughter, Eliza, speaks the Nez Perce tongue as well as she speaks English. We often use her as an interpreter."

"Some of our fellow missionaries in the Sandwich Islands would be shocked to hear that," Whitman said dryly. "I'm told they won't let their children associate with Hawaiian youngsters for fear they'll catch a fatal case of paganism. They even send their children back to Boston to be schooled."

Moving down the steep, winding, muddy trail as it descended several hundred feet to the Umatilla River, Spalding's horse lost its footing and fell, sliding a dozen feet down the slope before it could stop. Caught with his right leg under the animal, Spalding slid with it over the slick, rough lava rocks. Helping him extricate himself, Marcus Whitman exclaimed, "Clumsy brute! Are you hurt?"

Gingerly getting to his feet, Spalding limped a few strides, testing the leg. "Nothing is broken. Just seem to be skinned and bruised."

"Can you ride?"

"Oh, yes! But I'm glad we don't have far to go."

Though the hour was past midnight when they reached the flat on the north bank of the Umatilla River where the lodge of Dr. Whitman's staunch Indian friend Stickus was pitched, a lamp was lighted as they approached. Stickus came out to eagerly shake their hands, ordered one of his boys to unsaddle and care for their horses, then brought the two men into the tepee, which was warm and dry. His loyalty to Whitman went back to the first sermon preached by the missionary after his arrival at Waiilatpu, which had convinced Stickus that he wanted to live as a Christian. When he had become seriously ill a year or so later and a *tewat* failed to cure him, he sent for Dr. Whitman, who made him well, which increased his faith in the doctor. Hearing in the late summer of 1843 that Dr. Whitman was leading a large wagon train toward the trackless wilds of the Blue Mountains, he had hastened to ride east to the Snake River to meet them. Because of his skills as a guide, the train had gotten through.

Shedding their wet outer clothing, Spalding and Whitman spread their blankets on the floor of the lodge by a good fire and slept until morning. When they awoke shortly after daybreak Sunday, they were gratified by the sincerity with which Stickus conducted family devotions.

During the previous night's ride, Whitman had told Spalding about a warning given him by an emigrant name John Settle, who, with his family, had lived and worked at Waiilatpu during the winter of '46–'47. According to Settle, a group of "friendly" Indians had approached him early in November and urged him "to induce Dr. Whitman to leave the mission." Convinced that the dissident Indians intended to kill Whitman if he remained, Settle used every argument possible to get him to leave. When Whitman refused, Settle himself had packed up and left for the Willamette Valley.

Now Stickus was warning him that the Cayuses at Waiilatpu were plotting against him. "I will give you names of the men who talk of killing you," he said grimly. *"Tiloukaikt, Tamsucky,* and Joe Lewis. These are the leaders. And there are half a dozen more."

Whitman shrugged. "I appreciate the warning. But right now there are sick people to be cared for. I must visit the camps of Five Crows and Young Chief on the south side of the river."

"You will not like what you find in the camp of Young Chief," Stickus said gravely. "He has given his house to the Black Robes to use as a mission. They call it St. Anne."

"So I have heard. Well, it's a free country. While I'm there, I may talk to the priests about the advisability of asking the Cayuses to decide what kind of missionaries they want, Protestant or Catholic."

Because the leg caught under the falling horse still throbbed and ached, Spalding stayed in the Stickus lodge and rested while Dr. Whitman made his calls. Returning in late afternoon, Whitman said he had treated the Indian sick, then taken tea and talked with Bishop Blanchet and Fathers Brouillet and LeClaire.

"We had a good conversation. I suggested that it would be helpful if one of them came to Waiilatpu and talked to the Indians with me, showing them that despite our different religions we both have their welfare in mind. Father Brouillet said he would pay us a visit in a couple of days."

"I suppose it will do no harm," Spalding said.

"Now I must be heading home. Do you feel up to traveling?"

"No, I really don't. If Stickus doesn't mind, I'd like to stay here two or three days and let my bruises heal before making another long ride."

"You are welcome to stay as long as you like," Stickus said.

"Then I'm on my way," Whitman said. Giving them a tired smile, he extended his hand. "See you presently, Henry. May God be with you, Stickus."

"May He care for you, too, Dr. Whitman. Remember the bad men I told you about. I would be sad if they did you harm . . ."

5

At the age of thirteen, Catherine Sager was capable of judging events with the maturity of an adult while feeling their impact with the emotions of a child. The oldest of the five sisters, she insisted that they treat the Whitmans with loving respect, calling them "Father" and "Mother." As for her brothers, John, now seventeen, and Francis, fourteen, she was less successful in getting them to revere the Whitmans, for both boys still remembered their real parents and felt it would be disloyal to their memory to honor new parents so soon. In fact, John had grown so resentful of Dr. Whitman a year ago that he had run away and gone down to the Willamette Valley, returning only after Dr. Whitman promised to give him a piece of land and treat him like a grown man. To both boys, the term "Doctor" came much easier than "Father," though out of politeness they did call Narcissa "Mother Whitman."

Dr. Whitman got back to Waiilatpu from his trip to the Umatilla camps on Sunday night at ten o'clock. Worn out by long hours of household chores and caring for the numerous sick adults and children in what was called the "mansion," Mother Whitman had gone to bed. The two older boys, John and Francis Sager, had been given the responsibility of watching over Helen Mar Meek and Louise Sager, both of whom were seriously ill. Catherine herself, sick with a somewhat milder case of black measles, was sleeping on a settee in the living room. She woke up to Father Whitman speaking to her brothers.

"Go to bed, boys. I'll look after the girls the rest of the night."

Sleepily, Catherine watched as he went first to the bed of Louise, then to the bed of Helen Mar, where he stayed for some time. Taking her pulse, putting a hand on her cheek, bending close to look into her eyes, he sighed and shook his head, his strong, muscular shoulders sagging in despair. Going over to the bed where Mother Whitman lay, which was in a curtained-off area adjacent to the stairs going up to the attic rooms, he greeted her in a low voice. Catherine saw Mother Whitman sit up and heard her murmur a question.

"I'm afraid Helen Mar is dying," Father Whitman said somberly. "For those with Indian blood in their veins, it's always worse."

"Did you see Stickus?"

"Yes. He fears something bad will happen. He gave me the names of three men who are talking against us. *Tamsucky, Tiloukaikt,* and Joe Lewis."

"Oh, Marcus! What can we do?"

"Hope for the best and pray." He kissed her. "Go back to sleep, dear. If there's any change in the children, I'll call you."

After blowing out the candle, he crossed the room and sat down at the end of the settee on which Catherine lay, apparently deep in thought. His manner and portions of the conversation she had overheard disturbed her and kept her awake. Sensing her restlessness, he got up, patted her cheek reassuringly, and told her everything was going to be all right; then, drawing a chair close to the warmth of the living room stove, he sat gazing down at the dark, feverish face of Helen Mar. Soothed by his words and presence, Catherine at last fell asleep.

Monday, November 29, 1847, dawned cold and foggy, with fine mist suspended in air only a degree or two above freezing. Getting up, Catherine noticed that the curtains around Mother Whitman's bed were drawn. After she had gone into the kitchen and fixed breakfast for the children, Mother Whitman still not appearing, she filled a plate with food, poured a cup of coffee, and told Elizabeth to take it to Mother. When Elizabeth returned to the kitchen, she was troubled.

"Why is Mother crying?"

"I don't know. Is she?"

"When I pulled back the curtain, she was sitting in a chair beside her bed with her face in a handkerchief, sobbing as if her heart were breaking. She didn't touch her breakfast. She just motioned for me to put it down and leave."

"She's been working awfully hard, taking care of all the sick. If she wants to rest, let her."

The first piece of news brought over from the Cayuse village was grim and foreboding. During the night, three children in the lodge of *Tiloukaikt* had died of black measles. One or more of them were his own. When notified, Dr. Whitman offered to conduct a burial service. While waiting for the bodies to arrive, Whitman talked with Andrew Rodgers about the warning Stickus had given him.

"It's all piling up," he said wearily. "The epidemic of black measles, with its deadly effect on the Indians. The coming of the Catholics. The poison being spread by Joe Lewis. I just don't know what to do, Andrew, to improve relations with the Indians."

"Maybe cold weather will end the epidemic. But that won't help with the Catholics or Joe Lewis."

"Well, if things don't clear up by spring, I'm going to make arrangements to close the mission and move down to the Willamette Valley. We certainly can't continue here under these conditions."

Thinking that the half blood Nicholas Finley, who lived with his Cayuse wife in the nearby Indian village, would know if there was a plot against him, Whitman sent for the man and questioned him bluntly.

"I understand the Indians are to kill me and Mr. Spalding. Do you know anything about it?"

"You have nothing to fear, Doctor," Finley answered so quickly and glibly that Whitman felt sure he was lying. "There is no danger."

As always, the seventy-odd whites living in the various buildings on the mission grounds were up and about early, except for the eleven adults and children who were ill in bed. Judge L. W. Saunders, an emigrant from Oskaloosa, Iowa, whom Whitman had recently hired to teach in the mission school, decided most of his pupils were well enough to reopen the school. Isaac Gilliland, who had traveled west with Saunders, his wife, and their five children, was a tailor by profession; he had also been given work at the mission. That morning, he was working on a suit of clothes for Dr. Whitman, sitting cross-legged on top of a table while he plied his needle.

Picking up a rifle, Francis Sager went out to the corral where a steer was to be butchered; he was to be its executioner. John Sager was in the kitchen gathering twine and other materials with which to make a broom. Josiah Osborn was laying a floor in what used to be called the "Indian room" of the "emigrant house" but which now served as living quarters for his family. Peter Hall was doing carpenter work on an extension to the east end of the T-shaped "mansion house." Walter Marsh was grinding wheat into flour at the water-powered gristmill. Joseph Stanfield, a French-Canadian with Indian blood in his veins, was helping Francis Sager choose a steer to be slaughtered. Jacob Hoffman, Nathan Kimball, and W. D. Canfield were standing by to do the butchering.

By eleven o'clock, when the bodies of the three Indian children who had died during the night arrived at the mission, Mother Whitman had arisen and, without eating her breakfast, was caring for the sick. When Dr. Whitman accompanied the Cayuses to the burial grounds, he was surprised to note how few Indians attended the services.

"Strange they should stay away," he told Narcissa when he returned. "Usually many of them come. I suppose the beef butchering attracted them."

"You'd better take a look at Lorinda, Marcus. She's been crying again."

A pretty girl just past twenty, Lorinda Bewley was one of seven children in the family of John Bewley and his wife, which had arrived at the Whitman Mission that summer and decided to stay for a while. Suffering with what Dr. Whitman diagnosed as a recurrence of ague, complicated by some vague "female complaint" to which young unmarried women were susceptible, Lorinda had been put to bed in an upstairs room above the Whitman living quarters. After taking her pulse and temperature and listening sympathetically to her incoherent ramblings about a "presentiment of evil" she was having, Dr. Whitman returned downstairs, went to the medicine cabinet under the stairs, and mixed up a mild dose of laudanum, sugar, and water.

"Whatever ails her is not serious, I'm sure," he told his wife. "This will soothe her. Take it up to her and give her some woman talk."

Following the noonday meal, the men working outside resumed their tasks. Mary Ann Bridger, who had been sick with black measles but now was feeling better, began washing the dishes. Mrs. Osborn, in bed for three weeks, got up, dressed, and began moving about, though she was still very feeble. Her husband, Josiah, assisted her. Mother Whitman, a firm believer in frequent baths, even in cold weather, had poured hot water into a tub placed on the living room floor, and had insisted that Catherine undress and bathe. Finished and dressing now, Catherine was out of the tub, while Elizabeth had gotten into it. Tired from his long ride, Dr. Whitman took a book off the shelf, sat down by the stove, and began reading.

Going into the kitchen to get a glass of milk for Elizabeth, Narcissa Whitman was surprised and alarmed to find the room full of Indians. One of them rudely demanded the glass of milk she was carrying.

"You'll have to wait, this is for the child," Catherine heard her say sharply to the Cayuse.

As Mother Whitman came through the door from the kitchen to the living room, the Indian tried to force his way in after her, but she firmly shut the door in his face and bolted it. Pounding on the door from the kitchen side, the Indian began shouting in Cayuse, calling for the doctor, asking for medicine. Wearily, Dr. Whitman put the book aside, got up, and answered the knock. As he unbolted the door, the Indian again tried to force his way into the living room, but Whitman blocked the entrance with his powerful body.

"Medicine!" the Cayuse demanded angrily. "Want medicine!"

"Stay where you are and I'll get it for you," Whitman said. Closing and rebolting the door, he crossed the living room to the medicine cabinet, selected some pills and potions, then went back to the door. As he opened it, he spoke over his shoulder to Narcissa.

"Lock it after me. They're in an ugly mood."

Watching Mother Whitman bolt the door, Catherine Sager heard the clock strike two. In the kitchen beyond the door, loud, angry Indian voices were raised, with Father Whitman's soft, mild voice replying. Suddenly she heard the sharp explosion of a rifle shot. Mother Whitman turned pale.

"Good heavens! What happened?"

Jumping up in the tub, Elizabeth started screaming hysterically. Wrapping a towel around her, Mother Whitman said; "Hush, child! Dry yourself and get dressed. I'll help you."

Although Mother Whitman's first impulse had been to rush into the kitchen to see what had happened, just as Catherine's had been to open the living room door and run outside, they both managed to control themselves, realizing that the important concern right now was the safety of the people in this room.

"Mrs. Osborn, go to your room and stay there," Narcissa Whitman ordered. "Mr. Osborn, can you nail the latch on the front door shut so it can't be opened from the outside?"

"Reckon so."

With a carpenter's apron full of nails but no hammer handy, Josiah Osborn picked up a flatiron and was starting to drive a nail above the latch when the door was suddenly flung open, and Mary Ann Bridger burst in. She seemed paralyzed with horror, and unable to speak. Narcissa seized her by the shoulders.

"What happened? Did they kill the doctor?" she screamed.

"Yes!" Mary Ann sobbed.

"My husband is killed!" Catherine heard Narcissa cry over and over. "He is killed and I am left a widow!"

Soon Mary Ann was able to relate what she had seen. She had been in the kitchen when the shot was fired. The Indians crowded there included *Tiloukaikt* and *Tomahas,* the latter being the one who had demanded the medicine. When Whitman entered the room, he sat down at a table facing *Tiloukaikt,* Mary Ann said; then, while *Tiloukaikt* had the doctor's attention, *Tomahas* stepped up behind him, drew a pipe tomahawk from under his blanket, and struck the doctor's head. Dr. Whitman fell partly forward. A second blow on the back of the head brought him to the floor. Leaping to his feet and drawing his own tomahawk, *Tiloukaikt* bent over the doctor and chopped at his face time and again, mutilating it so badly that the features could not be recognized.

While Dr. Whitman was lying on the floor, an Indian had shot him in the neck, causing profuse bleeding. This was the shot heard by those in the living room.

As soon as John Sager, who was in the kitchen, became aware of the attack on Dr. Whitman, he grabbed a pistol and shot twice, wounding two of the Indians. *Tamsucky* then shot John. Severely wounded in the neck, John managed to push part of the scarf he was wearing into the wound, in an attempt to stanch the flow of blood. Hearing shouts outside, where violence also had begun, the Indians in the kitchen all rushed out to join the melee, leaving Marcus Whitman and John Sager, both mortally wounded, lying on the floor. At that point, Mary Ann Bridger fled, running around the north end of the building.

Meanwhile, Judge Saunders, following the noon meal, had assembled his pupils in the schoolroom, in another wing of the building. While out at recess, the thirteen-year-old half-blood boy John Manson saw eighteen or twenty Indians standing around watching three men dressing a beef. They all wore blankets strapped around their waists with belts. When Mr. Saunders rang the bell, the students went back into the schoolroom. Very soon thereafter, a number of shots were fired.

Looking out the window, Saunders saw Nathan Kimball, one of the butchering crew, running toward the mission house. His left arm was hanging limp and bleeding. Horrified, Saunders cried, "I must go to my family!"

In the living room of the mission house, Catherine Sager was standing at the window, watching what was taking place outside. Unarmed and working alone at the gristmill, Walter Marsh was shot down in the first moments of the attack. But Jacob Hoffman put up an effective resistance.

Picking up an ax, he swung it wildly as half a dozen yelling Cayuses closed in on him, managing to keep them at bay and wounding several before they overpowered him. Before Catherine's terror-glazed eyes, one of the wounded Cayuses, whose right foot had been split with the ax, pounced on Hoffman's body and disemboweled him.

Meanwhile, standing beside Catherine, Mother Whitman saw Judge Saunders running toward the kitchen door, apparently meaning to find out what had happened there. She waved at him and screamed, "Go back! "Go back!"

He turned around, his attention drawn by what was happening in the yard, saw the Cayuses overwhelming Jacob Hoffman, and ran back toward the schoolroom. Just as he got to the steps leading up to the door, a Cayuse brave seized him. Saunders shook him off. Another came at him. Again Saunders fought free. Then a rifle shot sounded. He staggered. There came another shot, and another, and suddenly he was down, with a dozen or so Cayuses plunging knives into his body, striking at his head with their tomahawks and war clubs, mashing it into pieces. Sickened, Catherine closed her eyes and sobbed as she buried her face in Mother Whitman's shoulder.

Making his escape from the Indians who had attacked him, Nathan Kimball crossed the yard and was let into the mission house through the west door. As he clasped his bleeding arm, he cried out, "The Indians are killing us! I don't know what the damned Indians want to kill me for. I never did anything to them! Get me some water!"

Catherine Sager realized that her ten-year-old sister, Elizabeth, was staring strangely at Mr. Kimball. Suddenly Elizabeth giggled. To Catherine's sister, hearing a normally very religious man swear was a greater shock than the brutal killings, which were beyond her understanding. From the look on her face, she seemed to expect that Mother Whitman would rebuke him for using profanity in the presence of children. She seemed quite surprised that, instead of scolding Mr. Kimball, Mother Whitman got water and began washing his wounded arm.

Andrew Rodgers, the young bachelor teacher, had been down at the Walla Walla River, getting a pail of water, when the shooting began. Hidden by the trees and bushes along the banks, he could have escaped detection and fled to Fort Walla Walla for safety. Instead, he rushed back to the mission house, running a gauntlet of gunfire from the Indians. Shot through the wrist and grazed behind the ear by a tomahawk, he made it to safety.

Mother Whitman's concern now was for the fate of her husband, Catherine knew. With the Cayuses gone from the kitchen, Narcissa unbolted the door from the living room side and went into the room. She was horrified to find Marcus and John Sager lying on the floor in pools of blood. At that moment, three women who were living in the emigrant house—Mrs. Hall, Mrs. Hays, and Mrs. Saunders—burst in through the north kitchen door. With their help, Narcissa half carried and half dragged Marcus into the living room and placed him on the settee. Catherine watched her fasten the door, return to the settee, and place a pillow under his head. Kneeling over him, she tried to stop the blood that was flowing from the wound in his neck, using a towel and wood ashes from the stove.

"Do you know me?" she asked.

"Yes."

"Are you badly hurt?"

"Yes."

"Can I do anything to stop the blood?"

"No."

"Can you speak with me?"

"No."

"Is your mind at peace?"

"Yes."

By now he was speaking only in monosyllables. His words became so incoherent Catherine could not understand them. Again and again, Narcissa cried out, "That Joe! That Joe! He has done it all!"

Several times during the next hour, Joe Lewis came to the door of the living room and tried to force his way in. Even though he had a gun in his hand, when Mother Whitman opened the door, blocked it with her body, and demanded, "What do you want, Joe?" he turned on his heel and left. Soon after Andrew Rodgers entered the room, Narcissa went again to the east door to look out through its window. As she stood there, an Indian who was on the other side of the yard near the entrance to the schoolroom raised his rifle, took careful aim, and fired. Struck in the right shoulder, she clapped her hand to the wound, and fell backward to the floor. Catherine screamed, ran to her, knelt, and cradled Narcissa's head in her lap.

"Mother! Are you badly hurt?"

"Don't worry about me, dear. Look after the poor, helpless children who are depending on us." Closing her eyes, she began to pray fervently. "Lord, save these little ones! O Lord, please save them!"

The gentle Andrew Rodgers, too distracted to speak, was making sweeping motions with his hands, urging the adults and children in the room to go upstairs to the attic. Catherine protested.

"What about the sick children? Aren't we going to take them up, too?"

"Of course!" Rodgers said. "We'll carry them up one at a time!"

When Helen Mar Meek and Louise and Henrietta Sager had been carried upstairs to join those who had walked up under their own power, there were thirteen frightened people in the small room: the two wounded men, Kimball and Rodgers; five women, with Lorinda Bewley still in her sickbed; and the four Sager girls, plus Helen Mar Meek and Mary Ann Bridger.

Meanwhile, Josiah Osborn, laying the floor in the Indian room of the mission house where he and his family were living, remembered that the floor boards were not nailed down. Lifting several of them, he hid his wife, himself, and their three children under the floor, the three-foot space above giving them plenty of room.

"We lay listening to the firing," he later said, "the screams of women and children—the groans of the dying—not knowing when our turn would come. We were, however, not discovered."

Nine-year-old Nancy Osborn said, "In a few minutes our room was full of Indians, talking and laughing as if it were a holiday. The only noise we made was by my brother, Alexander, two years old. When the Indians came into the room and were directly over our heads, he said: 'Mother, the Indians are taking all our things.' Hastily she clapped her hands over his mouth and whispered he must be still."

In the schoolroom, the children quickly shut and locked the door. Francis Sager suggested that they climb up into a loft which had been built over part of the room. Since there was no stairway or ladder available, the children moved a table under the door of the loft and piled some books on it to make it reach higher. One of the older boys then climbed up and helped the girls to enter. Among them was Matilda Sager, who later said, "Frank told us all to ask God to save us. I can see him now, as he kneeled and prayed."

The children had been hiding in the loft for an hour or so when the half blood Joe Stanfield came into the room below and called for the two Manson boys and David Malin. They came down and were taken to the lodge of Nicholas Finley, which was located to the north of the main mission house. Stanfield assured the boys that because they were part Indian, they would not be harmed. Next day, Finley took the three boys to Fort Walla Walla, where they were turned over to William McBean.

Soon after Stanfield had taken the three half-blood boys to Finley's lodge, Joe Lewis entered the schoolroom looking for Francis Sager, against whom he had a special grudge. Discovering Francis and the other children in the loft, Lewis demanded that they all come down at once. When they did, he marched them out into the yard and lined them up to be shot. Since the departure of the Manson boys, ten-year-old Eliza Spalding was the only person that could understand what the Indians were saying. Convinced that they were all going to be killed, she covered her face with her apron so that she would not see them shoot her.

"There they stood in a long row," Catherine said, "their murderers leaning on their guns, waiting for the word from the chief to send them into eternity. Pity, however, moved the heart of the chief [probably *Tiloukaikt*] for, after observing their terror, he said: 'Let us not kill them.' "

The children then were taken into the Indian room. As they passed through the kitchen, Francis saw his brother, John, lying mortally wounded on the floor. He leaned over and on a sudden impulse pulled at the scarf John had stuffed into the wound. Opened up, the wound began to bleed copiously. John tried to speak but could not. He died soon afterward.

"I will follow him!" Francis said, sobbing

"If you are on our side," some of the Indians taunted Joe Lewis, "you must kill this boy to prove it."

Joe Lewis grabbed Francis by the nose, jerked him forward, and called him "a bad boy." In their hiding place under the floor, the Osborns heard Francis pleading for his life.

"Oh, Joe, don't shoot me!"

Then came the crack of a gun, as Lewis proved his loyalty to the red men. Francis fell at the entrance of the north door leading out of the Indian room.

In the meantime, Mrs. Saunders, not knowing what had happened to her husband and to the Whitmans, and fearful for the safety of all the

women and children, decided to make a desperate appeal to Chief
Tiloukaikt through Nicholas Finley. John Manson was at the lodge when
she arrived, and later gave an account of what happened.

"Soon Mrs. Saunders came up to the lodge where Mrs. Finley, an Indian woman, her sister and several other Indian women were standing.
Besides the Cayuse Indian women, there were some Walla Walla Indian
men. The women seemed friendly to Mrs. Saunders.

"About four hundred feet away from the lodge was a hill that had three
Indians on it. One of the Indians rode down to kill Mrs. Saunders, but
Mrs. Finley expostulated with him and he rode off. Then Chief *Tiloukaikt*
rode down, shaking his hatchet over his head. He threatened Mrs. Saunders with it, but again Mrs. Finley urged him to desist and he rode off.
Then Edward *Tiloukaikt,* the oldest son of the Chief, rode down very
rapidly, shaking his tomahawk over his head and that of Mrs. Saunders
with fury. She had sunk down on a pile of matting in front of the lodge.
But the Indian women shamed him and talked to him. Then he rode off.

"Mrs. Saunders then came over to me and kneeled down. She begged me
to interpret for her to the Chiefs, as she did not understand the language of
the natives. She said: 'Tell the Chiefs that if the Doctor and men were bad,
I did not know it. My heart is good and I want to live. If they will spare
my life, I will make caps, coats, and pantaloons for them.' "

John Manson interpreted for her as she pleaded with *Tiloukaikt* for the
life of her husband and for the women and children.

"What do they say, John?" she asked anxiously.

"They are talking about it."

After some consultation, *Tiloukaikt* and the other chiefs agreed that
none of the women and children would be killed. Mrs. Saunders then
begged him to let all who were in the main mission house go to the emigrant house. *Tiloukaikt* gave his consent.

"Won't you go home with me, John?" she asked.

"I will ask."

Saying a curt "No," *Tiloukaikt* ordered Stanfield, who was also there, to
take Mrs. Saunders back to her quarters and get her some meat. John
Manson continued:

"Then Mrs. Saunders rose from her knees and went with Joe Stanfield.
They went to Dr. Whitman's house. Very soon, several shots were fired
there. Mr. Finley came and told us that three more had been killed . . ."

After searching the main floor of the Whitman home for Mrs. Whitman
and other members of the family, the rampaging Indians finally came to
the door leading to the attic room. This had been locked from the inside,
but the Indians soon smashed it open.

"We thought our time had come," Catherine later said.

While the Indians were still breaking down the door, Nathan Kimball said that if they only had a gun, they could keep them at bay. Someone remembered that there was the barrel of a broken gun in the attic room. Andrew Rodgers got it and held it over the railing of the stairwell. As soon as the Indians, who began ascending the stairs, saw the gun barrel, they hastily retreated. All was quiet for half an hour.

"We began to think that the Indians had left," Catherine said, "when we heard footsteps in the rooms below, and a voice at the bottom of the stairs called Mr. Rodgers. He would not answer for a time. Others finally prevailed on him to speak, remarking, 'God maybe has raised us up a friend.' "

The Indian was *Tamsucky*. It had been he, Narcissa was sure, who had tried to break into her bedroom one night after her husband left for the East in October 1842. Catherine recognized him as one of the Indians who had killed Judge Saunders, so she advised caution. But Narcissa was so eager to grasp any offer of aid in this hour of desperation that she was ready to listen to any friendly voice. After some consultation, the adults in the upstairs room decided that they should listen to what *Tamsucky* had to say.

"He told Rodgers that he had just arrived on the mission grounds, knew nothing of the terrible events which had taken place, and was offering his help," Catherine recalled. "Mr. Rodgers told him to come upstairs. He replied that he was afraid we had white men there who would kill him. Mr. Rodgers assured him of his safety. He then asked for Mother, and was told that she was badly hurt. Mr. Rodgers finally went to the doorway and talked with him and succeeded in having him come where we were. He shook hands with us all and seemed very sorry Mother was hurt; condoled with her until he won her confidence."

Tamsucky then passed on the terrifying information that the Indians were planning on burning the mission house down and that Mrs. Whitman and those with her should leave immediately for the lodge of an Indian who lived ten miles away. Saying that she was in no condition to travel, Narcissa refused to go. *Tamsucky* then told her to go to the emigrant house and spend the night there.

Eager to return to their families, the three women—Mrs. Hays, Mrs. Hall, and Mrs. Saunders—hastily left. Going with them was Lorinda Bewley, who had arisen from her sickbed. Rodgers helped Narcissa down the stairs. She was so weak from the loss of blood that she had to lie down on the settee. With her was Elizabeth Sager, who noticed how Narcissa averted her face when she saw her husband, who was still alive but unconscious. The sight of his bloody, mutilated head was too horrible to endure.

Remaining in the upstairs room because he did not trust *Tamsucky* was Nathan Kimball, along with Catherine, Louise, and Henrietta Sager, Helen Mar Meek, and Mary Ann Bridger.

Downstairs, the Indians ordered Rodgers to help carry Narcissa Whitman to the emigrant house. They moved from the living room through the kitchen and out the north door. Elizabeth Sager, who was following, noted that her brother John's body was lying across the doorway. As soon as the settee bearing Narcissa cleared the doorway, several Indians standing in the yard started firing their guns. As Elizabeth remembered:

"I was still on the sill when a shot from a row of Indians standing there struck Mrs. Whitman on the cheek. I saw the bullet as it hit her. Mr. Rodgers set the settee down on the platform at the doorway, saying, 'Oh, my God!' and fell. He, too, had been struck by a bullet."

As Elizabeth turned to flee to the upstairs room to rejoin her sister Catherine, she passed through the living room, where she slipped in a pool of blood. Upstairs, she stammered out her story of what had happened.

All the adults and children in the room were stunned into silence by the horror of what had happened.

"The terror of that moment cannot be expressed," Elizabeth said later. "There were no tears, no shrieks."

After a volley of bullets had been fired into the bodies of Narcissa Whitman and Andrew Rodgers, one of the Indians turned over the settee and dumped Narcissa's body into the mud. With fiendish delight, another Indian lifted up her head by grabbing her hair, and lashed her face with his braided leather quirt. Narcissa died at the time of the attack or shortly thereafter. Though mortally wounded, Andrew Rodgers lingered for several hours in a conscious condition.

"As soon as it became dark, the Indians left for their lodges," Nancy Osborn recounted. "Everything became still. It was the stillness of death."

The only sound breaking that stillness, Nancy recalled, was the groans of the dying. Dr. Whitman died about nine o'clock that evening; Rodgers, a little later.

"All we could hear were the dying groans of Mr. Rodgers, who lay within six feet of me. We heard him say, 'Come, Lord Jesus, come quickly.' Afterwards he said faintly, 'Sweet Jesus.' Then fainter and fainter came the moans until they ceased all together."

Killed by the Cayuses that bloody day were nine people—six men, two boys, and one woman. More killings were to come.

6

For Catherine Sager, Monday night was filled with terror. Though only thirteen years old, she was trying to be a mother to her three younger sisters and the two half-blood girls, as well as nurse for the wounded adult, Nathan Kimball. Three of the girls were ill and Kimball was in too much pain to be of any help.

"The Indians seemed to be making preparations to set fire to the house. We heard them ask for fire and splitting up kindlings. We fully expected to perish in the flames but this was more desirable than to be killed by the savages. Night came on. The Indians seemed to have left. We sat on the bed hardly daring to breathe in our fright. I took all the children on one bed. Their clothes were saturated with blood where they had lain on the bed with Mrs. Whitman. I tried to soothe them, but they were perishing for water. They cried almost all night."

Finally, one by one, the children fell asleep, leaving Catherine and Kimball still awake. After hearing the yowls of the cats, which had not been fed, and the striking of the hours by the clock in the room below, Catherine, out of utter exhaustion, at last lapsed into sleep.

When day began to break, Kimball awakened Catherine and told her that he was going to try to go to the river for a pail of water. Before leaving, he asked Catherine to bandage his arm, which was paining him greatly.

"But we have no cloth for bandages," Catherine objected.

"Sure we do. Tear up one of the bed sheets."

"Oh, we can't do that! Mother Whitman wouldn't like it."

"Child, don't you know that Mrs. Whitman is dead and will never have any use for the sheets?" Kimball scolded. "Do what I tell you and bandage my arm."

Reluctantly, Catherine tore up a sheet.

Disguising himself as a blanketed Indian, Nathan Kimball took a pail and headed for the river. He reached it in safety, but as he was about to return he noticed some Indians nearby. Fearful of being detected, he hid in a clump of bushes flanking the river, remaining there all day. Near sundown, thinking the Indians were gone, he picked up the pail of water and started back to the house. Just as he was climbing over the rail fence,

Edward *Tiloukaikt,* eldest son of the Cayuse chief, saw him and immediately shot him.

As he fell, the Indian gave a brutal laugh.

Evidently death came to Kimball instantly. He thus became the tenth victim of the massacre.

Attracted by the crying of the children early that Tuesday morning, some Indians came to the foot of the stairway leading to the attic and inquired what was the matter. Catherine begged them to get water, which one did. He also got them some bread. Because the children were crying for more water, which the Indian refused to get, Catherine decided to go for it herself.

"I could not bear to hear the piteous calls for water."

Going downstairs, she found her shoes where she had left them the day before, picked up a pail, and went to the river. As she returned, "some Indians were sitting on the fence. One of them pointed his gun at me. I was terribly frightened, but walked on. An Indian sitting near him knocked the gun up and it went off in the air."

Although she had borne up well until now, her narrow escape and sight of the bodies in the house and yard combined to bring on a fit of weeping with the other children when she returned to the upstairs room.

"We were weeping over the slain when Joe Stanfield came in. He told us to stop that noise; that they were dead and it would do them no good, and if the Indians saw us crying, they would be mad."

Stanfield told Catherine to take the children to the emigrant house. Since three of the children were too ill to walk, Catherine carried six-year-old Louise, and Elizabeth managed to carry four-year-old Henrietta. These four, with Mary Ann Bridger, started for the emigrant house. Helen Mar Meek had to be left behind, but Catherine assured her that she would return and get her. The people in the emigrant house saw the four children approaching and rushed out to meet them.

"For a few moments, we wept together," Catherine said. Accompanied by one of the women, Catherine hurried back to get Helen Mar. "We found her sitting on the bed, surrounded by Indians, screaming at the top of her voice."

She thought she had been deserted.

Sometime during the day, Tuesday, all the survivors of the massacre were brought together in the emigrant house. Included were the Canfield family and two sick men, Crocket Bewley and Amos Sales. They numbered some forty people.

Meanwhile, other survivors had escaped, some of them suffering terrible hardships.

The carpenter, Peter D. Hall, had been working in the room being added to the east end of the mission building when the attack began. When the sound of firing was heard by the Indians outside, several of them rushed to attack Hall, one carrying a gun; he raised it, aimed, and pulled the trigger. It misfired. Hall, a physically strong man, grappled with the Indian and succeeded in tearing the gun out of his grasp. By pointing it at the Indians, he managed to keep them at bay until he crossed the yard and reached the river. Plunging boldly into the icy water, he swam for the opposite shore. None of the shots fired at him by the Cayuses hit him.

Shielded by the protective willow trees and bushes which lined the river-banks, he cautiously made his way toward Fort Walla Walla, twenty-five miles away. Traveling all night, he reached the fort early Tuesday morning. He was the first to give Hudson's Bay Company Agent William McBean news of the attack on Waiilatpu.

Since he had fled immediately after the massacre began, Hall's information was fragmentary. He reported that "the doctor and another man were killed." He could give McBean no details regarding the identity of the murderers or how the attack originated. In his excited state, he was sure that his wife and children and all the white people at Waiilatpu had been slaughtered. Not at all happy to see him, McBean found Hall greatly agitated, fearful that the Indians would seek him out at the fort and kill him. McBean said:

"He finally resolved to leave and make for The Dalles. I remarked to him that it was rash and imprudent. The fort being enclosed, doors locked day and night, and fortified with two bastions, he would be safer in it than he would be on the open plain. My arguments had no force. I then asked him if he left a wife and children at the Mission. He replied that he had, but supposed them all killed. I observed that it was only a supposition— they might still be living, and that it was wrong to leave them without ascertaining their fate. With tears in his eyes, he begged and entreated me to let him go, being sure to reach The Dalles.

"Finding he was determined, I provided him with a coat, shirt, provisions and other necessaries for his voyage, and advised him to take the route less frequented by the Indians, across the Columbia, and to travel only during the night, when he would have a better chance of evading any camp by noticing their fire. I saw him safely across and the last tidings I had of him was that he had safely reached within a few miles of the Deschutes. But unfortunately having taken a canoe from the Indians and being near a rapid, which he attempted to run, the canoe overturned and he was drowned."

His body was never found.

Anxious to get more information about what had happened at Waii-latpu, McBean sent his interpreter, a man named Bushman, Tuesday morning to make inquiry there. Meanwhile, Nicholas Finley was preparing to leave the mission and take the three half-blood boys to Fort Walla Walla. Learning about it, Mrs. Saunders hastily wrote a note to McBean for Finley to carry in which she listed the names of eleven people she thought had been killed. Catherine, in her account of what happened on Tuesday, said that when Bushman arrived at Waiilatpu, he was so frightened by what he saw and heard that he "came only to the door and as soon as they assured him that it was so, he left."

Catherine saw Joe Stanfield busy digging a grave in the mission cemetery "three feet deep and wide enough for all to lay side by side." Until the bodies were collected on Wednesday morning for burial, they lay where each person had fallen. Some bodies had been covered with blankets.

Around two o'clock Tuesday afternoon another white man was killed by the still-bloodthirsty Cayuses. Living at the sawmill on Mill Creek fourteen miles east of the Whitman Mission were two families that cut down trees on the slopes of the Blue Mountains and milled them into timbers and lumber. Unaware of what had happened, a workman named James Young drove a team of oxen loaded with lumber from the mill site toward the mission. As he passed a Cayuse camp a mile or so from Waiilatpu, the unsuspecting man was shot down and killed. In their frenzied anger, his murderers even slaughtered the two oxen. Later, Stanfield buried the body where it fell. Hall and Young were the eleventh and twelfth victims of the massacre. There were still two more to die.

Bushman made the fifty-mile round-trip, Fort Walla Walla to Waiilatpu and back, in the same day. Next morning, McBean wrote a letter to the officials of the Hudson's Bay Company in Vancouver, relating what had happened. Pledging Bushman, who was taking the letter downriver, to absolute secrecy lest rash, premature action by the settlers endanger the lives of all the whites residing upriver, McBean specifically warned him not to tell Dr. Whitman's seventeen-year-old nephew, Perrin, who was working at The Dalles, about the massacre.

At Fort Vancouver, the letter was to be given to the man best qualified to deal with such an explosive situation, William McBean said.

That man was Peter Skene Ogden.

Never mind that the "Prince of Good Fellows and Terror of All Indians" was a Britisher living in a country now American; that he was pudgy and old and his muscles and bones were filled with an old man's aches and pains. No person living in the Pacific Northwest was as respected by the Indians of the interior as he. If the situation could be resolved without a massive shedding of white and Indian blood, he would know what to do . . .

7

Also escaping the massacre was W. D. Canfield. Being latecomers to Waii-latpu, he and his family were forced to accept makeshift accommodations in the blacksmith shop. When the attack began, Canfield was butchering a beef with Hoffman and Kimball. Catherine Sager told what happened:

"He saw his family standing in the yard and ran over toward them. As he did so, he was wounded in the side by a rifle bullet. Snatching up his youngest child, and calling his family to follow him, he rushed into the blacksmith shop. Going upstairs, he concealed himself under some old lumber and rubbish, where he lay all night."

The Indians did not pursue him. During the early part of Monday night, the half blood Joe Stanfield, who secretly was sympathetic to the whites, came and talked to him. Convinced that the Cayuses did not intend to kill the women and children, but sure that his own life would be in danger if he remained here, he decided to go to Lapwai, where he would warn the people at the Spalding Mission of what they could expect if the dissident faction of the Nez Perces joined in the uprising. Joe Stanfield gave him a good description of the 120-mile trail, which he had never been on before.

After traveling a night and a day in a northeasterly direction, he fell in with an Indian and his boy driving cattle. Since they were Nez Perces and friendly, he traveled with them to Lapwai, which he reached Saturday, December 4. There he found Mrs. Spalding, her three children, and a woman named Mary Johnson. Temporarily absent from the mission, though in the area, were her brother, Horace Hart, who had recently come out from Ohio, and a man named Jackson. After being received into the home, Canfield asked, "Has Mr. Spalding yet come?"

"No," Mrs. Spalding answered. "But we expect him any day."

"I have heavy tidings. They are all murdered at the doctor's."

After a long silence, Eliza Spalding got to her feet and said in an un-faltering voice, "I was not prepared for this, but go on, sir. Let me hear the worst."

"Mrs. Whitman and many others have been murdered by the Cayuses. Without doubt, your husband shared their fate."

When Eliza Spalding said that she must inform the Indians at Lapwai of what had happened, Canfield protested, for he feared that they might do what the Cayuses had done. But Mrs. Spalding had faith in the character of the Nez Perces. Summoning two of her most loyal Indian friends, Timothy and Eagle-from-the-Light, she told them what had happened. Sending a messenger a few miles up the valley to William Craig's home, she asked what she should do. Craig immediately replied, "Come here. We will protect you."

By then it was Sunday. Hart and Jackson had returned; both they and Canfield urged her to move at once to the protection of the William Craig home. But so strong were her religious convictions of strict Sunday observance, she refused to do so, saying, "We will rest on the Sabbath, for he that obeyeth that commandment shall be rewarded."

Her reward before the day was over was the arrival of a friendly Indian from Waiilatpu, who gave her the good news that her husband had been in the Umatilla area at the time of the massacre, that he had been told about it, and that he had escaped from a party of Cayuses seeking to kill him. Supposedly, he was headed for the safety of the Willamette Valley. So far as ten-year-old Eliza was concerned, she was a captive and still alive, for her services as an interpreter were valuable to the dissident Indians.

Monday morning, December 6, William Craig and a large party of Nez Perces arrived to escort the Spalding family to the Craig home. Shortly after they left the mission, a rowdy band of Nez Perces—later said to be members of Old Joseph's band—looted and set fire to the buildings. When told of it, Mrs. Spalding did not believe for a minute that her husband's dear friend in Christ Chief Joseph would stand for such a thing.

Her good friends Timothy and Eagle-from-the-Light already were on their way to Waiilatpu, where they intended to take young Eliza out of the hands of the hostiles and return her to her mother's arms . . .

Visiting Waiilatpu in early October, the nationally known artist John Mix Stanley had missed seeing the Whitmans because they had gone over to the Umatilla River to meet an emigrant train. Because he planned to spend several weeks at the Tshimakain Mission in the Spokane country, Stanley promised to return to Waiilatpu late in November. Accompanied by his Spokane Indian guide, Solomon, who spoke English, Nez Perce, and Chinook jargon, as well as his own tongue, John Mix Stanley camped Tuesday evening, November 30, on the lower Walla Walla River, twenty miles from the Whitman Mission. Moving on, next morning, the artist and his guide-interpreter were within six miles of the mission when they met an Indian boy and woman who gave them the frightening news of the massacre. He would surely be killed, the woman warned, if he rode on to Waiilatpu.

Hastily reining their horses around, Stanley and Solomon headed back toward Fort Walla Walla. Before they had ridden very far, they were over-taken by an armed Cayuse brave, who demanded of Stanley, "Are you a Boston man?"

"No, no!" Solomon answered quickly, for he knew if Stanley admitted to being an American, the Cayuse would kill him. "Not Boston man."

"What, then?"

As quick-witted as his guide, John Mix Stanley, who came from Ohio, said glibly, "A Buckeye."

To the Cayuse, this was a kind of man he had never met before. "Oh," he grunted. "Englishman?"

"Yes, a Buckeye is sort of an Englishman. But definitely not a Boston man."

Satisfied with the identification, the Cayuse let them go in peace. Leaving the trail and hiding until nightfall, lest they meet other hostile Indians, the two men reached Fort Walla Walla Thursday morning, December 2. When McBean told them what he knew about the massacre, Stanley immediately sat down and wrote a letter to the Walkers and Eells, missionaries at Tshimakain, informing them of it, and dispatched Solomon to carry it to them in all haste. Told by McBean that the Cayuses had sent parties to the Umatilla to find and kill Spalding, and that the hostiles were rumored to be preparing attacks on white settlements as widely separated as Lapwai and The Dalles, the artist decided to linger at Fort Walla Walla until the situation stabilized.

In doing so, he became involved with the lives of an entire family . . .

In their escape from Waiilatpu, Josiah Osborn, his wife, their nine-year-old daughter, Nancy, their four-year-old son, John, and their two-year-old son, Alexander, suffered a harrowing nightmare of hardships. While hiding under the floor of the Indian room, they had heard the shooting of Mrs. Whitman, Andrew Rodgers, and Francis Sager, followed by the prolonged dying groans of Rodgers, which had lasted until late in the evening. Mrs. Osborn had just that day arisen from the sickbed in which she had lain for three weeks. John, barely recovered from the measles, was too weak to do much walking; Alexander was too small to toddle far over rough ground. Even so, the Osborns decided that an effort must be made to slip out of the house after dark and walk the twenty-five miles to Fort Walla Walla through the freezing night.

As Nancy remembered it, they left about ten o'clock that Monday night. Groping around the Indian room for clothing, blankets, and food, they could find but little and did not linger long.

"Taking John on my back and Alexander in my arms, we started," Osborn said. "We could see no trail and not even the hand before the face.

We had to feel out the trail with our feet. My wife almost fainted but staggered along."

In addition to carrying his two sons, Osborn also had to carry some of the bedding and provisions. Nancy helped with what she could, but Mrs. Osborn was too weak to aid in any way. When they came to the ford of the Walla Walla River, they found the water waist-deep and icy cold. Osborn had to cross it five times, taking each of the little boys, his nine-year-old daughter, and finally his wife to the other side. Of this last trip, he said: "My wife in her great weakness came near washing down, but held to my clothes, I bracing myself with a stick."

After traveling two miles or so, Mrs. Osborn fainted. Since they could go no farther, they lay down in the cold mud, concealed by the trees and bushes, and tried to sleep. When daylight came, they could hear Indians coming and going along the nearby trail. The temperature was near freezing. All day Tuesday was spent in hiding. Osborn said, "The day seemed a week."

On Tuesday night, November 30, they continued their slow journey. Now they left the river with its tangle of willows and shrubbery, and ventured to walk on the trail. Several small streams had to be waded. Mrs. Osborn fainted again. Of their misery that night, Osborn said:

"We crawled into the brush and frozen mud, to shake and suffer from hunger and cold without sleep. The children, too, wet and cold, called incessantly for food, but they were so shocked and frightened they did not speak loud."

Another day was spent in hiding. When Wednesday night came, Mrs. Osborn was too weak to stand. She urged her husband to take one of the boys and go to the fort for help. They were then at least fifteen miles from their destination. At first Osborn rejected any suggestion of leaving his wife and the children, but she insisted. Finally he agreed to go, as this seemed the only possible way all could be saved. Taking John, whom he had to carry, with him, Osborn started for Fort Walla Walla. Since Osborn himself had recently had the measles, he found it necessary to rest frequently. He arrived at the fort early Thursday morning, December 2. To his dismay, he was given a cool reception by William McBean.

"He gave me about a half pint of tea and two small biscuits," Osborn said. "When we had got warm, I asked for assistance to bring in my family, but was unable to procure any."

Since McBean had sent his interpreter, Bushman, to Fort Vancouver with news of the massacre, he had only two hired men and two visiting Catholic priests with him at the fort. He had heard the rumor that one band of Cayuses was heading toward Lapwai to kill the Spaldings, while a second was going to The Dalles to kill Perrin Whitman. McBean was frightened by the possibility of the Cayuses attacking Fort Walla Walla, especially if they learned that he was harboring one of the Americans and his family who had escaped from Waiilatpu.

"I begged Mr. McBean for horses to get my family," Osborn said, "for food, blankets and clothing to take to them, and to take care of my little child till I could bring my family to his fort. Mr. Hall had come in Monday night, I heard, but McBean would not have an American in his fort and had put him over the Columbia River. He would not let me have horses, or anything for my wife and children. He said I must go to the Saint Anne Mission and seek refuge with the Catholic missionaries."

The St. Anne Mission was fifty miles away to the southeast. Getting there would mean passing back through the heart of Cayuse country. In desperation, Osborn appealed to the priests.

"I next begged the priests to show pity, as my wife and children must perish, and the Indians would no doubt kill me, but with no better success. I then begged to leave my child, but they refused."

It was at this moment, when every desperate plea for help had been rejected, that the "Buckeye" artist, John Mix Stanley, and his Spokane guide-interpreter, Solomon, arrived at the fort. When Osborn asked Stanley for help, the artist's response was immediate and positive. He would be glad to give Osborn food and clothing, he said. He also offered the use of his two horses. Because he felt it urgent to send Solomon to Tshimakain immediately, he could not let the Spokane Indian act as a guide for Osborn. But surely, he said, McBean would send one of his hired men along to help Osborn find his family.

Cravenly, McBean proposed a compromise. If Osborn would promise to take his family to the St. Anne Mission on the Umatilla, he would supply a Walla Walla Indian as a guide. Even if Osborn did not find his family, McBean said, he must go to the Catholic mission, not return here. To make sure that Osborn would be accepted and cared for at St. Anne's, McBean said magnanimously, he would have one of the priests write a letter introducing Osborn to Bishop Blanchet.

Since there was no alternative, Osborn accepted.

Wanting to save his four-year-old son, John, from the ordeal of another trip, Osborn asked Stanley if he would look after the child. Certainly, Stanley said, he would be glad to. No, McBean said with incredible callousness, the child goes with you or I will not supply the guide.

Fearful of being seen by hostiles, Josiah Osborn, his son, and the Walla Walla Indian guide waited until after dark Thursday evening, December 2, before setting out. By midnight they reached the spot where he thought he had left his family. Search as he would, he could not find them. He dared not shout for fear of discovery by hostiles. But with the coming of daylight

Friday morning, he did find them—"almost perished with hunger and thirst."

After giving them food, drink, and warm clothing, Osborn put his wife and three children on the horses, and, with the Walla Walla Indian guide, the family set out for the St. Anne Mission. They had traveled only a couple of miles when they were confronted by a Cayuse, who threatened to kill them.

"Would you shame your people by killing a sick old man with a sick wife and children?" the guide said contemptuously. "Have you not shed enough innocent blood?"

"If they turn back, I will not kill them," the Cayuse said sullenly. "But if they insist on going to the Umatilla, they will be killed."

Regardless of the promise he had made to William McBean, Osborn knew he had no choice but to go back to Fort Walla Walla. Reaching the post Saturday morning, the Osborns at first were refused admittance. When Mrs. Osborn declared that she "would lie down and die at the gate, but would not leave," McBean reluctantly let them in and provided them with a room.

"We had hardly got warm before McBean came in and wanted me to leave my family with him, and go down to the Willamette Valley by myself. But I refused to leave the fort and would not go."

So the Osborn family stayed at Fort Walla Walla as guests of the grudging Hudson's Bay Company until the rescue party led by Peter Skene Ogden took them downriver a month later. According to a statement made by John Mix Stanley, Agent William McBean would not even provide them with blankets until Osborn signed a promissory note guaranteeing payment. Because of his exposure and suffering during the two trips with his father, four-year-old John Osborn took sick and died shortly thereafter—the third child lost by Josiah Osborn and his wife. For the rest of their lives, they would remember Waiilatpu and Fort Walla Walla with bitterness . . .

8

Because of the injuries suffered when his horse slipped and fell, Henry Spalding had lingered two days on the Umatilla after Dr. Whitman's departure Sunday afternoon. Dining with Bishop Blanchet and Father Brouillet Monday, he told Brouillet that he intended to start back to Waiilatpu on Wednesday morning.

After baptizing some Indian children near death in the Umatilla camps, Father Brouillet left St. Anne Mission Tuesday morning and rode to Waiilatpu, as he had promised Whitman he would do. Arriving at *Tiloukaikt*'s village early in the evening of that day, November 30, he was horrified by what he saw.

With the assistance of Mrs. Saunders, who now was acting as the third mother of the five Sager sisters, and Joe Stanfield, who dug a mass grave, Father Brouillet gave the victims a Christian burial service, reading the Roman Catholic rites in Latin.

"Father Brouillet came back to the house to say a few words of encouragement," Mrs. Saunders said. "I offered coffee and food. He accepted the coffee, but refused the food, saying he had some with him and that he must hurry away to intercept Mr. Spalding before he should reach the Mission."

Attempting to meet Spalding and warn him of the danger he faced was risky, Father Brouillet knew. As a Catholic and a King George man, he was for the time being immune to Cayuse wrath. But they had sworn to kill Spalding and knew where he was. If they discovered Father Brouillet in the act of helping Spalding evade the fate they had decreed for him, the priest's own life might be forfeit.

Riding with him as he left Waiilatpu was a Cayuse Indian named *Camaspelo*—"Big Belly"—whom Young Chief had assigned as a guide and interpreter. As they passed through the Cayuse camp, a tall, slim, arrogant-mannered young Indian joined them. With a harsh laugh, he grunted something to *Camaspelo* in their Cayuse tongue, to which the interpreter replied with stiff civility.

"He says you ride like an old woman," *Camaspelo* said. "Even so, he will keep us company."

"Frankly, I'd rather he didn't. If we meet Spalding—"

"Do not say that name so he can hear you! He is Edward *Tiloukaikt,* son of the chief who plotted the massacre."

"Can you get rid of him?"

"No. But perhaps I can draw the poison out of his sting."

Unsure what was meant by that remark, Father Brouillet fell silent, anxiously gazing ahead across the bare, rolling hills for sight of a rider coming in their direction. After three miles or so, *Camaspelo* gave the sign to rein in their horses. When they had done so, he asked Edward *Tiloukaikt* to share a smoke.

"They prepared the calumet," Brouillet observed, "but when the moment came for lighting it, there was nothing to make fire. 'You have a pistol,' *Camaspelo* said to Edward *Tiloukaikt.* 'Fire it and we will light.' This was done and then Edward absent-mindedly neglected to reload his pistol."

A few minutes later, the three men saw Spalding galloping toward them. Shaking Father Brouillet's hand, Spalding asked, "Have you been to the doctor's?"

"Yes."

"What news?"

Giving Edward *Tiloukaikt* a sidelong glance, Father Brouillet answered tersely, "Sad news, I fear."

"Have more of the sick children died?"

From the way Edward was glowering at Spalding, Father Brouillet suspected that the young Cayuse was debating whether to kill him now or ride back to the Cayuse camp to confer with his elders. Not wanting to upset either Edward or Spalding, Brouillet spoke to *Camaspelo* in French, which the friendly Indian understood while Edward and Spalding did not.

"Beg him, in my name, not to kill Mr. Spalding."

After the translation of his appeal into Cayuse, Edward hesitated, grunted a sullen reply, then wheeled his horse around and rode away.

"He says he cannot take it upon himself to spare Spalding's life," *Camaspelo* said grimly. "He is going to consult with his father and the other Indians."

"Thank heaven! That gives us a little time!"

Quickly Father Brouillet told Spalding what had happened. As if struck with a physical blow, the missionary reeled in the saddle, his face going chalk-white. "The Cayuses have killed the doctor! Oh, God, they will kill me if I go to Waiilatpu! What shall I do?"

"From what I have heard, they're sending war parties out in all directions to kill all the Americans they can find. I would advise you to head west to The Dalles. If you reach there in safety, you can warn them to expect an attack."

Giving the Reverend Henry Spalding what food he had—half a loaf of bread and a small chunk of cooked beef—Father Brouillet shook his hand. "Go with God, dear brother! I'll pray for you!"

Without a word, Spalding reined his horse around and rode at a long gallop directly west through the gray, chill, overcast day. Trying to pretend that nothing out of the ordinary had happened, Brouillet and *Camaspelo* rode on toward the St. Anne Mission. Within twenty minutes, three armed Cayuse braves overtook them and started haranguing the interpreter in angry tones. As they did so, they kept staring at the priest, threatening him with hostile gestures. But they made no move against him, spinning their horses around presently and riding off in the direction Spalding had taken.

"I told them it was not you who warned *Tai-tam-nat* Spalding," *Camaspelo* said. "I told them I warned him. They threatened to kill me."

"Thank God they didn't!"

"They fear Young Chief and Five Crows. But now I am troubled, Father. I told a lie. Will I go to hell?"

"I think not," Father Brouillet said with a weak smile. "Tonight, I will pray for your absolution . . ."

At that time of year, the Walla Walla Valley was often covered with a dense blanket of near-freezing fog. Closing in on Spalding now as he rode west along the trail toward The Dalles, it formed a protective cover so impenetrable that he could not be seen a dozen feet away. Recovering from the initial shock of the tragic news, he conquered his impulse to think only of his own safety, and changed his plans. After he had ridden a few miles in a westerly direction, his concern for his family at Lapwai—coupled with the firm belief that the Christianized Nez Perces there would not turn against the whites—induced him to ride north, then east up the valley of the Touchet River, until he was traveling in the opposite direction from that his pursuers thought he had taken.

Riding all night Wednesday, hiding during the daylight hours on Thursday, then riding after darkness came that night, Spalding covered some forty miles before weariness forced him to lie down and rest. Because he neglected to hobble his horse, it got away, leaving him afoot in freezing December weather, still ninety miles from home. For food, he had the bread and meat that Father Brouillet had given him, but this was soon gone. His ill-fitting shoes, a gift from a missionary barrel sent out to Lapwai, pinched so badly that he was forced to discard them and wrap his leggins around his feet. Still lame from his recent injury, he limped painfully. His blankets were too heavy to carry, so he dumped them. On Friday night, he walked thirty miles. After resting the next day:

"Saturday night I made thirty miles more. My feet suffered from the frozen ground. I avoided the places of encampment and forded the streams far from the trail, lest the Cayuse might be waylaying. I secreted myself on the Sabbath—and hunger, pain in my feet, and weakness were very great; I wanted sleep, but could get none, for the cold. From the moment I stopped traveling in the morning until I started at night, I shook to the center of every bone with cold."

Feeling that Timothy could be trusted if any Indian could, he headed for the Nez Perce village located near the mouth of Alpowa Creek on the south side of the Snake River, reaching it after dark Sunday evening. A heavy rain was falling as he cautiously sought out Timothy's lodge.

Because of the rain and cold, most of the dogs that usually roamed about an Indian village at night had sought shelter inside the tepees, so Spalding was able to creep close to what he thought was Timothy's lodge. The Indians inside were holding religious services; he could hear them singing and praying.

"In the prayer, I heard the speaker name Doctor and Mrs. Whitman as killed, and myself as probably. But he named no one killed at my place. Oh, what an angel of mercy to the human family is hope!"

Though encouraged that the Nez Perces in this village still clung to the Christian faith, Spalding was afraid to reveal himself to anyone but Timothy. Not finding him, and being discovered and snarled at by dogs, he made a hasty retreat from the village, limping down to the sandy beach of the dark, wide, rapids-filled river.

By good fortune, he found a canoe, rowed across to the north shore, and made his way east over an extremely rocky trail. Going up the Clearwater, he found another canoe, crossed to the south bank of that river, and by dawn was just five miles from home. There he was discovered by a Nez Perce woman, who, after not recognizing him at first because of his haggard appearance, finally did, and notified her husband. Soon the half-frozen, exhausted, starving man was given dry clothes, hot food, and a warm bed.

Spalding had not found Timothy in the Alpowa village because Timothy had gone to Waiilatpu to procure the release of young Eliza. When she saw the kindly old Christian chief, her friend ever since her birth, she wept for joy, blending her tears with the ones he was shedding unashamedly.

"Poor Eliza!" he said as he picked her up in his arms. "Don't cry! You shall see your mother!"

Despite the respect the Cayuses had for Timothy and much as they desired his services as a spokesman for peace, no argument he could make would induce them to release the ten-year-old girl. In a sense, she was the most valuable hostage they held, for of all the captives she was the most fluent in the Indian tongue, having heard and spoken it all her life; thus she was extremely useful as an interpreter who could be trusted to tell the truth in their negotiations with the whites. But at least Timothy could tell her anxious parents that she was safe.

Reunited at last with his wife and three of their children at Lapwai, Henry Spalding concentrated on doing what he could to preserve the lives of young Eliza and the other captives. His immediate fear was that Americans living in the Willamette Valley would raise a force of volunteers and send it upriver to punish the Indians. In a letter to Bishop Blanchet, he wrote:

> My daughter is yet a captive, I fear, but in the hands of our merciful Heavenly Father. Two Indians have gone for her. We do not wish the Americans to come from below to avenge the wrong. The Nez Perces held a meeting yesterday. They pledged themselves to protect us from the Cayuses, if we would prevent the Americans from coming up to avenge the murders. This we have pledged to do, and for this we beg for the sake of our lives at this place and at Mr. Walker's. By all means keep quiet, and send no war reports; send nothing but proposals for peace.

Ever since the Joint Occupancy Treaty had been terminated and the country south of the 49th Parallel ceded to the United States, the Hudson's Bay Company factors of the area had devoted their energies to winding up business affairs. Conflicts between Indians and Americans in the region were not their concern. But in Fort Vancouver, the Company headquarters, Peter Skene Ogden reacted to the tragedy with the coolheadedness that had long marked Company dealings with the Indians.

Two decades had passed since Ogden had made his grueling treks across the Snake River country. And the years had taken their toll. Domesticated at last by his lovely Salish Indian wife, Julia, who had gone with him on most of his travels, borne him ten children, and now was making a comfortable home for him within the walls of the most civilized post in the Pacific Northwest, he could have said this was not his problem, sent Oregon's Governor Abernethy a sympathetic note, and gone back to his paperwork.

Being Peter Skene Ogden, he did no such thing.

Instead, he ordered three bateaux filled with trade goods drawn from Company stores. He sent a brief note to the governor requesting that he make no move that might jeopardize ransom negotiations. Then he stepped into the lead bateau and headed upriver.

His protective force, if such it could be called, consisted of sixteen French-Canadians—men notorious for their lack of enthusiasm when it came to fighting Indians—and his well-earned reputation for never making a promise he did not keep . . .

9

For the survivors, the ordeal was far from over. In all, forty-seven captives were being held by the Cayuses, and during the chaotic week following the massacre not a day passed that their lives were not endangered. Though the nominal head of the Cayuse tribe, Chief *Tiloukaikt,* had promised on the second day that there would be no more killings, his control of such bloodthirsty men as Joe Lewis, *Tamsucky, Tomahas,* and *Ish-ish-kais-kais* was very shaky.

Called Frank Escaloom by the whites, to whom he had once proclaimed himself a Christian, *Ish-ish-kais-kais* had become savagely violent, shooting Judge Saunders, killing the tailor Isaac Gilliland, wounding Narcissa Whitman, and killing Nathan Kimball as he was returning from the river with water. Now he was demanding that he be given one of the young white women to take to his lodge. *Tamsucky* wanted a white woman, too. Chief *Tiloukaikt's* son Edward was rebelling against his father, for he had lost face among the young men when he had failed to kill Spalding; he vowed to regain it by either slaying a captive, taking a white woman, or both.

Opposing the younger leaders' rash demands that all the whites be killed were warnings given by Stickus that he would not sanction murder, by Timothy and Eagle-from-the-Light that the Nez Perces would defend the American missionaries in their area, and by a mild-mannered, religious, older Cayuse chief called "Beardy" because of the unusual growth of hair on his face among a people normally without beards.

With the harvest of grain, fruit, and vegetables finished, and the mission well supplied with beef cattle, milk cows, sheep, and swine, both the captives and the Indians dipped freely into the stores of supplies laid up at the mission to meet the needs of the coming winter. All day long and late into the night, the Indians crowded into the rooms occupied by the women and children, requesting food and clothing. Young Eliza Spalding was exhausted by the demands for her services.

"All day long she was here and there interpreting every silly thing the natives wished to say to the captives," Catherine said, "sitting for hours at the mill in order to interpret for the men at work. The exposure, with anxiety for the fate of her father and mother, weighed on her till she gave out. Taking a fever, she lay very low for days."

By the conciliatory nature of his actions, Chief *Tiloukaikt* appeared to regret the violence committed by his people and began to act as if he wanted to make peace with the white man's God. At the sawmill fourteen miles east of the mission, the two families grew concerned over the prolonged absence of James Young, who had headed for the mission with a wagonload of lumber Tuesday, November 30, and had not been heard from since. After dark on Sunday evening, December 5, his brother, Daniel Young, arrived at Waiilatpu, somehow managing to pass the Cayuse village without being detected. At the emigrant house, Mrs. Saunders gave him the sad news of his brother's death. She suggested that if any Cayuses who did not know him found him there, he might escape their wrath by pretending to be an Englishman. But Chief *Tiloukaikt,* who soon discovered his presence, was not fooled.

"You have done a bad thing," *Tiloukaikt* said, "in traveling on the Sabbath. The women in this house also have done a bad thing, sewing and making shirts on the Lord's Day. This must cease."

If the captives found it strange that *Tiloukaikt* condemned traveling and sewing on Sunday after he had countenanced murdering the white missionaries, they had the good sense not to point out the inconsistencies in his reasoning. Truth was, the Cayuses were beginning to realize how dependent upon the skills of Americans they had become. Though they had developed a taste for bread, their lack of interest in working at the gristmill caused Dr. Whitman not to bother teaching them how to grind wheat and corn into flour. Learning that Daniel Young's father was a miller, *Tiloukaikt* sent the young man back to the sawmill under the watchful eyes of three armed Cayuse braves, with orders to bring the two families living there down to Waiilatpu.

"If they and the other white people work well," he promised Mrs. Saunders, "you all will be permitted to go to the Willamette Valley in the spring."

Implied in the promise, Mrs. Saunders knew, was the condition that no army of American volunteers from downriver come marching into Cayuse country determined to seek vengeance for the killings. If that happened, there was no doubt in her mind that every man, woman, and child being held hostage would immediately be executed.

Under the safe-conduct given by *Tiloukaikt,* the millwright Elam Young, his wife, and his two grown sons, along with Joseph Smith, his wife, and their younger children, arrived at the mission; they were housed in the emigrant house, and went to work in the gristmill.

Meanwhile, the always hungry Cayuses kept the white women busy

cooking dishes for them that their own wives lacked the ingredients, sea-
sonings, or culinary knowledge to prepare. Still suspicious of the existence
of a white plot to poison them, even though Dr. Whitman was dead, the
Indians insisted that one of the white cooks eat a bite of whatever dish she
had prepared, just to make sure it was safe. In her well-intentioned attempt
to cement the friendship of Beardy, whom she had induced to stay with
the women and children each evening until after the young men had returned to their lodges, Mrs. Saunders very nearly precipitated the kind of
violence she was trying to avoid.

"I found some dried peaches in the storeroom," she told Catherine. "Bet
he's never eaten peach pie before. Not the way I make it, anyway. He's in
for a treat."

Finding the first piece of peach pie delicious, Beardy politely asked for
another, another, and another—which Mrs. Saunders happily supplied.
Unhappily, the dried peaches kept expanding when blended with the gas-
tric juices of Beardy's well-stuffed stomach. As a result, he became violently ill.

"He vomited the peaches and thought it was blood," Catherine said,
"and came at once to the conclusion that he had been poisoned. He resolved to have us all put to death. As soon as he recovered, he made his
decision known to his people. We were informed that they would kill us
the next day. The Indians came armed and with dark brows. Taking my
little sister in my arms, I quietly sat on the floor behind the stove determined to meet my fate with her."

Before the executions could take place, an Indian woman named Kath-
erine, who was the wife of a Hudson's Bay Company employee and could
speak some English, arrived at the mission. When she learned what had
happened, she laughed and told Beardy his ailment was his own greedi-
ness. After being convinced that he had no one to blame but himself, he
calmed down and treated the whole incident as a joke.

But neither Beardy's efforts to protect them nor *Tiloukaikt*'s promise
that there would be no more bloodshed prevented three young single
women from being raped and two more young men from being killed.

Five years ago, when *Tamsucky* had tried to break into the bedroom of
Narcissa Whitman, he had been frightened away by white employees of
the mission. But none of the whites had the power to frighten him now.

"One evening an Indian came to the house and seemed to be looking for
someone," Catherine said. "We learned that it was Miss Lorinda Bewley.
She was sick with the ague, and was lying in bed. He went to the bed and
began to fondle over her. She sprang up and sat down behind the stove. He
sat down by her side and tried to prevail upon her to be his wife. She told
him that he had a wife, and that she would not have him. Finding that

neither persuasion nor threats availed, he seized her and dragged her out of the house, and tried to place her upon his horse. He failed in this. He tried to stop her screams by placing his hand over her mouth. The contest lasted for some time, when, becoming enraged, he threw her with violence upon the ground. After perpetrating his hellish designs upon her, he ordered her to go to the house. The poor, heartbroken girl came in shaking with agitation."

Among the several white people who witnessed the brutal attack through the windows of the house was Lorinda Bewley's brother, Crocket. A year older than she, he and Amos Sales, who was about his age, had been sick in bed for a week with camp fever that had made them very weak.

"While the brute was thus maltreating his sister," Catherine said, "Mr. Bewley, unable to stand the screams, got up to go to her rescue. At our earnest request, we sent him back to bed."

Emboldened by *Tamsucky's* sexual attack on Lorinda Bewley, Edward *Tiloukaikt* the next day, Wednesday, December 8, persuaded two Cayuse braves, *Wai-e-cat* and *Clokamas,* to join him in killing Crocket Bewley and Amos Sales. Though the lives of the two young white men had been spared at the time of the massacre, the two were sitting up in bed now and feeling a little better; thus, by Edward *Tiloukaikt's* standards, they were fair game.

"One day Edward *Tiloukaikt* came into the room," Elizabeth Sager said. "He had taken a bed post and fixed it up as a war club. Eliza Spalding and I and some of the other children were in the room. Crocket Bewley and Amos Sales were lying in bed. They had the camp fever. Edward *Tiloukaikt* raised his war club and hit Crocket Bewley on the head. We children screamed and ran out of the room. Edward *Tiloukaikt* came out and said, 'Come on back, you must stay in the room till we are finished.'

"We had to go back while the Indians beat Amos Sales and Crocket Bewley over their heads till they had killed them. When they had battered their heads for quite a while, they dragged them out into the yard. Next day Joe Stanfield came with a wagon and a yoke of oxen and buried them."

The day before, Crocket Bewley had helplessly watched his sister being raped. Today, she watched in paralyzed horror as he and Amos Sales were beaten to death. Afterward, Catherine Sager said, Lorinda "hid under a bed and gave vent to her grief."

But for her, more horror was to come.

In his camp on the Umatilla River, Five Crows, who by the authority of Agent Elijah White had been appointed head chief of the Umatilla, Cayuse, and Walla Walla tribes, took no part in the massacre and did not condone the violence done by the Cayuses. But since the deed had been done and a number of unmarried young white women were in need of protection, he judged it an act of Christian decency that he take Lorinda Bewley, whom he admired, into his lodge and give her food, warmth, and shelter. After all, as he confided to his half brother Young Chief, he, like his other half brother, Old Joseph, had been baptized by the Reverend Henry Spalding in the mission church on June 16, 1843, and had been given the Christian name Hezekiah. Furthermore, he could proudly boast that he was among the twenty-one natives admitted to membership in the Presbyterian Church during the eleven years of the mission period.

At the time, Five Crows had no wife. A wealthy man, he owned over a thousand horses and many cattle, and could give a wife lots of material things to make her happy. He knew that a number of white mountain men and Hudson's Bay Company employees had taken Indian wives. Why shouldn't a well-to-do chief like himself take a white wife? No reason at all, he decided. So before he heard about *Tamsucky* raping Lorinda Bewley and Edward *Tiloukaikt* clubbing her brother to death, he sent an Indian servant to Waiilatpu with orders to fetch her to his lodge.

When Lorinda learned of the intention of Five Crows to make her his wife, she went to *Tiloukaikt* and pleaded with the chief.

"Please don't make me go to Five Crows! Let me stay at Waiilatpu with the other women."

"You will be safer at the camp of the chief," *Tiloukaikt* answered, shaking his head. "All the Indians will be glad to protect the wife of Five Crows."

"But I don't want to be his wife."

"That does not matter. What matters is that here I cannot help you. If you stay here, you will become the property of all the men who want a white woman. You will do well to marry such a great chief as Five Crows."

Even though she was still sick with fever, the Indian sent to get her insisted on starting back to the Umatilla that same day, December 9.

"There was no escape," Catherine said. "The poor girl had to go. We offered her all the comfort we could. But what is comfort under such circumstances? We saw the weeping girl ride away."

Perhaps it was just as well Lorinda left when she did, for only a short time later *Tamsucky* arrived, accompanied by Joe Lewis, a team and wagon, and a coil of rope. Having failed to abduct her alone and on horseback, he intended to bind her and take her back to his lodge in the wagon.

"They ransacked the house well," Catherine said, "not believing that she was gone."

The incident proved the correctness of *Tiloukaikt's* statement that if

Lorinda had remained at Waiilatpu, she would have become "the common property of all."

It was midafternoon when Lorinda and the Indian servant left Waiilatpu, so they had to spend the night in the open in the sparse shelter of a clump of bushes under a creek bluff, in a couple of blankets. The night was cold, with a raw southwesterly wind driving flurries of snow before it. By the time they reached the Umatilla village at noon, December 10, Lorinda's body was numb and she was shaking with alternate chills and fever.

At first, Five Crows was kind. Lifting her off her horse, he carried her into his lodge and laid her down on a bed of robes and blankets. A fire warmed her and she was given a good meal of meat stew, vegetables, and hot tea. Seeing that she was still unhappy, Five Crows asked, "Why do you shake and cry?"

"Because I am sick and don't want to be here."

"Would you rather be in the house of the Black Robes?"

"Yes! Oh, yes! Anywhere but here!"

"Very well. You may go to the house of the white men—for the rest of the day. Perhaps a few hours there will make you feel better. Tonight, I will come for you."

At the St. Anne Mission, which was located not far from the camps of Young Chief and Five Crows, Lorinda found seven white people in residence; Bishop Blanchet, Father Brouillet, two other priests, and three French-Canadians. Terrified by Chief Five Crows' statement that he would come for her tonight, Lorinda begged the bishop for protection.

"Either let me stay here or send me to Fort Walla Walla. Don't let him take me to his lodge."

"I'll do all I can for you," Bishop Blanchet said uneasily. "But you must realize we're in a precarious situation here."

"He says he's a Christian. Can't you tell him to act like one?"

"Unfortunately, he is not of the Catholic faith, Miss Bewley, so I have no moral authority over his behavior. But I assure you I'll do all I can."

Shortly after dark, Five Crows came to the mission to get her. She refused to go. Angrily, Five Crows told the priests that they were to blame for her obstinancy, and were giving her bad advice, and he was getting tired of it. Then he left.

Exhausted, ill, and emotionally drained, Lorinda was so dazed by the traumatic events of the past few days that she could not think coherently. "Tell me, please—where do I sleep?"

Motioning her to be silent with a firm, admonishing gesture, Bishop Blanchet crossed the room and conferred with the French-Canadians and his fellow priests. Though she could hear them clearly enough, even though they were keeping their voices down, she could not understand them, for they were speaking in French. Presently, Bishop Blanchet broke off the conference, came back to her, and spoke solemnly.

"We are agreed, Miss Bewley."

"On where I should sleep?"

"Yes. We are agreed that you'd better go to Five Crows' lodge."

"You can't mean that!"

"You'd better go. If you don't, he will do us all injury."

This was not happening, Lorinda thought frantically. Father Brouillet was not placing a coat over her shoulders, a fur hat on her head, and mittens on her hands, while at the same time murmuring platitudes about these being perilous times during which people did what they had to do. She was not being led by one of the French-Canadians through the snow-filled darkness to the lodge of Five Crows, who greeted her first with a kindly smile, then with a grunt of disgust as her body went rigid; she became hysterical, and began to scream.

"Take her back!" the Indian ordered. "She's no good to me screaming and shaking."

Returned to the Catholic mission, she remained there for three days and nights, unmolested by Five Crows. But just as she was beginning to believe that he had given up on the idea of taking her into his lodge, he appeared Tuesday evening, December 14, declaring that his patience was at an end.

"I want her now!" he said. "If she refuses to come with me willingly, I will take her by force."

While the priests watched without lifting a hand or saying a word to stop him, he did just that.

"She refused to go with him and he resorted to force," said Catherine Sager, one of the few people in whom Lorinda later confided her experiences during the next two weeks. "She held onto the table until her hands were skinned, but what is the strength of a frail woman in the hands of a savage, lustful man? She was taken to his lodge, and in the morning after *family prayers*, he sent her back to the Priest's house."

For two weeks, from December 14 to 28, Lorinda Bewley spent the nights with Five Crows and the days at the Mission of St. Anne. "I would return early in the morning to the bishop's house," she said, "and be violently taken away at night. The bishop provided kindly for me while at his house."

How Five Crows provided for her while in his lodge she discreetly left unsaid.

10

Meanwhile at Waiilatpu, several young men in the Cayuse village were casting lustful eyes at two teenage white girls, Mary Smith, fifteen, and Susan Kimball, sixteen. Even before the massacre, Edward *Tiloukaikt* had been smitten with one of the girls.

"Edward tried to buy Mary Smith," Mrs. Saunders said, "when he saw her at Umatilla when her family was on their way to the mission. She was a beautiful brunette and the young chief offered five horses for her."

According to Catherine Sager, *Tamsucky* called a meeting of several young Indian men and young white girls the evening after Lorinda Bewley had been taken away. With brutal logic, he pointed out the helpless condition of the young women.

"There are a lot of vagabond Indians around," he said, "who would be happy to take a young white woman into their tepees. Therefore, it would be best for each of the white girls to select a young Indian man to be her husband, who would protect her. Are you willing?"

"No!" the young women answered firmly. "We do not want Indian husbands!"

"Will you be taken by force, then? We can do that, you know."

With the memory of what had happened to Lorinda Bewley fresh in their minds, Mary Smith and Susan Kimball faced reality and reluctantly consented.

"The chief told them they were wise now," Catherine Sager said, "and called on the young men that wanted wives to come forward. Two did so: one named Clark; the other Frank. Both were influential and rich, and both were able to speak some English. The girls were told to choose between these young men. Mary Smith took Clark. Susan Kimball took Frank. Miss Kimball wept all the time."

For some reason, the young Cayuse named Clark, who was one of *Tiloukaikt*'s sons, changed his mind, deciding that he did not want a white wife after all. Eagerly, his brother Edward stepped forward and claimed Mary as his wife. Frank Escaloom—*Ish-ish-kais-kais*—took Susan. Since he had killed her father, she had good reason for weeping.

"Chief *Tiloukaikt* was opposed to any of the Indians taking white wives," Catherine said. "But by this time he had lost control over his son Edward, who was in various ways usurping his authority."

Judged by the guarded comments made later by both Catherine Sager and Mrs. Saunders, much that happened between Indian men and white women went unreported.

"In conclusion," Catherine wrote, "I would like to say that I have endeavored to present things in their true light. What has been related in the foregoing pages, is for the most part what fell under my own observation. In giving a history, I have had to touch upon a delicate subject—one that I have always avoided in conversation—namely, the treatment of the young women by the Indians. I have endeavored to present them in such a manner as to spare the feelings of those concerned. For this reason I have not related many things that would be interesting."

Of all the Indian leaders in the area, *Camaspelo*—"Big Belly"—best understood the enormity of what the dissident Cayuses had done and what the consequences of the massacre would be for their future. Though not a participant in the bloodshed, he knew that to the Americans living in Oregon an Indian was an Indian, just as to the Indians living here a white man was a white man. Blood must pay for blood, he realized. The knowledge was so depressing that on one occasion he said, "I am so fearful and discouraged, I am thinking of killing all my horses and leaving the country. All the Indians are expected to die."

But when Bishop Blanchet received the letter from Spalding begging the Catholic priest to exert his best efforts in behalf of peace, *Camaspelo* agreed that calling a council of Cayuse chiefs to discuss ways and means of preventing a murderous war might be worthwhile. With his approval, messengers were sent to the various tribal leaders, requesting them to assemble at St. Anne's Mission on Monday, December 20.

Meeting with Bishop Blanchet, Father Brouillet, and three other priests at ten o'clock that morning were the principal Cayuse chiefs, *Tiloukaikt*, Young Chief, Five Crows, and *Camaspelo*, along with a number of subchiefs and the two Nez Perces who had brought Spalding's letter. Spalding and the Nez Perces proposed a four-point program, Bishop Blanchet told the assembly, to the following effect:

1. That Americans should not come up to make war.

2. That they should send up two or three great men to make a treaty of peace.

3. That when these great men should arrive, all the captives should be released.

4. That they would offer no offense to Americans before knowing the news from the Willamette Valley.

After presenting these proposals, Bishop Blanchet invited the chiefs to speak. *Camaspelo,* who talked first, was brief, saying that while he had taken no part in the killings, he knew that Indians living in the area would suffer if war came; thus he hoped that the whites would accept the proposals, which he approved.

Father Brouillet recorded the essence of what was said. He noted that *Tiloukaikt,* who spoke next, talked for two hours. *Tiloukaikt* began by saying that "he was not a great speaker, and that his talk would not be long," then launched into a detailed review of the history of the Cayuse nation "since the arrival of the whites in the country down to the present time."

Leading the list of grievances held by the Cayuses against the whites were the deaths of the Indians killed by the Sioux while traveling east with William Gray in 1837, the death of *Halket,* a nephew of Young Chief, who succumbed to disease at the Red River Mission in January 1837, and the death of Elijah Hedding, the Christianized son of Walla Walla Chief *Peopeo Mox-mox*—"Yellow Bird"—who had been killed by a white man while on a horse-selling expedition to California in the fall of 1844.

Also mentioned were Whitman's refusal to pay rent for the land used by the mission, his sympathy for the increasing tide of American emigrants passing through Cayuse country, and the mistreatment of Eastern Indians by whites as related to the Cayuses by Joe Lewis.

When he had finished, Five Crows and Young Chief spoke more briefly and with less bitterness. But Edward *Tiloukaikt,* when given his chance to talk, emphasized the terrible loss of life suffered by the Cayuses because of the introduction of the white man's diseases.

"He gave a touching picture of the afflicted families," Father Brouillet wrote, "in seeing borne to the grave a father, a mother, a brother, or a sister; spoke of a single member of a family who had been left to weep alone over all the rest who had disappeared."

He repeated the accusation that Whitman and Spalding had plotted to poison the Indians in order to get their lands and their horses—a plot that Andrew Rodgers admitted was true, Edward claimed, just before he died.

After all the chiefs had had their say, they asked Bishop Blanchet to add two more proposals to the four being sent to Oregon's Governor Abernethy, namely: "That the Americans should forget the lately committed murders, as the Cayuses will forget the murder of the great chief of Walla Walla committed in California; and that Americans may not travel any more through their country, as their young men might do them harm."

Suppressing his serious doubts that the Americans would even consider the two proposals, Bishop Blanchet included them in the six-point manifesto, then wrote an introduction in which he referred to the conviction held by the Indians that Whitman actually had been poisoning them. He mentioned the fact that six Cayuses had been buried on Sunday, November 28, and three more on the morning of the day the massacre began.

"They were led to believe that the whites had undertaken to kill them all," the bishop wrote. "These were the motives which led them to kill the Americans."

Signing the document were *Tiloukaikt, Camaspelo,* Young Chief, and Five Crows.

Even before the ink was dry on the laboriously crafted manifesto, a messenger arrived from Fort Walla Walla with surprising news. Aware of its far-reaching significance, Bishop Blanchet announced it to the assembly.

"The great man sent to negotiate the release of the captives is not an American. He is an Englishman. He has just arrived at Fort Walla Walla, with full authorization to do whatever needs to be done to assure the release of the captives. He is Peter Skene Ogden . . ."

Summoned to meet with Ogden as soon as possible, all of the Cayuse chiefs except Five Crows, who feared he would be asked to give up Lorinda Bewley, rode with Bishop Blanchet to Fort Walla Walla, where the white-haired, plainspoken, highly regarded Hudson's Bay Company factor opened the council at 9:30 A.M., Thursday morning, December 23.

"We have been among you for thirty years without the shedding of blood," Ogden said. "We are traders of a different nation from the Americans. We supply you with ammunition, but not to kill the Americans, who are of the same color, speak the same language, and who worship the same God as ourselves. Their cruel fate causes our hearts to bleed. Why do we make you chiefs, if you cannot control your young men?"

"I am one of those young men," Edward *Tiloukaikt* said sullenly. *"Tai-tam-nat* Whitman was a *tewat,* who was poisoning our people."

"When Indians all over Oregon are dying of measles and other diseases, that is a foolish thing to say. How could Dr. Whitman be responsible for the deaths of so many in such widely scattered places?"

"We were told he was responsible. Joe Lewis said it."

"I did not come here to argue with rash young men," Ogden said coldly. "I came here as an official of the Hudson's Bay Company. I left Fort Vancouver before the Americans had been notified of the killings."

"What will the Americans do?" *Tiloukaikt* asked anxiously. "Will they come upriver and make war on us?"

"I cannot say. If you wish it, on my return I will see what can be done for you. But I do not promise to prevent war. Deliver me the prisoners to return to their friends. I will pay you a ransom. That is all."

The talks went on all day, stalling time after time on Cayuse demands that Ogden guarantee that the Americans would not make war on them—which he would not do—and his demand that all the captives, including Lorinda Bewley and the whites at Lapwai, be brought to Fort Walla Walla within six days before the ransom would be paid—which the Cayuses were reluctant to do without a no-war guarantee.

"Fifty blankets, fifty shirts, ten guns, ten fathoms of tobacco, ten handkerchiefs, and one hundred balls and powder."

These were the goods, Ogden told the Cayuses, that he would pay them upon their delivery of the captives. In addition, if the two Nez Perces present at the meeting would go without delay to Lapwai, 140 miles east, and arrange for the Spalding family, Mary Johnson, Horace Hart, W. D. Canfield, and Mr. Jackson to be escorted to Fort Walla Walla, he would give them "twelve blankets, twelve shirts, two guns, twelve handkerchiefs, five fathoms of tobacco, two hundred balls and powder, and some knives" for their trouble.

What he did not tell them was that, after drawing the goods valued at $130.31 from Company stores, he intended to write Sir George Simpson that, should the Company not approve the expenditure, "to avoid any remarks being made, let it be placed to my private account."

Leaving Fort Walla Walla the evening of December 23, the two Nez Perces made the 140-mile ride to Lapwai in two days despite the scant hours of daylight and the bitter-cold winter weather. Ogden urged Spalding to waste no time in getting his people to Fort Walla Walla. If they delayed, he said, he might be forced to head downriver with the Waiilatpu captives as soon as they were delivered to him in order to avoid retribution from the Cayuses. In reply, Spalding wrote:

"We will come as soon as we can, but I beg you not to leave before we arrive, for I have just learned from the two Nez Perces who returned from Fort Walla Walla that the Cayuses have resolved should they learn that the Americans purpose to come up to avenge the death of those who have been massacred, that they will immediately fall upon myself and family and all Americans in the country and kill all."

This was not news to Peter Skene Ogden; this was precisely what he feared.

Over the strenuous objections of *Tamsucky, Tomahas,* Frank Escaloom, and his son Edward, Chief *Tiloukaikt* returned to Waiilatpu and told them he intended to release the captives. When informed Christmas Day that they could leave for Fort Walla Walla on Wednesday, December 29, Mrs. Saunders asked if they could take along their personal belongings.

"Yes, take all," he said impatiently, "and heaps of food for a long journey."

Five wagons were needed to carry their baggage, food, and the women and children. Leaving at daylight on the twenty-ninth, the wagons pulled by horses took the lead, while those pulled by the slow-plodding oxen fell behind.

"We had gone but a short distance," Catherine said, "when a squaw came out of her lodge nearby and told us to hurry, that the natives were going to kill us."

The day was cold and rainy. While they were fording the Touchet River, halfway to the fort, the wagon in which Catherine Sager and Mrs. Saunders were riding got thoroughly drenched by the high water which washed over the side of the bed. On the far side of the river, they stopped, got out, and started to build a fire by which to warm themselves and dry their clothes. *Tiloukaikt* and Beardy rode up and urged them to keep moving.

"Hurry, hurry!" the two Indians said. "No camp! Get to the fort!"

With Beardy moving the oxen along and *Tiloukaikt* keeping a wary eye on the trail behind them, they traveled all day through the cold downpour of rain, reaching Fort Walla Walla a little after dark. Ogden greeted them warmly.

"Thank God you are all safe!" he exclaimed fervently as he ushered them into a large room where a fire was burning in the fireplace. "I feared you had been killed!"

To the surprise and delight of the released captives, they had a joyful reunion with the Osborn family, who had been living at the fort since a few days after the massacre, and with Lorinda Bewley, who had arrived that afternoon. This was Lorinda's story:

"On the 28th of December, in the morning, while I was at Five Crows' lodge, an Indian rode up leading a horse and handed me a note from Mr. Ogden, stating the joyful news that he had finally succeeded in redeeming all the unfortunate captives; that he had redeemed me. I had nothing to fear and nothing to do but to accompany the Indian as fast as I could, comfortably, to Fort Walla Walla."

The Indian was *Camaspelo*, whose well-reasoned arguments, added to what Ogden wrote, had convinced Five Crows that he must let Lorinda Bewley go. He did so with surprising good grace.

"I could hardly believe my eyes," Lorinda said. "I bowed my knees with a grateful heart, and thanked my Savior for his great mercy to me. Five Crows prepared tea and a good breakfast for me, and put a new blanket and buffalo robe upon the saddle to make it comfortable for me to ride and for sleeping at night, and a thick shawl around me, and assisted me on my horse, and bade me goodbye kindly and with much feeling, and gave me food for the journey."

With the captives being held by the Cayuses now surrendered, Ogden

kept his promise and paid the ransom goods on Thursday, December 30.
After the goods had been distributed, he allowed the Indians to celebrate
with a dance inside the fort enclosure, though he made sure that the
former women and children captives stayed in locked rooms with guards
on the doors.

"After the dance," Mrs. Saunders said, "the only Indians allowed in the
fort were the old ones and those known to be friendly. Even these had to
leave at sundown. A large band of Cayuses were camped just outside the
fort. This was the cause of no small anxiety to both Ogden and McBean."

Adding to the anxiety of the two Hudson's Bay Company officials was
their knowledge that ten American volunteers under the command of Major H. A. G. Lee had come upriver from the Willamette Valley to The
Dalles, arriving there December 21. Ostensibly, their purpose was to protect lives and mission property. But once the captives were out of harm's
way, their position quickly could be converted into an advance base for a
punitive expedition against the Cayuses. If the dissident Indians learned
about the presence of the volunteer force, they very well might renege on
the promises they had made, overwhelm the small force at the fort, kill the
captives, and launch a war.

Though Ogden had urged Spalding to bring his people to Fort Walla
Walla as soon as possible, transporting six adults and three children with
all the food, clothes, and supplies they would need for a 140-mile journey
in cold winter weather was not easily accomplished. But by December 28
the caravan departed from Lapwai. Escorting the whites were forty well-
armed Nez Perce braves, led by the ever-faithful Timothy.

Becoming increasingly concerned over the belligerence of the dissident
Cayuses, who were hearing new rumors from downriver every day, Ogden
declared that if the people from the Lapwai Mission did not arrive by
Saturday, January 1, 1848, he would not take the chance of lingering at the
fort longer, but would start without them. On Saturday noon, a Nez Perce
scout, riding ahead, brought word that the Lapwai party was only a few
hours behind him.

"Great was the rejoicing!" Mrs. Saunders remembered.

Among those who rejoiced were the reunited Canfield family and the
Spaldings, with their daughter, Eliza.

Only the presence of the forty armed Nez Perces prevented one of the
dissident Cayuses from precipitating a new outbreak of bloodshed. Catherine said:

"Early in the day *Tamsucky* came to the fort with his gun in his hand,
evidently going to kill Mr. Spalding. Taking his stand by the side of the
gate, he seemed to be waiting for Mr. Spalding to pass on. Mr. S. came
right in to see his daughter, who stayed in the fort. He kept his eyes on

Tamsucky as he passed by. Seeing so many Nez Perces there armed, *Tamsucky* became alarmed and left by the opposite gate."

Though the downriver trip would begin next day, Sunday, January 2, none of the missionary people objected to traveling on the Sabbath—not even Mrs. Spalding. But she was deeply touched by the farewell given her by the gentle Timothy; after knowing the Spalding family for eleven years, and becoming the mission's first convert to Christianity, he had a premonition that he would not see her again in this world. Holding aloft the book of the New Testament that she had translated—the Gospel of Matthew— and that she had helped print, and had given to him, he spoke with tears in his eyes.

"Now, my beloved teacher, you are passing over my country for the last time. You are leaving us forever, and my people, Oh, my people, will see no more light. We shall meet no more in the schoolroom, and my children, Oh, my children, will live only in a night that will have no end. I now look on your face for the last time. But this book in which your hands have written and caused me to write the words of God, I shall carry in my bosom till I lie down in the grave."

The party being taken downriver by Peter Skene Ogden and his sixteen French-Canadian boatmen was a large one, taxing the capacity of the three bateaux. In addition to the forty-seven captives from Waiilatpu and the nine from Lapwai, there were eleven at the fort who wanted to go down the river. These included the Osborn family of five, the artist John Mix Stanley, the two Manson boys, Bishop Blanchet, and two of his priests. The other two priests decided to remain at Fort Walla Walla in the hope that they might soon return to one of their newly established missions. In all, the number of people embarking in the bateaux totaled eighty-four.

But one small boy who wanted to go was left behind. This was David Malin Cortez, the half-Portuguese, half-Indian child Narcissa Whitman had taken in a few years ago because he had no parents, had been badly mistreated, and wasn't wanted. Now nine years old, he was still unwanted. So he was left behind. Catherine Sager, who had become fond of him, said:

"The last look I had of him was when we moved away from Fort Walla Walla, leaving him standing on the bank of the river crying as though his heart were breaking."

Reaching Fort Vancouver on Saturday, January 8, the survivors were given a warm welcome by Chief Factor James Douglas. Already plans were afoot to mount a military expedition to apprehend the Cayuse murderers and punish the tribe for what it had done. Ironically, the first group of people to be terrorized by the Oregon Volunteers were the recently ransomed captives.

After spending the weekend at Fort Vancouver, the former captives were taken by boat across the Columbia River to Portland. Assembled on the dock there was a company of fifty men, under the command of Colonel Cornelius Gilliam, getting ready to leave for The Dalles. With them were Governor Abernethy and Captain William Shaw, the man who had delivered the seven Sager orphans to the Whitmans in 1844. When the boats containing the former captives approached the Portland dock, the Oregon Volunteers gave them a typically noisy frontier greeting.

"As we pulled in toward the wharf at Portland, a lot of men on the wharf fired a salute," Elizabeth Sager said. "We children were terrified. We crawled under some canvas and tried to hide in the bottom of the boat. We thought they were trying to kill us."

Seeing the terror of the children, Gilliam and Shaw hastened to comfort them.

"They told us," said Elizabeth, "that they were firing the guns in our honor."

So far as the Cayuse tribe was concerned, the Volunteers wanted blood vengeance. Counting four-year-old John Osborn and ten-year-old Mary Ann Bridger, both of whom died a few weeks after reaching the Willamette Valley, nineteen people with white blood in their veins were victims of the massacre. The Cayuse tribe—which numbered around four hundred—had lost one hundred and ninety-eight souls, most of them children.

But by the rules of white justice, the score was not even yet. The murderers must be apprehended, given a fair trial in a white man's court, convicted, and hanged. Even if that meant waging two years of brutal war . . .

11

So far as John Crane was concerned, it was a stupid damn war. But some of his ex–mountain men friends relished it. The legislature of the Provisional Government had been in session when Governor Abernethy received Peter Skene Ogden's letter telling about the massacre. Next day, it authorized raising a regiment "not to exceed 500 men" for the purpose of marching into Cayuse country to apprehend the murderers. Since their term of service was to be ten months, this was tantamount to a declaration of war against the Cayuses.

On December 14, a "peace commission" was appointed consisting of three men: Joel Palmer, Robert Newell, and Major H. A. G. Lee. It was directed to proceed "immediately to Walla Walla and hold a council with the chiefs and principal men of the various tribes on the Columbia, to prevent, if possible, the coalition with the Cayuse tribe in the present difficulties."

"Which is a polite way of saying we ain't to make peace with the Cayuses," Doc Newell told John Crane, "just do our damndest to make sure none of the other tribes join them in making war on us."

Because news of the Whitman Massacre would cause a national reaction once word of it reached the East, the suggestion that a special messenger be sent to Washington City was quickly endorsed. Joe Meek volunteered to make the trip.

"Been travelin' back an' forth across the country fer more years than I care to remember. Happens President Polk is married to a cousin of mine. Won't be no chore fer me to git an invite to the White House, where I can tell the bigwigs all about how bad this part of the country wants to become a territory of the United States."

For the past ten years, many memorials had been sent to the nation's capital urging that the jurisdiction of the United States be extended to Oregon—with no results. Now a new "Memorial to Congress" was drawn up, stating the case with even more urgency.

"Having called upon the government of the United States so often in vain, we have almost despaired of receiving its protection, yet we trust that our present situation, when fully laid before you, will at once satisfy your honorable body of the great necessity of extending the strong arm of guardianship over this remote, but beautiful portion of the United States domain."

When asked to join Doc Newell, Joe Meek, and the force of Oregon Volunteers heading upriver, John Crane said he'd be glad to go along and lend what aid he could as a guide, scout, or interpreter. But he doubted that the Cayuses would stand still and do battle.

"Biggest job you'll have," he told Doc Newell, "will be to convince the Volunteers that there's a sight more friendly Indians upriver than there are hostiles. Hell, the Nez Perces have proved how friendly they are. But if some trigger-happy clodhopper of a farmer, who don't know a Nez Perce from a Fiji Islander, takes a shot at one and by greenhorn luck happens to kill him, we'll have a real war on our hands."

"Hear tell Bill Craig stood by the Spaldings," Doc Newell said. "Ain't that a switch for him?"

"He's mellowed some," John said. "And he is a white man. It'd be a good idea, Doc, for you and me to look him up, once we get Joe headed for the States." He looked questioningly at Meek. "Any idea when you'll try crossing the Blues?"

"Depends on the weather" Meek answered, shaking his head. "The snowdrifts up there are ass deep to a twenty-foot-tall giraffe through January and February. But come March, a Chinook ought to melt 'em to where I can make it. Once I git over the crest and down onto Snake River Plain, I'll breeze through without much trouble, I'm thinkin'. Doc Whitman made it in winter. So can I."

The first shots of the Cayuse War were fired near The Dalles early in January when a small group of Volunteers overtook a mixed bag of Cayuse and local Indians that had stolen three hundred cattle left in the area by emigrants the previous fall. In the skirmish, the Volunteers failed to recover the cattle, but did manage to kill three Indians, wound a few more, and capture sixty Indian horses.

"If gaining sixty scrub Injun ponies while losing three hundred fat beef cattle is what you call a victory," Meek said caustically, "you Volunteers better hope for a few defeats."

"Hell, I ain't a Volunteer," Doc Newell protested. "I'm a peace commissioner—with a paper that says so. Trouble is, I can't make peace till the shootin' stops."

Moving up the Columbia toward Cayuse country, the Volunteers exchanged long-range shots with the hostiles on several occasions, with no significant effect. In an abandoned Indian village in the Deschutes area, the Volunteers set fire to a dozen empty lodges. In retaliation, the Cayuses burned down all the buildings at Waiilatpu except the gristmill—which they needed to grind their grain—then rode over to the Umatilla River and set fire to the St. Anne Mission.

From what John Crane could learn from friendly Nez Perce scouts, the Cayuse leaders were divided. Favoring war to the bitter end were *Tamsucky, Tomahas,* Five Crows, and most of the younger men, while Stickus, Beardy, and *Camaspelo* wanted a negotiated peace. Some of the Cayuses were boasting that "Americans are easy to kill," citing as examples the massacre victims they had clubbed to death. Believing that the Americans were poor fighters, young warriors from several inland tribes joined the hostile Cayuse faction, seeking glory and scalps, bringing the number of fighting men to four hundred by late February, when the Oregon Volunteers at last forced them into a decisive battle in the Umatilla area.

One unpleasant surprise to the hostiles was the fact that a number of ex–Hudson's Bay Company employees, French-Canadians, and half bloods had joined the Volunteers and were fighting on the side of the Americans. Included in Colonel Gilliam's regiment, which now numbered five hundred, were seventeen-year-old Perrin Whitman; W. D. Canfield, one of the released captives; and half-blood Tom McKay, who, with John McCleod, had escorted the Whitman-Spalding party from rendezvous to Fort Walla Walla in 1836. Serving with Tom McKay, who was a Captain of Volunteers, was his brother, Charles, ranked a lieutenant.

"Hear tell the hostiles are itchin' for a battle," John told Doc Newell. "Tom McKay tells me a Cayuse *tewat* named Gray Eagle is braggin' his medicine is so strong no bullet can hurt him. If he is shot, he says, he'll 'puke up the bullet.' "

"Sounds like a real good trick, if he can do it. Hope we get to see him try."

In a sharp, bloody battle next day, Gray Eagle got an opportunity to test his magic. Spotting Tom McKay fifty yards away during the heat of the skirmish, Gray Eagle gave a whoop of derision, lifted his rifle, and cried, "There's Tom McKay! I will kill him!"

But McKay fired first. A crack shot, he watched as Gray Eagle, struck squarely between the eyes by the bullet, toppled off his horse. Beside him, Charles McKay said laconically, "Reckon he'll puke it up?"

"Not likely. I shot him above his pukin' spot."

"Well, now, I got my sights on Five Crows. Let's see if I can get him."

Charles McKay fired. Struck in the right arm by the shot, Five Crows reeled back and retired from the battle.

Counting their casualties when the battle was over, the Cayuses and their allies were shocked to discover eight dead and five badly wounded. With this stark lesson that the Americans could and would fight, all the allies deserted the Cayuses and headed for home. Divided and demoralized, the Cayuses abandoned organized resistance, broke up into small groups, and retreated into the wilderness of the Blue Mountains.

With the weather moderating now, Joe Meek and the nine ex–mountain men who planned to travel east with him headed into the Blues March 4, escorted through Cayuse country by a hundred Volunteers. Meanwhile, Colonel Gilliam and the rest of the soldiers marched to Waiilatpu. Near the mission's charred ruins a military post called Fort Waters was built, from which, for the next few months, details ranging from squad to company size rode out in search of hostiles to capture or kill.

"Mostly, all they catch are friendly Injuns," Doc Newell complained, "which, after being mistreated and having their horses and cattle stolen, ain't in no mood to help me locate the hostiles and negotiate peace. Have you heard from Bill Craig?"

"Yeah. He says *Tiloukaikt* has been seen in Nez Perce country, hiding out with relatives."

"There's a five-hundred-dollar reward being offered for him, *Tamsucky,* or *Tomahas* by the Provisional Government. I'm authorized to write a voucher for a live body. Will they turn him in?"

"No Nez Perce would turn in a relative, Doc, you know that. But they ain't comfortable having him around for long, Craig says, so he keeps moving on. Craig thinks our best chance to end the war is to put pressure on the Cayuse chiefs who want peace to round up the ringleaders and give them up. He says Lawyer, Timothy, and Old Joseph have been trying to persuade Stickus, *Camaspelo,* and Five Crows to surrender the ones who planned the massacre."

"Hear tell Joe Lewis is heading down Salt Lake way. Seems the Mormons have promised to supply the guns and troops he needs to run the Volunteers back to the Willamette. Or so Lewis claims."

"My guess is the Mormons won't give Joe Lewis the time of day," John said, shaking his head. "If you don't need me here for the next couple of weeks, I've a notion to ride up to Lapwai and see Bill Craig. You're welcome to come, if you like,"

"You run along. I'd better stay here, just in case peace breaks out. Give Bill my regards."

At Lapwai, John Crane told William Craig about the rumor of the Mormons supplying the Cayuses with arms and troops. It had just been another fanciful story cooked up by the lying half-breed, Craig said, aimed to persuade Edward and Clark *Tiloukaikt* to travel with him until away from their friends.

"Seems when he got 'em in the neighborhood of Fort Hall," Craig told John, "he cut their throats while they slept, stole their horses, guns, and gear, and then hightailed it north to the Flathead country. Nicholas Finley, another breed, joined him there. A pair to draw to, I'd say, if murderous devils is what you're after."

"Finley gets around. A month ago, he was over at Fort Colville, encouraging the Indians there to join forces with the Cayuses and whip hell out of the Oregon Volunteers. But he turned tail and scooted when that didn't work out."

"Hear tell the Injuns burned Waiilatpu."

"All but the gristmill. Which reminds me, Bill. Doc Newell sends his regards. He says to tell you that if you're in danger here and need a soldier escort out of the country, Colonel Gilliam will be happy to send up a hundred Volunteers to look after you."

"Say, that sure is kindly of him!" William Craig said, throwing back his head and laughing heartily. "But from what I hear of the Volunteers, I'm a sight safer amongst the Nez Perces than I would be with them. When you go back, John, tell Colonel Gilliam that. Tell him if *he* needs some good fighting men, I'll send him the forty Nez Perce bucks that escorted the Spaldings to Fort Walla Walla. Ain't no hostiles in this part of the country willing to tangle with them."

"Speaking of the Nez Perces, you recollect I told you about my half brother, Tall Bird?"

"Peo-peo-Kuhet? Sure, I know him well. He's a mighty fine man."

"Any idea where he'd be now?"

"Likely in the Wallowa winter village near the mouth of the Grande Ronde, just half a day's ride from here. Would you like to meet him?"

"I surely would."

"As easy done as said. We'll ride over that way tomorrow."

12

Though Tall Bird did not mention it to William Craig and John Crane, he had seen his half brother on two occasions the past couple of summers, when the Wallowa band had met wagon trains in the upper Grande Ronde Valley to trade with the emigrants. The first time, he had been surprised by the changes ten years had wrought in John's appearance and manner. This yellow-haired, handsome, quiet-spoken man working as a guide for the wagon train bore little resemblance to the sodden, disheveled drunk who had repelled him so at the Green River rendezvous.

William Craig had explained it, of course, saying news of the deaths of his mother, father, and the mother of his son had driven John to seek solace in alcohol. Tall Bird had long since forgiven him for that. Still, Tall Bird two summers ago did not feel the time was right to establish a relationship with his half brother, for this was too private and sensitive a bond to be made in the presence of so many strangers.

Last summer, though, when he again saw John, he had been at the point of getting him off alone and telling him who he was when sickness broke out among the children in the train. Before Tall Bird could talk to him, John cut the trading short and hurried the emigrants on to Waiilatpu, so that Dr. Whitman could examine the youngsters.

But he was here now, brought to the winter village by their mutual friend, William Craig, who had gone back to Lapwai in a couple of days. Showing him around and introducing him as his *Suyapo* "brother" gave Tall Bird a good feeling inside. As much at ease in the Nez Perce tongue, sign language, and Chinook jargon as Tall Bird was in English, French, and the regional native languages, John communicated well with the Wallowa Nez Perces. Like most ex–mountain men, he had a gracious, unhurried sense of propriety and manners—traits important to the dignity of the proud *Nimipu*.

The first person Tall Bird introduced John to was his mother, Moon Wind. Now sixty years old, she had gotten a little plump, her face had become fuller, and her hair was streaked with gray. But she still was a beautiful woman. As she took both of John's hands in hers and smiled up at him, her dark eyes filled with tears.

"Moki Hih-hih never came back. But now you are here and have met your brother."

"Hattia Isemtuks," John said softly in Nez Perce. "What a beautiful name! And a beautiful lady to bear it."

"Ahh taats! What a flatterer you are!"

"My father loved you and your son very much. He said he wanted me to love you, too. Now that we've finally met, I want you to know I do."

"Peo-peo Kuhet, have you showed your brother the page in the Holy Book where *Moki Hih-hih* wrote down our names and the date you were born?"

"Not yet, Mother. But I will."

Long treated as his most precious possession, the forty-two-year-old New Testament given him by the white father he had never seen was sacred to Tall Bird. When he removed it from its waterproof case and showed John Crane the inscription written on its flyleaf, he was pleased that his half brother should be moved so deeply.

"He wanted to come back, you know," said John. "It was a great disappointment to him that he couldn't."

"He suffered a crippling illness, my mother was told."

"Sure, there was that. But it wasn't the illness that kept him in St. Louis. It was what he regarded as a sign from God that he had sinned and must pay for it by giving up his dream of becoming a trader in the Nez Perce country. He was a very religious man."

"I know," Tall Bird said simply. "This he told me."

"How could he tell you?" John asked with a puzzled frown. "You never saw him."

"Oh, but I did! In my *Wy-a-kin* vision, he came to me in the mountain dawn across a bridge of mist and ice. In appearance he looked so much like you that I would have recognized you at once, even if not told who you were. In my *Wy-a-kin* vision, he said I would go on a long journey in search of the Book of Heaven, but I might not reach its end because of sickness and death on the bank of a big river. These things came to pass. He told me I must learn to read the book he gave me and live by its teachings. This I have done. He told me I must follow the path of peace and never kill a fellow being. This, too, I have done."

"He tried to make a missionary out of me, with no luck," John said wryly. "Guess he was working on the wrong son."

"Since the missionaries came, the *Nimipu* have listened to their teachings. Many have joined *Tai-tam-nat* Spalding's church—as have Timothy and Joseph. But they are worried now. How much longer will the Americans make war on the Cayuses to avenge the killings at Waiilatpu? How much more Cayuse blood must be shed to pay for the murders?"

"Under American law, there can be no peace until the instigators of the massacre are arrested, brought to trial, and punished."

"The word 'instigator' is new to me. What does it mean?"

"A person who plans a killing, who talks in favor of it, who persuades others to shed blood."

"Such people are known to the *Nimipu*," Tall Bird said, nodding. "By marriage and kinship, many of us are related to Cayuses. But to us it would be a betrayal of those ties to turn over a relative to white justice."

"Well, somebody's got to do it. If the Cayuses want peace, they'll have to give up half a dozen bucks with blood on their hands. Once they've been brought to trial, the whites will end the war."

"I shall tell Chief Joseph and Timothy that," Tall Bird said. "Perhaps they can bring peace . . ."

John Crane stayed a week with Tall Bird and the Wallowa Nez Perces in their winter village on the lower Grande Ronde. Like the week he had spent with his son Luke a year ago, it was a rewarding time of establishing ties of blood kinship closer and warmer than any he had known since leaving home fourteen years ago. Moon Wind became his "mother"; her older brother, Red Elk, now almost blind and badly crippled with swollen joints, but still proud of his relationship with *Moki Hih-hih,* became his "father"; and Tall Bird became his "brother." Most pleasing of all, the four children of Tall Bird and Flower Gatherer accepted him as a member of the family.

Both the oldest son, now twenty-one, and the oldest daughter, nineteen, were married, with cooking fires of their own. They were well-mannered young people who apparently had given their parents few problems as they were growing up, and thus were loved, appreciated, and taken for granted. On the contrary, the second-oldest son, sixteen, *Peo-peo Amtiz*—"Swift Bird"—and the youngest daughter, nine, *Peo-peo Uenpise*—"Singing Bird" —were so lively, outgoing, and personable that no one could ignore them.

"In these times, it is not easy to be a sixteen-year-old boy," Tall Bird told John solemnly, as they watched a dozen Nez Perce youngsters set up cairns of stone and pole flags to mark out a course over which they presently would race their horses. "Since he first began to toddle, Swift Bird has loved physical competition—wrestling, footraces, war games, hunting games, and horse races. He is so fast, strong, and nimble, he almost always wins. The more difficult the contest, the more he enjoys it."

Noting that the course laid out began on a sandbar at the river's edge, crossed through swimming-depth water, led steeply upward along a slope covered with treacherous lava rubble, turned downward to the river in a frighteningly abrupt descent, again crossed the river, then ended at a rock cairn on the sandbar, John shook his head.

" 'Pears to me like the winner of this race will be its survivor—if any. Tell you one thing—Swift Bird is a born horseman. Wish my son, Luke, could meet him."

"This is the son who lives in St. Louis?"

"Yeah. He's six months younger than your boy—and just as active. He's a great rider, too."

"Why does he not live with you?"

"Because he's in school in St. Louis and I'm on the go a lot. He wants to be an officer in the United States Army. To do that, he has to go to school."

"Before the white man came, our young men trained to be warriors, too. Fighting the Shoshones, the Blackfeet, and the Sioux—these were times of glory for the young men. Hunting buffalo east of the mountains also was exciting to them, for always there was the zest of being in a land far from home, where an enemy might attack at any time. To a sixteen-year-old boy, hunting and war are far more interesting than peace. Swift Bird would much rather listen to his uncle Red Elk tell about killing Blackfeet and buffalo than listen to me tell about my journey east in search of the Book of Heaven."

"I know," John said sympathetically. "He's pestered me to tell him all the details of the Waiilatpu Massacre and the war against the Cayuses. Not that he approves. But the action excites him."

Among the Nez Perces, children were welcome at every family's cooking fire, John learned, and were treated as a son or daughter no matter what their relationship to the family might be. From his first meeting with nine-year-old *Peo-peo Uenpise*—"Singing Bird"—he found himself adopted as a very special person, her *Pekelis Suyapo*—"White Grandfather." The happiest child he had ever seen, she was constantly humming to herself, putting words to her improvised songs, telling herself and anyone near what she was doing and how she felt about it. Though scolded by her mother that it was rude to climb on John's lap, snuggle up against his chest, and ask him to tell her a grandfather tale, she negated the reprimand by asking, "Do you think me rude, Grandfather?"

"Course I don't."

"Tell Mother that. Then tell me a grandfather tale about little white girls who live in tepees that roll on wheels."

Before leaving the village, John promised to accept Tall Bird's invitation to visit the Wallowa band in its summer camp in the beautiful high meadow country as soon as peace came to the land. It was a country, Tall

Bird said, whose purity of air, sunshine, lakes, mountains, streams, and grass exceeded all the other regions in the West.

"Come and stay as long as you like, brother. You are part of our family now."

Meanwhile, Joe Meek had reached Washington, where he was warmly treated by President Polk, by Congress, and by the press. Appointed United States Marshal for Oregon Territory, whose enabling act Congress quickly passed, he returned to Oregon with the good news that a regiment of Mounted Riflemen was on its way to assist the new territory in bringing peace to the area. Thus assured of federal support, Governor Joseph Lane sent a strongly worded message to the leaders of the Cayuse tribe: *Give up the murderers or we will carry on a war of extermination.*

Shortly thereafter, five Cayuses were surrendered and brought down-river to Oregon City, where United States Marshall Meek took custody of them.

They were: *Tiloukaikt, Tomahas, Kia-ma-sump-kin, Clokamas,* and *Ish-ish-kais-kais.* All five, said their chiefs, "have blood on their hands."

"Gonna give 'em a fair trial before he hangs 'em, Joe says," Doc Newell told John Crane. "He's strong for law and order, Joe is."

An indictment for murder was issued against each of the five prisoners May 21, 1850, with the trial beginning the next day. Twenty-two prospective jurors were challenged and excused in an effort on the part of the defense to exclude all older Oregon citizens who might be Indian haters. Three hundred spectators jammed the courtroom each day to observe the proceedings.

Testifying for the five accused Cayuses were Stickus, Young Chief, and *Camaspelo.* Called as prosecution witnesses were young Eliza Spalding, Catherine and Elizabeth Sager, Lorinda Bewley, and a number of other white residents at Waiilatpu.

At the beginning of the trial, the defense counsels argued that at the time of the massacre, the laws of the United States had not been extended over the area occupied by the Cayuse tribe. In reply, the court ruled that by an 1844 Act of Congress all the territory west of the Mississippi River was "embraced within and declared to be Indian Territory; and as such, subject to the laws regulating intercourse with the Indians."

Seeking to lessen the guilt of the murderers by showing that Marcus Whitman had been warned repeatedly of the danger he faced because of the practice of the Cayuses of killing their own medicine men when one of their patients died, the defense called two prime witnesses. The first was Dr. John McLoughlin, former Hudson's Bay Company factor at Fort Vancouver, now retired and an American citizen. The second was Stickus, the

Cayuse chief who had long been Dr. Whitman's staunch supporter and friend. Both men said that Whitman knew that a *tewat* who failed to cure a patient was in danger. Stickus said, "I told him to be careful, for the bad Indians would kill him."

The court refused to admit the relevance of such testimony.

After two days of hearings, the case went to the jury. The charge given the jurors by Judge Pratt was brief. In the opinion of John Crane, who listened to it with a great deal of interest, it was devastating to the defendants.

"You should bear in mind," Judge Pratt said, "that the Cayuse nation, which had voluntarily surrendered the five prisoners, knows best who were the perpetrators of the massacre."

After deliberating for only one hour and fifteen minutes on Friday afternoon, May 24, the jury returned a verdict of guilty against each of the five. Judge Pratt then sentenced the five Cayuses to be hanged on Monday, June 3, 1850. Watching the Indians as the sentence was translated to them, John Crane saw them shake and tremble, the stoic calm with which they had endured the proceedings up until now completely shattered.

"It ain't that they're cowards," Doc Newell muttered to him, shaking his head in sympathy for the Indians. "They wouldn't mind being shot— but being hanged is to die like a dog, they feel, not as a man."

As the execution date drew near, the Catholic clergymen, whom the Cayuses regarded as allies and friends, gave them spiritual consolation. At nine o'clock on Monday morning, the day the multiple hangings were to take place, Archbishop Blanchet and Father Veyret conducted low mass for the Indians in their private quarters, then baptized each of the five, naming *Tiloukaikt,* Andrew; *Tomahas,* Peter; *Ish-ish-kais-kais,* John; *Clokamas,* Paul; and *Kia-ma-sump-kin,* James. After the baptism, the five were confirmed and became members of the Catholic Church.

"That'll set old Spalding on his ear," Doc Newell told John Crane when he heard about it. "He's already telling people he thinks the Catholics put the Cayuses up to the massacre so they could steal Dr. Whitman's land and converts. Now he'll say this proves it."

Though it was not a prospect he particularly relished, John agreed to accompany Doc Newell to the hangings, for this once-in-a-lifetime event was to be a public affair in which their old friend United States Marshal Joe Meek would play a leading role. A gallows with five nooses and five trapdoors through which the condemned men would drop when Marshal Meek severed a single control rope with his tomahawk, had been constructed on the east bank of the Willamette River, near the island on which the five Cayuses were being held prisoner. Every man, woman, and child that could walk or crawl would attend, Doc Newell predicted.

"Are the Cayuses still cringing from death by hanging and begging to be shot instead?" John asked Doc Newell.

"Yeah. Joe says he can't change the sentence. But he's gonna give 'em something that will straighten their spines."

"Any notion what it will be?"

"Well, it's an Injun thing, I'm guessing, cooked up by him and Jim Bridger. Mary Ann Bridger died, you know, a couple of months after she got to the Willamette Valley, just as Helen Mar Meek died at Waiilatpu. He and Bridger swore to take revenge. But what that's got to do with the hangings, I can't say."

Five minutes before two o'clock in the afternoon, the doomed Indians were marched toward the foot of the scaffold by a guard of twenty riflemen. The murmuring of the crowd rose in volume, then died. John knew that this final act of man's brutality toward man must take place before peace could come to this land he had chosen for his home; yet a wave of pity swept over him as he watched the five Cayuses approach the scaffold. All were trembling uncontrollably, dragging their feet, paralyzed with fear. Standing where they must pass close by were Archbishop Blanchet and Marshal Meek. In the silence, John heard the archbishop ask *Tiloukaikt* if he was at peace.

"Yes," *Tiloukaikt* answered. "I am at peace with God."

"You have signed a statement that you are not guilty of the crimes of which you have been convicted. Yet you gave yourself up. Why did you do it?"

"Did not the missionaries tell us that Christ died to save His people?" *Tiloukaikt* asked. "So die we, to save our people."

After passing the priest, who murmured consolation and a prayer for each man, the five Cayuses walked by Joe Meek, who was standing just beyond. As they did so, John saw Meek touch each Indian on the arm to get his attention, make a quick series of hand signs, and say something in a voice so low that his words could not be heard two paces away.

As a result, a curious thing happened. Each Cayuse straightened, stood tall, looked proud, and walked with a firm, manly step to the scaffold platform, where he stood unflinching on the trapdoor as the noose was adjusted around his neck.

Promptly at 2 P.M., United States Marshal Joseph Meek cut the rope controlling the trapdoors. Five Cayuse souls newly named Andrew, Peter, John, Paul, and James entered eternity.

Peace had come at last to the upriver country.

Later that afternoon, John Crane, Doc Newell, and their old friend Joe Meek sat in a riverfront tavern sharing a few drinks in celebration of a very special day.

"One question, Joe," Doc said. "What was it you told them poor devils that put such iron in their backs?"

"Why, I just told 'em," Meek said quietly, "that they'd murdered my daughter, Helen Mar, and Jim Bridger's daughter, Mary Ann. For that, I told 'em, I was taking blood vengeance, as any father has a right to do."

"About what I'd guessed," John Crane murmured, nodding. "If anybody could understand a father taking revenge for the loss of a child, they would . . ."

PART THREE

Pe-wa-oo-yit—First Treaty Council 1851–1859

1

With the Indian war over and the prospects good for a sizable emigration from the States next year, John Crane told his wife, Felicia, in early August 1850 that he reckoned he'd head east to Independence and see if he couldn't pick up a guiding job. She owed him a favor, he figured. Because her late husband had established only squatter's rights to the square mile of land he had claimed, John had filed on it when the Provisional Government was formed in 1843, then solidified his title under the Donation Claims Act following the organization of Oregon Territory last year. As current male head of the household, title to the land was in his name, of course, so when he agreed to give Faith, Hope, and Charity and their respective husbands a quarter section of land apiece, his wife was pleased with his generosity.

"Far as land is concerned, all I want is twenty-five acres or so to graze a few horses on," he said. "Let the kids farm the rest of that quarter, too, though title to it should stay in my name so you'll have the land the house sits on, case something happens to me."

"You're a good-hearted man, John, though you'll never be a farmer. Go back to your guiding, if you want. I know you're restless here."

"Well, the pay is good, Felicia, and we can always use the money. Hear tell my old friend Captain Bonneville is commandant of a new post on the Oregon trail, Fort Kearney. That's in the Nebraska country. Kind of like to see him again. Likely I'll stop at Fort Bridger, too, and chew the fat with Jim. He'll be interested to hear about the Cayuse hangings."

"Will you visit your Wallowa Indian relatives?"

"Sure," John said lightly, wondering for the umpteenth time why he'd ever told her about Tall Bird. In her rigidly structured moral world, any white man that would bed an Indian woman and admit to being the father of her child was an object of scorn. She judged all Indians to be "Siwashes," which was what the squat, dirty, vermin-infested, unattractive natives of the lower Columbia area were called. But it was a prejudice he knew it was useless to try to change.

"Guess I'm kind of like Bill Craig—more red than white under the skin."

"I'm not criticizing you, John. It's just that dirty Indians repel me and wild Indians scare me."

"Wish you could meet my niece, Singing Bird. She'd charm you. Maybe I'll bring her home for a visit."

"Oh, John, don't ever do that! I'd be—well, I'd be shamed!"

"Not as much as I'd be," he said coldly. "But don't worry. I'll never take that happy little girl where she ain't welcome."

Finding the Wallowa Nez Perces in their summer village on a grassy plain near the forks of two cold, sparkling streams, John had to agree with Tall Bird's boast that this was one of the most beautiful high country regions of the West. Stirrup-high grass covered the valley floor, giving sustenance to thousands of Nez Perce horses. Fine stands of pine, fir, and larch grew on the lower foothills, with jagged brown peaks capped with snow rising into the rich blue sky. Spawning now in the white gravel beds above a spectacular six-mile-long gorge were forty- and fifty-pound salmon, whose battered bodies literally covered the river from bank to bank as they struggled upstream in their frenzy to commit their final creative act.

"The big dark salmon are not good to eat when they begin to spawn," Tall Bird said. "They are poor-fleshed and about to die. But soon the redfish will come up the Wallowa River. They are the best-tasting salmon of all, even though they are much smaller. We will feast when they come."

"With all the game I've seen in this country, 'pears to me like you can feast anytime you take the notion. Lord, what grass! To a rancher, this'd be cow heaven!"

"We are beginning to build up our own cattle herds. *Tai-tam-nat* Spalding and William Craig have shown us the value of raising beef herds rather than taking long trips to the buffalo country."

"You say your son Swift Bird is there now?"

"Yes," Tall Bird said, a cloud veiling his eyes. "At eighteen, he is a man, taking charge of his own life. To him, seeing new country, hunting buffalo, and fighting Blackfeet are far more exciting than staying home."

"When I was his age, I got a lot of excitement out of chasing girls," John said wryly. "Don't girls interest him?"

"Oh, yes, he likes girls, too. In fact, he talks of marrying one who lives in the Kooskia village when he comes back from the buffalo country."

"Anybody I'd know?"

"I doubt it. The Kooskia band lives at the eastern edge of *Nimipu* country, on the South Fork of the Clearwater. Their chief is an old warrior named *Ap-push-wa-hite*—'Looking Glass.' He has a son who bears the same name, a few years older than Swift Bird. The girl is a granddaughter or niece, I believe. She will cost five good horses."

"As father of the groom, will you get a chance to inspect her to make sure she's sound of wind and limb?"

"I will take Swift Bird's word for that," Tall Bird said with a smile. "What about your son? Is he a soldier now?"

"Not yet. He's just finished his first year at West Point."

"Is he interested in girls?"

"Probably—though he's not confided in me. For a young man his age, he has a strong sense of direction and purpose. Before he undertakes anything as serious as marriage, he'll have to graduate from the Academy and be assigned to a military post with decent quarters for a wife, he says."

"You have a wife in the Willamette Valley, you told me, who has three married daughters. Do they have families?"

"Yeah," said John. "The girls are all married to good men and are raising a passel of kids. But they're not blood kin to me like yours are, so I don't really feel close. Felicia is a good woman but she's never understood my liking for the Nez Perces—and she never will. I made her title to the farm legal by filing on it under the Donation Claims Act, then signed over a quarter-section to each of the kids."

Tall Bird frowned. "I have heard of this Claims Act but I do not understand it. How does it work?"

"Why, it's simple enough. Under its terms, any white male citizen of Oregon over the age of eighteen is entitled to lay claim to a square mile of land, simply by marking its boundaries and filing papers in a territorial land office."

"Does he build a fence around it and keep people out?"

"He don't have to—but he can. The land becomes his, you see, with him able to do what he pleases with it."

"To the *Nimipu,* this is a strange concept. To us, land is to be used, not owned. We have learned to fence small garden plots to prevent livestock from damaging vegetables, grain, and fruits, of course. But the rest of the land is simply there to be used by all the people. We do not understand how white men can pass laws saying a piece of it can be owned by an individual."

"I know. But like it or not, that is the law. Come to think about it, Tall Bird, the way the Donation Claims Act is set up, you could file on a section of land yourself. The law says 'Any white or half-white male over the age of eighteen' is entitled to file. You're half-white—and can prove it. Might not be a bad idea for you to file on a piece of land up here in the Wallowa country. It could be valuable someday."

Tall Bird looked thoughtful. Sitting their horses on the crest of a low divide from which a wide expanse of grass-covered valley floor, rivers, and mountains could be seen, the two men were dwarfed by the immensity of the country. Tall Bird moved his hands in a circular, encompassing gesture.

"Do you mean to say I could take a piece of land from the heart of this valley, make it my own, and forever after keep all other people from riding across it?"

"That's the law."

"Any white or half-white man could do that?"

"Yes."

"But an Indian could not?"

"Afraid not. White men made the law."

"What it means, then, is that someday white men who are strangers to the Wallowa country may come here, file claims, and chop the country up into mile-square pieces, building fences and cabins, keeping the *Nimipu,* who have grazed their herds, hunted, and fished in the rivers and lakes for ten thousand summers, from using the land as they always have used it— by taking its bounty without scarring its breast."

"Sure, that could happen," John said. "But I doubt that it ever will. Still, it wouldn't hurt for you to file on a piece of land. When you've picked out the claim you want, let me know. I'll help you draw up the papers."

John Crane stayed a full week in the summer village of the Wallowa Nez Perces, riding with Tall Bird, Chief Joseph, and other members of the band over the beautiful, rugged, varied country of the region, which ranged from the ten-thousand-foot-high mountains in the south to the awesome depths of Snake River's Big Canyon in the east. With the run of redfish into Wallowa Lake reaching its peak, Indians from other Nez Perce and related bands came to the area, set up tepees, then patiently waited their turn for the opportunity to catch their share of the rich, tasty fish. Watching their behavior, John marveled at how strictly both the local Indians and the visitors respected one another's rights.

"How do they know which family is entitled to fish in a particular spot for a certain length of time?" he asked Tall Bird.

"Someone in the family usually remembers. If they do not and a dispute arises, they ask Chief Joseph to decide what is to be done. When he tells them, they do it."

"With no argument?"

"Why should they argue? They know there are plenty of redfish for all. They know he will be fair. So they accept his decision and wait their turn."

Taller than the average Nez Perce, Old Joseph was in his early fifties, handsome, quiet-spoken, and still deeply religious though the white missionaries were gone. His son, Young Joseph, now ten years old, was slim and large-boned, giving promise of being even taller than his father. Though he had not yet gone on his *Wy-a-kin* quest, he was showing a maturity beyond his years, Tall Bird said, and no doubt would be accepted as chief of the Wallowa band when his father chose to give up the authority.

In the lodge each night during John's stay, Singing Bird snuggled against her *Pekelis Suyapo* and insisted that her "White Grandfather" tell her another tale. Never having had children of his own, he felt ill at ease at first, not knowing what kind of a story would be suitable for the ears of a little Indian girl. When he protested that he was not a good teller of grandfather tales, Flower Gatherer, the child's mother, laughed.

"You will be by the time Singing Bird gets through teaching you. She knows exactly what she wants."

"Monster tales are what she likes best," Tall Bird said. "Like the devil-fish in Wallowa Lake who eats maidens."

"What I was told as a kid were Bible stories," John mused. "Some of 'em were awful bloody. Like David and Goliath . . ."

With August half-gone and first frosts painting the aspens and tamarack of the high country autumn-gold, John told Tall Bird it was time he moved on. Saying that he had given thought to filing on a piece of land, Tall Bird asked him to ride out from the village between the forks of the two rivers and look at the land he had chosen. Lying several miles west of Wallowa Lake, taking in both valley grassland and foothill timberland, the rising, rolling terrain was split by a small, rapids-filled stream tumbling down out of the mountains to the south.

"What do you think, brother?" asked Tall Bird.

"Kind of out of the way, ain't it? Seems to me a piece of land near the lake or along the river, where the trails run or camps are made, would be a sight more inclined to increase in value."

"I mean to live on it, not sell it."

"Yeah, you've got a point there. It's the kind of land men like you and me would live on. If it's what you want, I'll help you file on it. Just one piece of advice. When you file, use your white name—Mark Crane. To make sure it's legal, I'll attach an affidavit that you're my half brother."

"That is good. For if anything happens to me, I want the land to be yours. You are family now . . ."

2

For the next three years, the winds of change blew with increasing velocity over Oregon Territory. Crossing the wide expanse of land between the Willamette Valley and Independence in an easterly direction during early fall, then turning around and recrossing it in the opposite direction in late spring and summer, John Crane marveled at the ever-expanding number of people determined to make their fortune and future in the Far West. Sure, the discovery of gold in California had stimulated the tide of adventurers flowing in that direction. But the farm seekers, the cattle raisers, the businessmen looking for opportunities in lumber, fish, or sea enterprises, still were inclined to take the right-hand branch of the Overland Trail where it forked a few days' travel west of Fort Hall and head for the fabled land called Oregon.

As first organized, the territory had stretched from the 42nd Parallel on the south to the 49th Parallel on the north, and from the Continental Divide on the east to the Pacific Ocean on the west—a piece of land roughly 500 miles wide by 700 miles long, totaling 350,000 square miles.

Not counting Indians, which of course no one did because they weren't citizens, most of the population lived in the Willamette Valley west of the Cascades, with a few families and intrepid businessmen beginning to turn north from the Columbia River now that control of Fort Vancouver had passed from British to American hands.

Because westering Americans with gumption enough to leave their homes in the East were the kind of people that insisted on controlling their destiny, it did not surprise John Crane that their first demand wherever they settled was for local government in which they could have a voice. Replying to that demand in 1853, President Franklin Pierce made a separate entity, Washington Territory, of the land lying north of the Columbia River, with its eastern border the same as that of Oregon Territory: the crest of the Rocky Mountains. As its first territorial governor he appointed a thirty-four-year-old army officer, Isaac Ingalls Stevens.

"Major Stevens graduated from the Academy fourteen years ago," Luke Crane wrote his father from West Point, and continued:

But he made such a name for himself here that he still is pointed out as a model to be emulated by cadets in the Corps of Engineers. He graduated first in his class, designed and built a number of fortifications along the East Coast and in the South, and served with great distinction in the Mexican War. I am sure he will do well as Governor of Washington Territory. I only wish I were in a position to become a member of his Survey party.

As matters now stand, it appears that I will graduate in the top ten percent of my class, which I hope will please you. My first assignment, I have just been informed, will be to Fort Gibson, Indian Territory. If you're not familiar with that area, it lies southwest of Missouri and is the wilderness region to which the Five Civilized Tribes were relocated following their removal from the East during the 1830s. Though I haven't as yet had the pleasure of meeting any of these red gentlemen, I'm told they are called "civilized" because just before scalping you they say "Pardon me!"

Because of his son's comments on Governor Stevens's record and the fact that Stevens had been an officer in the Corps of Engineers until he resigned to take the presidential appointment, John Crane followed the news of his progress with more than casual interest. A small-statured, black-haired man, with alert dark eyes and a neatly trimmed mustache-goatee, Governor Stevens seemed to be aggressive, energetic, and politically ambitious.

On his way out from St. Paul to his new office in the capital—being established at the southern end of Puget Sound—he might as well survey a northern route for a transcontinental railroad, he told President Pierce. While doing this, he would also contact Indians encountered along the way, with the aim in mind to come back later, treat with them, and "extinguish title to their lands."

Within two years, he had accomplished both objectives.

In this whirlwind tour west of the Cascades he had little trouble getting the small but numerous tribes living there to agree to reservations in or near where they had lived for generations. They were already "settled" Indians to a degree. Their homes were the forests, the streams, and the saltwater beaches on the rainy side of the mountains, where they need not roam far to find sustenance or neighbors with whom to trade. Furthermore, they were intimidated by the large numbers of white people who had moved into their country, built cabins, cleared fields, and established farms. Most important of all, they had been tamed and their numbers drastically thinned by the greatest civilizing force of all—smallpox and other white man's diseases.

But the tribes east of the Cascades—the horse Indians—were quite another matter. In order to deal with them, John Crane knew, Governor Stevens would have to convene large numbers of well-armed warriors belonging to the most powerful tribes in the Pacific Northwest, impress them with the strength of the American government, shower their leaders with substantial gifts, and negotiate treaties that would put them in their place forever and open the rest of their lands to settlement by the whites.

The spot chosen for the meeting was an ancient, traditional Indian council ground in the heart of the Walla Walla Valley, six miles east of the abandoned Whitman Mission. Invited to the treaty talks were members of five tribes: Nez Perce, Cayuse, Umatilla, Walla Walla, and Yakima. The time set for the talks was late May 1855. Given advance notice that the council was to take place, John Crane agreed to be there and act as interpreter for the Wallowa band of Nez Perces.

"Chief Joseph says we will never sell our homeland," Tall Bird wrote. "But if the council with the white leaders is to make clear which land we live on and which land the whites may settle on, we will be glad to take part. All we want is to live in peace with our neighbors, Chief Joseph says, whether they be red or white."

Because this was to be the most important council held east of the Cascades, elaborate preparations for it had been made, John learned when the party reached the Walla Walla Valley. A wall tent had been set up on level, open ground on the north bank of Mill Creek, facing the Blue Mountains. In front of it a large arbor of poles and brush was erected to shade the white and Indian leaders from the sun, a structure the Nez Perces called a "*tukash.*" Enough open space was nearby for a large number of Indians to seat themselves on the ground where they could see the participants in the talks and hear what was said as it was relayed to them through interpreters and criers.

Ranged along the creek were the tents of the civilian packers and the military guards. A log-walled house had been built to contain the food supplies and gifts for the Indians. A large herd of beef cattle grazed nearby, with enough potatoes, sugar, coffee, bacon, flour, and beans on hand to give each Indian attending the council daily food rations for several weeks.

The arrival of the Nez Perces in midmorning, May 24, was a dramatic, breathtaking spectacle. While the main body of Indians stopped a mile away, half a dozen of the leaders rode forward to meet the commissioners, accompanied and introduced by William Craig. Among them were Lawyer, Timothy, Joseph, Old James, Eagle-from-the-Light, and Tall Bird. Shaking Tall Bird's hand, John asked him if he knew how many Nez Perces were in the party.

"Twenty-four hundred, by my count," Tall Bird said. "When the chiefs told the *Nimipu* that the white commissioners wanted to talk about dividing the land, most of our people decided to come and hear what was said."

"Is Swift Bird here?"

"No. He is still with Chief Looking Glass, killing buffalo and Blackfeet east of the Bitter Roots. A message was sent to Looking Glass, telling him about the council, but we do not know if he will come. Lawyer hopes he will not, for they have never been friends. All Lawyer can do is talk, Looking Glass says. All Looking Glass can do is fight, Lawyer says."

Limping to the top of a nearby knoll, Chief Lawyer waved his cane above his head in a circling gesture, signaling for the arrival spectacle to begin. Strung out single file, riding their best horses at a dead run, brandishing their war shields, spears, and guns, yipping, and shouting battle cries, the garishly painted and dressed Indians came charging across the plain toward the group of white and Indian leaders as if making a hostile attack. Circling, weaving in and out, the seemingly endless stream of superbly mounted men kept the white men frozen to the spot for a good twenty minutes before the last of the riders passed. Then, in response to another signal from Lawyer, a hundred or so Nez Perces swung off their horses, a corps of drummers squatted down, and a circle of howling, contorting dancers performed a bloodcurdlingly realistic going-to-war dance. When it ended, the Nez Perce leaders joined the whites in smoking the pipe of peace, while across the wide expanse of valley floor tepees began to rise as the women made camp.

Because talks could not begin until the other tribes arrived, several days passed before the opening of the council. Provisions were issued to the Nez Perces at the rate of one and a half pounds of beef, two pounds of potatoes, and one half pound of corn a day. Unlike the friendly Nez Perces, the Cayuses, Walla Wallas, and Umatillas arrived quietly and went into camp without a salutation of any kind. Hearing that they were refusing to accept provisions from the whites and were pitching their lodges a mile distant to the south, where they were screened by a line of trees from the camp of the whites and the Nez Perces, John Crane was concerned.

"What are they mad about?" he asked Tall Bird. "They even turned down a gift of tobacco, I heard. That's a pretty blunt insult."

"All I know is what Five Crows said: 'You will find out by and by why we won't take provisions.' My guess is they're counting on the Yakimas to put up a bold front and force the commissioners to abandon the council. They feel that the Catholics, who have started a mission in the Yakima country, are their friends and will make the Americans stay in the Willamette Valley."

"I've heard talk that Governor Stevens intends to appoint *Kamiakin* head chief of the Yakimas. Do you know him?"

"Very well. He is half *Nimipu,* for his father was a member of the Asotin band. He was also a famous horse thief, unable to resist stealing every fast horse that caught his eye. To Indians, of course, horse stealing is an honorable pursuit—except when a person steals from his own people. This *Kamiakin's* father did; thus, was forced to flee to the Yakima country. There he married into the tribe and sired three sons. *Kamiakin* is the oldest and very much like his father."

When the large contingent of Yakimas arrived next day, they, too, refused to accept provisions from the commissioners. Father Pandosy, the Catholic priest who had come with them, told Governor Stevens that *Kamiakin* was not ill disposed toward the whites.

"It's just that he feels he can't speak for a people who have never been united as a tribe and have never had a head chief. In his country, there are fourteen related bands such as the Wishrams, the Celilos, the Wanapums, the Klickitats, and others which speak the same language and recognize one another's fishing and hunting areas. But the concept of being a tribe is alien to them."

"We've heard a rumor that he, Young Chief, and *Peo-peo Mox-mox* are plotting to lead an uprising aimed at murdering all the whites before the talks can even begin. Do you think there's any substance to it?"

"No, I don't. When the Oregon Volunteers came upriver to fight the Cayuses a few years ago, *Kamiakin* was urged to lead the Yakimas against the whites. He refused. He's a moody, headstrong, unpredictable man, Governor, but he's no fool. I don't think he'll commit his people to a war they can't win."

Designated as chiefs for the Nez Perces were Lawyer, Joseph, James, Timothy, and Red Wolf. For the Cayuses: Young Chief, Stickus, and *Camaspelo.* For the Walla Wallas: *Peo-peo Mox-mox.* For the Yakimas: *Kamiakin, Ow-hi,* and *Skloom.* Six interpreters were sworn in when the council convened May 29, but since the day was rainy and cool it was agreed to postpone the talks until the next afternoon, which, when it came, was sunny and clear. Governor Stevens made the opening speech, during which he told the Indians of the sincere concern for their welfare in the heart of the President of the United States.

"I went back to the Great Father last year to say that you had been good, you had been kind, he must do something for you. My brother General Palmer wrote to the Great Father in like manner."

Lieutenant Lawrence Kip, a recent West Point graduate who was in charge of the small military escort, murmured to John Crane, "How did

Joel Palmer get to be a general? I didn't know he'd even been in the Army."

"He fought with the Oregon Volunteers," John said. "Seems to be a rule after that kind of service all enlisted men become colonels, all the officers generals."

"I told the Great Father, these Indians have farms," Governor Stevens went on. "The Great Father said he wants them to have larger farms. I told him you had cattle and horses. He said he wants your cattle and horses to increase. I told him some of your grown people could read and write. He said he wants all the grown people and all the children to read and write. I told him that some of you are handy at trades. He said he wants to give all of you the means to learn trades."

Translating phrase by phrase, as the other interpreters were doing, pausing while strong-voiced Indian criers repeated the words in different dialects and tongues so that row after row of Indians seated in concentric semicircles on the ground could hear, John accepted the fact that this was going to be a long afternoon. As William Clark had written in his journal after going through such a session with the Nez Perces in Chief Broken Arm's village many years ago, the process was "tegious." But there was no other way it could be done.

Stevens turned the council over to Superintendent Palmer, who gave a long, detailed review of 360 years of conflict between the American Indians and the European settlers in the New World.

"They clearly show that the white man and the red man cannot live happily together," he said. "There should be a line of distinction drawn so that the Indian may know where his land is and the white man where his land is."

After a long day of interpreting, William Craig and John Crane retired to John's tent to rest and recuperate. Craig gave a mighty yawn.

"Won't Isabel be surprised when I tell her white people and red people can't live happily together? Wonder where our line of distinction ought to be drawn?"

"Care to wet your whistle with a small dram?"

"Be dramned if I wouldn't!" Craig chuckled. "The bullshit shoveled out today would drive a teetotaler to drink."

John poured generous drinks into two tin cups. "Do you think the Nez Perces will accept a reservation?"

"All according to where its boundaries are set. As long as they can live in their country and ain't restricted in where they can travel, they'll be agreeable. Least, Lawyer, Timothy, and Old James will. How does Old Joseph feel?"

"The same way. He wants peace and he wants his homeland."

"Sure is a handsome son he's got, that Young Joseph. Gonna be even taller than his father, from the looks of him. What'd he be now, fifteen?"

"Around that. Tall Bird tells me he went on his *Wy-a-kin* quest a couple of years ago. While he was up in the mountains fasting alone, one of those heavy thunder and lightning storms came up that hit the Wallowas now and then. Gave him a real doozy of a name. *Hin-mah-too-yah-lat-kekt.* Know what it means?"

" 'Thunder Rolling over Distant Mountain Heights' would be close enough. But he'll be called 'Young Joseph' till the old man dies."

Taking the first of June off to recover from two days of speeches and to confer among themselves, the Indians returned to the council at noon, Saturday, June 2. With the preliminary groundwork laid, Joel Palmer got down to cases.

"I have said that the white man and the Indians could not live together in peace. It is but fifty years since the first white men came among you. Now we have a good many settlers in the country below you.

"You may ask, 'Why do they come?' Can you stop the waters of the Columbia River from flowing on its course? Can you prevent the wind from blowing? Can you prevent the rain from falling? Can you prevent the whites from coming? You are answered: 'No!'

"This land was not made for you alone. The fish that come up the rivers, the beasts that roam through the forests and plains, and the fowls of the air were made alike for the white man and the red man.

"Now while there is room to select for you a home where there are no white men living, let us do so."

Following the conclusion of Palmer's lengthy speech, the Indians were invited to open their hearts. *Peo-peo Mox-mox,* whose son had been killed by whites and his murderers never punished under the Code of Laws, made a caustic reply.

"I know the value of your speech from having experienced it in California. From what you have said, I think you intend to win our country, or how is it to be? Suppose you show me goods. Shall I run up and take them? Goods and the earth are not equal. Goods are for using on the earth. I do not know where they have given lands for goods."

After several Indians spoke in a similar vein, the council adjourned for the day. Both William Craig and John Crane noted that Lawyer had had nothing to say.

"My guess is he's waiting to see how *Peo-peo Mox-mox,* Young Chief, and *Kamiakin* feel," Craig said. "If any of the chiefs are going to balk, they'll be the leaders."

"Tall Bird says he still hears rumors of a massacre."

"A few hotheaded windbags, probably. None of the chiefs want war."

But something appeared to be in the wind, for when John Crane got up next morning he was surprised to find that during the night Chief Lawyer had removed his tepee from the Nez Perce section of camp and pitched it next to the tent of the white commissioners. Stevens told John Crane and William Craig what had happened.

"He came to me late last night and disclosed a conspiracy on the part of the Cayuses to suddenly rise up and massacre all the whites on the council grounds. 'I will come with my family and pitch my lodge in the midst of your camp,' he said, 'so that those Cayuses may see that you and your party are under the protection of the head chief of the Nez Perces.' And he did."

Though neither man cared to dispute Steven or Lawyer, both wondered if the plot really did exist. Craig shook his head.

"Lawyer is shrewd. Could be he exaggerated the threat so's he'd look good in the eyes of the commissioners. Obviously, if there was a plot, no band of Indians would attack an important Nez Perce chief. They'd have the whole tribe down on 'em."

"Tall Bird says there's been a lot of disagreement among the Nez Perce leaders. He says Lawyer may have gotten some of the chiefs so mad at him for favoring a treaty that he moved his lodge to the white section of camp for *his* protection, rather than theirs."

"Well, whatever the reason, he sure made himself points with Governor Stevens."

Whether or not violence had been planned, the talks June 4 were peaceful. After several of the chiefs had asked questions regarding where the proposed reservations would be located, Governor Stevens and Superintendent Palmer got down to specifics.

Two reservations were planned: one in Nez Perce country, the other in Yakima country. Placed on the Nez Perce Reservation would be the Spokanes, the Cayuses, the Walla Wallas, and the Umatillas, as well as the Nez Perces. Gathered on the Yakima Reservation would be the Colvilles, Okanogans, Palouse, Pisquose, Klickitats, and other bands, as well as the Yakimas. Ceded to the federal government by the Indians would be approximately thirty thousand square miles of land.

Why only two reservations for a dozen or more tribes of Indians? Governor Stevens explained:

"We want as many tribes together as can be taken care of by one agent. We can do more with the same means. Think over what I have said and hear the rest tomorrow."

3

As explained by Governor Stevens next day, June 5, the rest consisted of thousands of dollars' worth of tools, clothes, supplies, and equipment needed to make them "settled" Indians; houses and annuities for the head chiefs; schools and teachers for their children. Would the Indians be confined strictly to the reservations? Of course not!

"You will be allowed to pasture your animals on land not claimed or occupied by the settlers. You will be allowed to go on the roads, to take your things to market, your horses and cattle. You will be allowed to go to the usual fishing places and fish in common with the whites, and to get roots and berries and to kill game on land not occupied by the whites, all this outside the reservation."

A payment of $100,000 would be made the first year the tribes were on the reservation; a further payment of $250,000 would be spread over a period of twenty years. After that, John Crane mused sardonically, it apparently was assumed that a people who had lived as Indians in this part of the world for thousands of years would have mastered the art of living like white men and would be self-sufficient. However, these sums of money would not be given in cash. Governor Stevens asked the chiefs to listen carefully while he gave his reason for this.

"We can furnish you with nearly twice as many goods as you can get from the traders. We shall buy things you want in New York and San Francisco at cheap rates and good articles. The expense of getting them to you will not come out of your money; it will cost you nothing. At Fort Walla Walla, a flannel shirt costs you three dollars. We will give you three shirts for three dollars. You pay for a calico shirt at Fort Walla Walla one and a half and two dollars. We can furnish you calico shirts for fifty cents apiece."

Unimpressed by the bargains they would get in ready-made shirts, the disturbed Indians questioned the soul-wrenching fact that they were being asked to sell their lands. After admonishing the interpreters to translate truly, the Cayuse chief Stickus, who long had been friendly to the whites, expressed his feelings with great eloquence.

"My friends, I wish to show you my heart. Interpret right for me. How is it that I have been troubled in mind? If your mother were here in this country who gave you birth, and suckled you, and while you were suckling some person came and took your mother and left you alone and sold your mother, how would you feel then? This is our mother, this country, as if we drew our living from her.

"I name three places for myself: the Grande Ronde, the Touchet toward the mountains, and the Tucannon."

The lands lying along these streams had not been included in either reservation, which would thus force the Cayuses to leave the land of their birth; Stickus was saying that he would resist removal to the Nez Perce Reservation with every fiber of his being.

On that note, the meeting adjourned.

Though the boundaries being drawn for the Nez Perce Reservation satisfied the majority of that tribe, the leaders of the three tribes being uprooted from their lands expressed their resentment in bitter terms. Young Chief said:

"I wonder if the ground has anything to say? I wonder if the ground is listening? I hear what the earth says. The earth says, 'God has placed me here to produce all that grows upon me, the trees, fruit, roots, and grass.' It was from her that man was made. God on placing men on earth desired them to take good care of the earth and do each other no harm. God said, 'You Indians who take care of a certain portion of the country should not trade it off unless you get a fair price.' "

Growing impatient, Superintendent Palmer scolded the Indians sharply.

"Young Chief says he does not see what we propose to give them. *Peopeo Mox-mox* says the same. Can we bring these sawmills and these gristmills here on our backs? Can we build these schoolhouses and these dwellings in a day? It takes time to do these things.

"We don't come here to steal these lands. We pay you more than they are worth. Here in this little valley and in the Umatilla Valley there is a little good land, but between these two streams and all around is a parched-up plain. What is it worth to you or to us? Not one half of what we have offered for it. Why do we offer so much? It is because our chief has told us to take care of his red people. We come to you with his messages to try and do you good."

Interpreting that final phrase to the Wallowa band as William Craig relayed it to the Lapwai Nez Perces, John Crane winked at his ex–mountain man friend and murmured, "By God, he'll *do* 'em good, too."

The Indians still refused to give in. *Camaspelo* protested against moving from the fertile valley where he had established a productive garden, to the land of the Nez Perces, much of which was heavily timbered. He said:

"How do you show your pity by sending me and my children to a land where there is nothing to eat but wood? That is the kind of land up there; that is the reason I cry. Look at my hands! An old man's hands. I have them by hard work. I ask myself, have I labored in vain? What have I to be glad for?"

Realizing that the talks had reached a dead end, the commissioners saved face by saying that since the Nez Perces were satisfied and anxious to go home, the treaty with them could be signed tomorrow. Stevens said optimistically: "We shall meet as friends, I hope."

With that, the council adjourned.

Like all treaty negotiations, the vital compromises that unsnarled the most knotty problems were made during talks held after council hours between leaders of both factions—talks not recorded for posterity by the two official secretaries, James Doty and William McKay, who were present for the public sessions. After conferring one by one with the dissident chiefs in the tent of the commissioners late into the night, Stevens and Palmer agreed on a compromise plan by the terms of which a third, smaller reservation for the local Indians would be set up. Even Young Chief was satisfied.

"The reason why we could not understand you," he said when the council met next day, "was that you selected this country for us to live in without our having any voice in the matter. You took away all my country. Where was I to go? Was I to be a wanderer like a wolf? Without a home, without a house, I would be compelled to steal, consequently I would die. I will show you the lands that I will give you. We will then take good care of each other."

Placed on the third reservation, whose boundaries would include well-watered valley, foothill, and mountain land on the western slope of the Blues, would be the Umatillas, Cayuses, and Walla Wallas. A head chief would be appointed for the united tribes, with the same provisions for improvements, clothing, and annuities. In addition, it was agreed that a house would be built for *Peo-peo Mox-mox* on the Columbia River, where he had been accustomed to grazing his horses and cattle and trading with the emigrants.

With four of the tribes present now ready to sign the treaty, the commissioners turned their attention to *Kamiakin* and the Yakimas, who had been promised a large reserve in the area occupied by the fourteen bands that shared it. Getting word that the Nez Perce chief Looking Glass, who had been on a prolonged sojourn in the buffalo country, was nearby and would be arriving at the council grounds the next day, Governor Stevens was pleased.

"My friends, I am glad Looking Glass is coming. When he is close by, two or three of us will go and take him by the hand and set him down by his chief in the presence of his friend, *Kamiakin*. Let us now have *Kamiakin*'s heart."

"The forest knows me," *Kamiakin* said moodily. "It knows my heart. It knows I do not desire a great many goods. All that I wish for is an Agent, a good Agent, who will pity the good and bad of us and take care of us. I have nothing to talk long about. I am tired. I am anxious to get back to my garden. That is all I have to say."

Old Joseph, who had been listening quietly to what was being said at the council, now spoke for the first time. To John Crane, there was a gentle dignity and a human tolerance in his words:

"These people here are my children. I see them all sitting here. Talking slowly is good. It is good for the old men to talk straight. Talk straight on both sides and take care of one another. It is not us we talk for. It is for our children who come after us. It is good for the old people to talk together good and straight on account of our children on both sides, to take care of each other till the last day."

Speaking through a big, red-bearded white interpreter named Andrew J. Bolon, *Skloom* tried to do some bargaining for the Yakimas.

"Once I saw a white man take an ax and cut a mark on a tree, as if he had made a watch. He went to that tree and looked up and saw a star. He took a line and measured the land from that tree. All the land he had measured, he plowed. For this country that he had plowed up, he got eight hundred dollars for each mile.

"My friends, I have understood what you have said. When you give me what is just for my land, you shall have it."

In reply, Stevens said: "We do sell good lands for eight hundred dollars a mile, but not in this country. Looking Glass is coming. We shall stop talking and shake his hand."

With the talks suspended so that the Indians and whites could greet Chief Looking Glass, John Crane found pencil and paper and did a bit of arithmetic. He shared his conclusions with William Craig.

"Want to know what the Indians will be getting for the land they're giving up?"

"What?"

"According to my figures, ten cents an acre."

"The hell you say!" Craig exclaimed wryly. "Why, that'd make my claim worth all of sixty-four dollars!"

"Not in cash, Bill. Way Governor Stevens talks, you'd have to take it out in shirts. Which do you prefer—flannel or calico?"

Standing on a knoll with Tall Bird and William Craig, John Crane watched Chief Looking Glass and his party of half a dozen warriors as they rode at a gallop across the valley toward the headquarters of the council camp. Tall Bird's eyes were sparkling with anticipation, for he had heard that his son Swift Bird was a member of the group.

"Looking Glass is seventy years old," Tall Bird said. "But he has the strength of a man half that age. He and twenty lodges of his band have been living in the buffalo country for three years. At one time, I'm told, the Blackfeet raided his village and stole many of his horses. He and his warriors followed, caught the thieves, fought them, and recovered the horses. Looking Glass himself killed two Blackfeet and took their scalps."

"Swift Bird is with him, you say?"

"Yes. He married a niece of Looking Glass and now is blood brother to the chief's son, who is a few years older than he. I am told my son is a fierce warrior now. Which makes me proud in one way, sad in another."

"How do you suppose Chief Looking Glass will react to the proposal to put the Nez Perces on a reservation?"

"Not well," Tall Bird answered, shaking his head. "When word reached him that the council was taking place, he was camped in the Bitter Root Valley, near the eastern foot of Lolo Pass. The news made him so angry he decided he must come to the council. With a few chosen warriors, he crossed the mountains through snowdrifts that at times were shoulder-deep on the horses. He and his party have ridden three hundred miles in just seven days. I am told he is mad."

Indeed, he was very mad. Watching Chief Looking Glass lead his party through the camp at a gallop, with him, his son, and Swift Bird triumphantly waving scalps tied to the end of their war lances, John Crane knew that the worst kind of trouble had arrived. Pulling his horse to a sliding stop, Chief Looking Glass vaulted to the ground, scowled blackly at the rows of Nez Perce observers, then cried in a voice that needed no amplification by criers:

"My people, what have you done? While I was gone, you have sold my country! I have come home and there is not left me a place on which to pitch my lodge. Go home to your lodges! I will talk to you later."

Turning to Governor Stevens and General Palmer, he shook his scalp-decorated lance at them and shouted:

"I am head chief of the Nez Perces, not Lawyer. The boys talked yesterday. Now I will talk."

"Reckon the fat's in the fire," William Craig muttered to John Crane. "The council's blown plumb to hell."

Looking visibly shaken, Governor Stevens, who had tried to shake hands with Chief Looking Glass only to be bluntly ignored, announced without bothering to consult with General Palmer, "Today's talks are adjourned. We will meet again tomorrow morning."

4

To the stunned commissioners, it appeared that two and a half weeks of patient negotiating had been blasted into irreparable pieces. Young Chief, *Peo-peo Mox-mox,* and *Kamiakin* seemed to be ready to support Looking Glass and back off from tentative commitments they had made. Lawyer, who had lowered his head and walked away when Looking Glass harangued his people, as if acknowledging the old chief's supremacy, came late in the evening to Governor Steven's tent. In an aggrieved voice, he asked, "Why did you not tell Looking Glass that I, Lawyer, am head chief of the Nez Perces?"

"Because I considered his tirade the outpourings of an angry, excited old man," Stevens answered patiently. "Because I was sure his heart would become right if left to himself for a while."

"Then you still recognize me as head chief?"

"Your authority will be sustained. Looking Glass will not be allowed to speak as head chief. You, and you alone, will be recognized."

"Will you tell Looking Glass that?"

"I certainly will. Should Looking Glass persist, the appeal will be made to your people. They must sign the treaty agreed to by them through you as head chief. If they do not, the council will be broken up and you will return home, your faith broken, your hopes of a future gone."

According to what Tall Bird told John Crane later, a stormy council was held in the Nez Perce section of camp that night, a meeting that lasted until the small hours of the morning. Though no vote was taken, the *Nimipu* agreed that for the purpose of this council Lawyer would be recognized as head chief, and with Looking Glass and other leaders would sign the treaty.

In the camps of the Cayuses, Walla Wallas, Umatillas, and Yakimas, pressure was also brought to bear in favor of signing the treaties.

Sunday, June 10, no talks were held. Instead, Timothy preached a sermon in which he stressed the fact that God would punish whoever dared break the faith of the Nez Perces in attempting to persuade them not to sign the treaty.

"Seems the Almighty has taken sides," William Craig said dryly. "As

Reverend Spalding used to say, you can't make a Christian out of an Indian until you get him settled down."

A rumor flew around the camp that Governor Stevens, in a private session with *Kamiakin,* Father Pandosy, and interpreters Andrew J. Bolon and Dominique Pambrun, had threatened to unleash a war against the Yakimas if *Kamiakin* refused to sign the treaty. When John Crane asked Pambrun if this was true, Pambrun hesitated a moment, then nodded.

"Yeah, it happened. Governor Stevens told *Kamiakin* he was sick and tired of his stalling and he'd better sign the treaty or else."

"Or else what?"

"His exact words were: 'If you do not sign the paper, you will walk in blood knee deep.' Father Pandosy, who was sitting next to me, nudged my elbow and said, 'That is a great error. He should not make such a threat. Look at *Kamiakin.* He is in such a rage that he is biting his lips so that they are bleeding.' And *Kamiakin* was. But he kept still and agreed to touch the end of the writing stick, just as a gesture of friendship to the whites. But between you and me, the treaty is only a piece of paper to him."

Whatever significance there was to touching the end of the writing stick as it was placed on the *X—his mark* on the final page of the treaty, the Indian leaders of the five tribes all took part in the ceremony Monday morning, June 11. In order, they were:

Aleiva, or Lawyer
Head Chief of the Nez Perces, his X mark
Ap-push-wa-hite, or Looking Glass, his X mark
Joseph, his X mark
James, his X mark
Timothy, his X mark

and so on, until fifty-eight Nez Perces had signed the treaty. Led by *Peopeo Mox-mox,* thirty-six chiefs of what later would be known as the Umatilla Confederated Tribes (Cayuse, Walla Walla, and Umatilla) stepped forward and let their hands be guided as a pen made their mark. Finally *Kamiakin* and thirteen other chiefs signed a third treaty for the newly formed Yakima Nation, which had not existed until now.

With William Craig translating for him, the eloquent, religious Nez Perce Chief Eagle-from-the-Light concluded the nineteen days of talks with a brief speech whose tone was that of a prayer of benediction. He said:

"My forefathers are all dead. I only am left. There is but the encampment remaining. It is good to hear and think of each other. I do not want our hearts to come together wrong, but right, and remain so as long as we are people. The Lord will reward us both when our hearts are good and we look and care for each other."

In his report to the Commissioner of Indian Affairs back in Washington City, Governor Stevens boasted that he had just concluded the most successful council ever held with Indians in the West, one that would assure peace for years to come, settle the Indians on reservations where they would become civilized like white men, and open vast areas of lands to settlement by deserving emigrants from the East.

Now, Stevens said, he would move on toward the country of the Spokanes, Coeur d'Alenes, and Blackfeet, with whom he expected to make similar treaties before the end of summer. Ironically, the tough old Chief Looking Glass agreed to join him with a hundred young warriors who would act as an escort in the place of the Fort Dalles soldiers, most of whom, along with Lieutenant Lawrence Kip and General Joel Palmer, would be returning to Oregon. William Craig, whom Stevens had appointed as a "colonel" in the nonexistent territorial militia, was so intrigued with the prospect of talking peace with the Blackfeet that he agreed to go along as an interpreter.

"What about Swift Bird?" John Crane asked Tall Bird. "Is he going, too?"

"Oh, yes!" Tall Bird said. "He says it sounds exciting—and it's excitement he loves. He and Young Looking Glass always have to be in the middle of the action."

"At their age, so did I." Chuckling, John shook his head. "My son, Luke, will be green with envy when he hears about your son acting as an escort for Governor Stevens. From what he writes me, it's pretty dreary duty building quarters for troops and tame Indians down in Indian Territory. He'd give his eyeteeth to be out here."

"Are there buffalo in that part of the country?"

"No, most of the buffalo are gone where the Five Civilized Tribes have been settled. They're still plentiful in the western part of the territory, Luke says, but before the Indians can go on a hunt there they've got to get a permit from their agent and take a military escort along to make sure they don't make war against another tribe. As hunters, he says, they aren't very good. Their horses are poor and they're lousy shots."

"If this is true, they most go hungry much of the time."

"Oh, they eat well enough on government rations and beef issues. The most exciting day of the week, Luke says, is Saturday, when each band is given its allotment of live beef on the hoof. Instead of killing and butchering the steers in a pen, the Indians like to let the cattle run so they can have the fun of chasing and shooting them. Every once in a while, their shooting is so bad their beef issue gets away."

"Your son has a low opinion of Indians, I gather."

"Just of the ones he's seen. Most young professional army men are like that, I'm afraid. For instance, Lieutenant Kip told me he'd never seen an Indian that could shoot worth a damn. Indians never take care of their rifles, he said, don't know how to sight them, and haven't got the slightest notion of effective killing range. When I asked him which Indians he was talking about, it turned out the only ones he'd ever seen shoot were tame Indians living near the settlements. There, if they fail to down wild meat, they can always go to town and buy a steer or a hog. I told him he'd get his eyes opened if he ever went on a buffalo hunt with the Nez Perces. From what I've seen, they're better shots than white soldiers."

Tall Bird nodded. "Years ago, your father gave Red Elk the first rifle he ever owned. Before he let Red Elk shoot it, he taught him how to take care of it, load it, sight it, and understand its sure-kill range. When the *Nimipu* hunt in the buffalo country, they know their families will go hungry if they don't kill meat."

"With butcher shops few and far between."

"When the Blackfeet attack, a *Nimipu* rifle must be ready and his bullets must fly true."

"Or he's a dead Indian. I told Lieutenant Kip that, but I don't think I convinced him. The only way to make believers out of professional white soldiers is to have them face the Nez Perces in battle—which I hope never happens."

Following the breakup of the council, Tall Bird invited John Crane to return with him to the summer camp of his band in the Wallowa country. Because he'd passed up a guiding job, he guessed he could spare a couple of weeks, John said. Once there, he found the weather so fine and the company so congenial that "a couple of weeks" became two and a half months before he knew it. Contributing greatly to his pleasure in visiting the Nez Perces was the affection given him by his niece Singing Bird, who, at fifteen, was a stunningly beautiful young woman, with a personality that matched her name.

"Got a man picked out yet, *Peo-peo Uenpise?*"

"Yes, *Pekelis Suyapo.* A very handsome man."

"Anybody I know?"

"Certainly you know him, White Grandfather. He is you."

"Come on, Singing Bird. You can't marry me. We're related."

"Then I will never marry at all!" she declared. "I will be a maiden all my life. No, I cannot live long without you. When the next full moon comes, I will get into a canoe at midnight, row out to the middle of Wallowa Lake, and sing a love song to the monster. He will rise up out of the depths and devour me."

"You got your monster love song composed yet?"

"I'm working on it. Tonight, I will sing you the first verse."

Because the treaty council had been the most important event to take place in the inland country for many years, the continuing journey of the Stevens party was a frequent campfire topic, with stories passed along the Indian grapevine and brought back by travelers who had seen the white men and the natives with whom they were attempting to make treaties. Looking Glass, Eagle-from-the-Light, William Craig, Swift Bird, and a hundred *Nimipu* warriors had joined Stevens in the Coeur d'Alene country, where the governor had successfully concluded a treaty with the Coeur d'Alenes, Flatheads, Pend Oreilles, and Kootenays. Under its terms, these tribes had ceded twenty-five thousand square miles of land in exchange for a reservation one-tenth that size, and payment in goods, buildings, and annuities for the chiefs similar to those made at the Walla Walla council. Eager to inform his constituents of his success, Governor Stevens dispatched his express rider, W. H. Pearson, to Olympia, the capital of Washington Territory, with a report on what had been accomplished.

The essence of the report was: that treaties had been made with most of the tribes east of the Cascades; that all the land not included in the reservations had been ceded to the federal government; and that a vast area formerly claimed by the Indians now was open to mining exploitation and settlement by the whites.

Though Stevens had told the Indians and did say in the report that the treaties would not become effective until ratified by the United States Senate and signed by the President, that minor clause—if mentioned at all by newspapers and word-of-mouth publicity—probably would be totally ignored, John Crane guessed, by white miners and settlers . . .

5

General John E. Wool, military commandant of the Pacific District, had reluctantly approved the building of the army post Fort Walla Walla, in the summer of 1856, on the site where the treaties had been made; but it was his firm conviction that the best way to avoid conflict between the Indians and whites, was to keep the area east of the Cascades closed to settlement by Americans. Despite strong objections by Governor Stevens, General Wool's policy prevailed.

In the spring of 1856, the United States Senate ratified treaties made with the Blackfeet, Coeur d'Alenes, and other inland tribes. But because of the arbitrary army edict closing the interior country to access by whites, the treaties negotiated with the Nez Perces, Cayuses, Walla Wallas, Umatillas, and Yakimas stayed locked up in committee.

All through 1857 a peace of sorts lay over the land. Hearing that two white miners had been killed by Indians in the Colville area, Lieutenant Colonel Edward Steptoe, in command of the new military post of Walla Walla, decided early in May 1858 that the time had come to "show the flag" and demonstrate to the Indians of the interior country that the army was present not to make war but to keep the peace. With 159 men and a large packtrain, the colonel set out May 8, intending to make a leisurely march through the country of the Palouses, Spokanes, and Coeur d'Alenes.

"When the expedition started, one hundred mules were required to pack the camping outfit," a local historian later reported. "As the last one was loaded, it was found that no room remained for the ammunition."

The last statement was an exaggeration, William Craig told John Crane. In actuality, the three companies of dragoons and the partial company of infantry carried forty rounds per man, along with two mountain howitzers. But their arms were very poor.

"Two of the dragoon companies were armed with musketoons—short muskets with a very limited range, useless beyond fifty yards," Craig said. "The other dragoon company had Mississippi yager rifles, which carried well but could not be loaded on horseback. There were ten good carbines in the infantry company. Some of the men had revolvers, and others had only old-fashioned muzzle-loading pistols. The cavalry did not have sabers."

Reaching Snake River at the mouth of Alpowa Creek, the command was joined by Chief Timothy and three Nez Perce warriors, who agreed to go along and act as guides and interpreters. By May 16, the troops were ninety miles north of the Snake, deep in the heart of Coeur d'Alene country, and surrounded by increasing numbers of Indians who were strenuously objecting to what they regarded as a trespass on their lands. If the soldiers went any farther, the Indians said, they would attack. Because they greatly outnumbered his force, Colonel Steptoe told them that he would turn back the next morning.

Monday, May 17, the command broke camp and started the return march south. Daylight revealed hostiles hovering in all directions. Urged to parley by a Catholic priest, Father Joseph, who was acting as interpreter for the Coeur d'Alenes, Colonel Steptoe asked a Nez Perce warrior, Levi, to take part in the talk so that he would be sure of what was being said. Shortly after the parley began, Chief *Soltees,* who was speaking for the Coeur d'Alenes, solemnly assured the priest that no attack would be made on the whites; then, in response to a query from some of his people, he turned and shouted something to them in the Indian tongue.

"What did he say?" Steptoe demanded of the priest.

"I'm not sure," Father Joseph replied uncertainly. "Something about a delay—"

But Levi, the Nez Perce brave, was sure. Lifting his quirt, he struck the Coeur d'Alene chief over the head, at the same time crying out, "What for you tell Steptoe you no fight and then say to your people wait awhile? You talk with two tongues!"

When the parley broke up, the column of troops began the retrograde march. At first the retreat was orderly. Then, in response to visual and shouted signals, the Indians began firing on the soldiers from all directions. Without waiting for orders, a Captain Taylor and a Lieutenant Gaston led their company in a charge through the milling mass of Indians that opened a path to the south for the rest of the command. Riding with H troop and the pack animals, Colonel Steptoe led the way through the surrounding hostiles, heading for home.

As the morning passed and Indians continued to attack the column from all directions, the pace of the retreat quickened. Captain Taylor and Lieutenant Gaston, with their company, fought a desperate rearguard action. Weary, exhausted, with their ammunition running low, they still maintained their moving position protecting the rear of the fleeing column. In desperation they sent a courier asking Colonel Steptoe to halt the command and give the beleaguered men an opportunity to reload their guns. The request was ignored.

Out of ammunition, badly outnumbered, and deserted by the rest of the command, Captain Taylor, Lieutenant Gaston, and members of the rear guard were reduced to fighting the Indians hand to hand, using clubbed pistols and empty muskets against the knives, lances, bows and arrows, and guns of the Indians. It was in this battle that Private Victor C. DeMoy, a former French army officer who had served in both the Crimean and Algerian wars, began a legend when he cried as he swung a clubbed musket at the Indians, *"My God, my God, for a saber!"*

Wounded so badly that he could not ride or bear to be carried by a comrade on a horse, DeMoy asked that he be placed in a sitting position on the ground, with a loaded revolver in his hand. After killing or wounding several Indians, he used the last bullet on himself.

"Course, all I got to vouch for these stories," William Craig told John Crane, "is that this is the way Indian survivors told 'em to me. But likely they're true, for if there's one thing an Indian won't lie about, it's what he sees happen in a battle. If he's caught lying, he's shamed forever."

What certainly proved to be true was that the Steptoe command had suffered a defeat so severe that it could only be called a disaster. Hearing that Captain Taylor, Lieutenant Gaston, and a substantial portion of the rear guard had been killed, Colonel Steptoe finally halted the command on the slope of a hill, where the weary soldiers dug in and made a stand. At a council of war, it was decided to bury the howitzers and leave the balance of the stores and packtrain for the Indians, whose joy in looting their prizes might occupy them long enough to give the soldiers an opportunity to steal through their lines.

Sure that they had the troops surrounded, the Indians broke off the siege as darkness fell. They went into camp and spent the night dancing and celebrating. Checking on the supply of ammunition, Colonel Steptoe learned that the troops were down to only four rounds per man. There was nothing to do but run for it.

"Some say it was Timothy who saved what was left of the command," William Craig told John, "leading the soldiers through the lines of the hostiles over trails that only he knew. Others say he bribed some of the hostile chiefs to let the survivors go. It does seem clear that *Kamiakin,* who was running the whole show, warned the hostiles to keep a close watch over the soldiers. But the Coeur d'Alenes, Spokanes, and Yakimas were having so much fun dancing and celebrating that they paid him no mind."

Whatever act of heroism, carelessness, or chicanery was involved, the escape attempt was successful. Leaving behind the dead and badly wounded, muffling spurs, bridle chains, and anything metal that could clink, covering light-colored horses with dark blankets, and moving through the darkness with the silence of ghosts, the soldiers filtered one by one through the loosely manned lines of the hostiles until they were out of earshot, then mounted and rode for safety as fast as their horses would run.

Twenty-four hours and 70 miles later, what was left of the command reached the north bank of the Snake, opposite Timothy's village. Whether or not he had acted as guide and savior, a number of Nez Perces in his band crossed and stood guard between the weary survivors and possible attack, while the women cared for the wounded and ferried them across the river. Earlier, a lone Nez Perce brave had been dispatched as a messenger to Fort Walla Walla, 150 miles away. He returned to Timothy's village with Captain F. T. Dent and the company that had been left behind at the garrison.

Riding in from the east a day later was a contingent of Nez Perces led by Chief Lawyer, carrying a large American flag. Informed of what had happened by the incredibly swift Indian system of passing mirror or smoke signals from point to point, he had assembled a strong force of warriors, had brought them here, and was prepared to fight the enemies of his white friends.

But Colonel Steptoe and his weary soldiers had had enough. Seventeen officers and men had been killed, fifty had been wounded, and large quantities of arms, supplies, equipment, and pack animals had been deserted or lost.

Earlier that year, when Major Granville O. Haller had tried to impress the Yakimas with the might of the federal government by leading a command of eighty-four men north from The Dalles into Indian Reservation country, his troops had been attacked and defeated, with the loss of five men killed and seventeen wounded. Coupled with that fiasco, the Steptoe Disaster (as it came to be called) made the fighting ability of regular army troops look very bad indeed.

This was a state of affairs not to be tolerated by the War Department. Corrective measures must be taken at once . . .

6

So far as John Crane and his ex–mountain man friend William Craig were concerned, their share of Indian-fighting could be handled from now on by regular army troops, thank you, with no regrets from them. Being interested in bringing stability to the upriver country, both men welcomed the news that General John E. Wool had been removed as army commander of the Department of the Pacific in May 1857, with General Newman S. Clarke named as his successor. Because an uneasy state of peace existed east of the Cascades, Clarke had seen no reason to change the Wool policy of exclusion of American settlers from the interior country.

But the Steptoe Disaster drastically altered his attitude.

Moving his headquarters from San Francisco to Fort Vancouver, Clarke ordered the Hudson's Bay Company agents at Fort Colville to stop selling arms and ammunition to the Indians and to turn over all horses and mules taken from the Steptoe command and later sold to the Company. If the Indians wanted peace, they must return all property stolen or captured. Furthermore, they must identify and surrender for punishment any of their people who had committed acts of violence against the whites.

Failure to comply with these terms would result in only one thing—a war of extermination.

Made confident by their recent victories, the Indians disdainfully turned down the proffered peace terms. So General Clarke set the machinery in motion for the war of extermination to begin. Deeply involved in that war, John learned, would be two people linked to him by ties of blood or friendship: his Nez Perce nephew, Swift Bird, and the young army officer classmate of his son, Luke, whom he had met during the First Treaty Council talks in the Walla Walla Valley in 1855, Lieutenant Lawrence Kip.

In a letter to his half brother, Tall Bird wrote:

Why my son loves the excitement of war so much, I cannot say. But love it he does. Since we no longer fight the Blackfeet in the buffalo country, he and a number of the young men can talk of nothing but the adventures they had protecting Governor Stevens and daring the Coeur d'Alenes and Spokanes to fight. When Chief Lawyer asked for warriors to die with him to rescue the Steptoe command, Swift Bird was one of the first to volunteer. He was deeply disappointed that there was no battle. But now that the whites have declared war on all the hostiles of the inland country, he is determined to enlist in the company of Nez Perce soldiers being raised by Chief Lawyer. It disturbs me that he is doing so, but I cannot persuade him that the ways of peace are best.

In charge of this campaign, John heard, would be Colonel George Wright, a stocky, square-jawed, white-haired army officer of the old school, who was reputed to be a stern martinet. Lieutenant Kip was assigned to Company M of the Third Artillery and was to report the action to newspapers and military journals. He participated enthusiastically in both tasks.

Stationed at Fort Walla Walla when the young lieutenant arrived June 19 were four companies of the First Dragoons and two of the Ninth Infantry. Built near the site of the council, the post was well supplied with water, grass, and nearby timber.

On this expedition, Colonel Wright would be in command of a seven-hundred-man force, while Lieutenant Colonel Steptoe would be left behind with a hundred men to garrison Fort Walla Walla. In his inspections, reviews, and twice-a-day drills, Colonel Wright soon revealed himself to be a disciplinarian who would brook no slackness in performance.

"A few days ago sixty Nez Perces arrived," Kip wrote, "under an old chief named Lawyer, whom I knew at the council in 1855. Colonel Wright had a talk with the deputation of the tribe, and made arrangements by which they became our allies."

On August 5, Kip's unit received orders to march to the juncture of the Tucannon with the Snake sixty miles to the northeast, where the soldiers would spend a week erecting a fort. This was planned to be an advance base on the edge of hostile country, where troops could fall back if strongly pressed by the Indians. It would be called Fort Taylor, in honor of one of the fallen officers of the rear guard that had saved Steptoe's command from annihilation.

The main force left Fort Walla Walla on August 7. It was a formidable one, consisting of one company of dragoons, six companies of artillery, two twelve-pound howitzers, and two six-pound guns. Instead of short-range musketoons, the soldiers carried "rifle-muskets" which shot a minié ball that could kill at six hundred yards. This time, the dragoons wore sabers. Thirty thousand rations were transported on pack mules and in wagons.

Since it now was late summer in a semiarid land where little rain fell during June and July, the Indians had made the route to their country difficult by burning off a wide expanse of grass, forcing the column to march for miles through choking clouds of dust. With the fort nearly complete, and Colonel Wright and the rest of the command due the next day, Lieutenant Kip saw the glare of grass fires burning north of the river.

"The Nez Perces tell us the Indians are collected in large numbers at the Lakes, about five days' march from here, where they are going to meet us. We trust it is so, as it will give us an opportunity of finishing the war."

Once the Snake had been crossed, Kip wrote, the campaign would begin in earnest. This time, the soldiers were well prepared:

"Our transportation consists of six mules to a company, and a mule to each officer, besides the three hundred and twenty-five mules which the quartermaster has in his train. Our entire train, therefore, consists of about four hundred mules. Large wagons cannot go beyond Snake River. We shall attempt to take only one light vehicle, which Lieutenant Mullan needs for his instruments.

"Now as to our fighting force. The dragoons number one hundred and ninety; the artillery, four hundred; the infantry (as Rifle Brigade), ninety. Total, about six hundred and eighty soldiers, besides about two hundred *attachés,* packers, wagon-masters, herders, etc.

"Then we have thirty Nez Perces, and three chiefs to act as scouts and guides. They are placed under the command of Lieutenant John Mullan. These, our allies, have been dressed in uniforms to distinguish them during a fight from the hostiles. Like all Indians, they are particularly delighted with their clothes, and no young officer, just commissioned, thinks as much of his uniform as they do. They insist, indeed, upon having every minute portion, even to the glazed cap covers."

Having stopped to visit John Crane in the Willamette Valley on his way upriver, Lieutenant Kip had been intrigued by the fact that his West Point classmate, Lieutenant Luke Crane, and John's three-quarter Nez Perce nephew, Swift Bird, were both serving as United States soldiers. At the beginning of the present campaign, Kip made a point of meeting the young Nez Perce, finding him to be a handsome, stocky, muscular man who was eager to carry out whatever orders were given him, but a bit shy because of his lack of fluency in English.

"I go to mission school for a while," he admitted to Kip, "but I don't like it much 'cause I rather ride, hunt, and go to buffalo country."

"Who wouldn't?" Kip said with a smile. "From what I've seen of your riding, you'd make an excellent cavalryman. Did you know I went to school with your cousin, Lieutenant Luke Crane?"

"Is this the same school where Governor Stevens go?"

"Yes. It's called West Point."

"My father has told me about it. He says it is where young white men go if they want to be soldier-leaders in war."

"Luke rides well, too. Would you like to meet him some day?"

"If he would come here to my country, yes. I would take him on a buffalo hunt. But I never could go to his country. It is too far away. I would get lost."

Though the command planned to cross the Snake at daybreak August 23, a violent wind and rain storm delayed them for two days. First, the sand and dust blew so thickly that visibility was limited to a few feet. Then the rain fell in torrents, turning the sand and dust to mud, while at the same time extinguishing the grass fires on the far side of the river.

With the horses and mules swimming and the men and packs ferrying across the swift, dangerous river in flatboats, the command was transferred to the north shore in two days' time.

Some sixty miles north of the Snake, two of the Nez Perce scouts rode into camp the evening of August 30 with the news that a large body of Indians had been sighted ahead. The dragoons saddled their horses and rode out to investigate, while the artillery and infantry prepared for battle. But after a long-distance exchange of fire between the dragoons and what apparently was a contingent of scouts for the hostiles, both groups fell back with no damage done on either side.

On this day Lieutenant Kip recorded two casualties among his comrades: "This afternoon two men of the artillery died from eating poisonous roots."

The best he could make out after talking to the two dead soldiers' messmates, one of the men had claimed to be an expert on Indian food. Going to a nearby marshy area, he had dug up some camas bulbs, boiled them until they were soft and mushy, then shared them with two of his friends. Not liking the sweetish taste, one of the soldiers had spit out his first bite, eaten no more, and had not even gotten sick. The other two, after eating several of the bulbs, had developed violent abdominal cramps, gone into convulsions, and died.

"I thought camas were good to eat," Kip said in puzzlement to Swift Bird. "Aren't they a staple in the Nez Perce diet?"

First nodding, then shaking his head, Swift Bird searched for the words to express himself.

"*Camas,* two kinds. Purple flower, yes—*taats,* is good. White flower, no —*kapsis,* is bad." Lifting his right hand to his mouth, chewing, then swallowing as if in the act of eating, he clasped both hands over his belly and doubled up as if in violent pain. "I eat *kapsis camas—Ine-ketinkse*—I kill myself by poison."

"But there were no blooms on these camas plants, I'm told. The stalks above ground had shriveled and dried. How could anyone tell which were good and which were bad?"

"Let woman tell. She know."

"You mean let her eat one and see what happens?" Kip said incredulously. "Is that how you find out?"

"No, no! Just let her dig up and cook. She know."

What Swift Bird was trying to say, Lawyer explained, was that since it was the women who dug, prepared, and cooked all the native roots eaten by the *Nimipu,* they were taught from childhood which were good and which were bad, and could distinguish one from the other at any stage of growth. But with no such experts present, the two soldiers had paid for their lack of knowledge with their lives.

The next day, August 31, as the column marched north over fairly level country sprinkled with clumps of cedar, fir, and pine trees, groups of hostiles exchanged fire with the Nez Perces, who were acting as advance scouts. Though nominally under the command of Lieutenant Mullan, who found them bold and fearless, Kip noted:

"Their individuality is developed so strongly that it is difficult for him to induce them to obey orders. Each one fights on his own responsibility."

Because men and animals were tired, Colonel Wright decided to remain in camp at a spot some twenty miles south of the Spokane River for a few days. Reading this as a sign of indecision of the part of the soldiers, the hostiles grew more aggressive, swarming over the nearby hills, shouting taunts, inviting an attack. After placing the four hundred mules and the extensive stores under a strong guard in a secure location, Colonel Wright prepared for battle.

"After advancing about a mile and a half," Kip reported, "we reached the hill and prepared to dislodge the enemy from it. Major Grier, with the dragoons, marched to the left, while the party of Nez Perces, under the direction of Lieutenant Mullan, wound around the hill and ascended it to the right. The main column came next, with Colonel Wright and staff at its head, followed by Captain Keyes, commanding the artillery, the rifles, and the howitzer battery.

"As soon as the dragoons reached the top of the hill, they dismounted— one half holding the horses and the others acting as skirmishers. After exchanging a volley with the Indians, they drove them off the hill and held it until the foot soldiers arrived. On our way up, Colonel Wright received a message from Major Grier, stating that the Indians were collected in large numbers (about five hundred, he thought) at the foot of the hill, apparently prepared to fight. Colonel Wright immediately advanced the battalion rapidly forward, ordering Captain Ord's company to the left to be deployed as skirmishers.

"My place, as adjutant of the artillery battalion, was, of course, with Captain Keyes. We rode to the top of the hill, where the whole scene lay before us like a splendid panorama. Below us lay four lakes—a large one at the foot of the barren hill on which we were, and just beyond it three smaller ones, surrounded by rugged rocks, and almost entirely fringed with pines.

"On the plain below we saw the enemy. Every spot seemed alive with the wild warriors we had come so far to meet. Mounted on their fleet, hardy horses, the crowd swayed back and forth, brandishing their weapons, shouting their war cries, and keeping up a song of defiance. Most of them were armed with Hudson Bay muskets, while others had bows and arrows and long lances."

Thus the Battle of Four Lakes, as it would be called, began. Kip continued:

"Orders were at once issued for the artillery and infantry to be deployed as skirmishers and advance down the hill, driving the Indians before them from their coverts, until they reached the plains where the dragoons could act against them. At the same time, Lieutenant White, with the howitzer battery, supported by Company A under Lieutenant Tyler, and the rifles, was sent to the right to drive them out of the woods. The latter met with vigorous resistance, but a few dischargees of the howitzer, with their spirited attack, soon dislodged the enemy, and compelled them to take refuge on the hills.

"In the meanwhile the companies moved down the hill with all the precision of a parade. As soon as they were within six hundred yards, they opened their fire and delivered it steadily as they advanced. Our soldiers aimed regularly, though it was no easy task to hit their shifting marks.

"But minié balls and long range rifles were things with which now for the first time the Indians were to be made acquainted. As the line advanced, first we saw one Indian reel in his saddle and fall—then, two or three—then, half a dozen. The instant, however, that the braves fell, they were seized by their companions and dragged to the rear, to be borne off. We saw one Indian leading off a horse with two of his dead companions tied on it.

"But in a few minutes, as the line drew nearer, the fire became too heavy, and the whole array broke and fled toward the plain. This was the chance for which the dragoons had been impatiently waiting. As the line advanced they had followed behind it, leading their horses. Now the order was given to mount, and they rode through the company intervals to the front. Taylor's and Gaston's companies were there, burning for revenge, and soon they were on them. We saw the flash of their sabers as they cut the Indians down. Lieutenant Davidson shot one warrior from the saddle as they charged up, and Lieutenant Gregg clove the skull of another. It was a race for life, as the flying warriors streamed out of the glens and ravines and over the open plain, and took refuge in the clumps of wood or on the rising ground."

If the horses of the dragoons had been fresh, the troopers would have made a terrible slaughter of the hostiles, Kip felt, but after twenty-eight days on the march, the mounts were exhausted. Entirely blown, the horses halted, their riders dismounted, and the foot soldiers passed through the ranks, pursuing the Indians across the rolling, broken country for two miles—then they, too, ran out of strength and had to stop and rest.

Thus the battle ended for that day with the Indians routed and the soldiers victorious.

"What the Indian loss was, we cannot exactly say, as they carry off their dead," Kip recounted. "Some seventeen were seen to be killed, while there must have been between forty and fifty wounded. Strange to say, not one of our men was injured. One dragoon horse alone was wounded. This was owing to the long range rifles now first used by our troops, and the discipline which enabled them so admirably to use them."

For three days the command rested, with the Nez Perce scouts sent out to reconnoiter. During this time the weather changed, growing damp and cold. On September 5 the soldiers broke camp and, after marching north about five miles, saw Indians collecting in large bodies to their right. As the command emerged from rough, broken country and entered a broad prairie fringed by trees, the Indians attacked. This time the hostiles tried a new strategy, as Lieutenant Kip reported.

"We had nearly reached the woods when they advanced in great force, and set fire to the dry grass of the prairie. Under cover of the smoke, they formed round us in one-third of a circle, and poured in their fire upon us, apparently each one of his own account. The pack train immediately closed up.

"It was curious to witness the scene—the dust and smoke, and the noise and shouting of the Mexican muleteers driving forward to the center four hundred overloaded animals, while the troops were formed about them with as much order and far greater rapidity than if no danger threatened. Then on the hills to our right, if we could have had time to have witnessed them, were feats of horsemanship which we have never seen equalled. The Indians would dash down a hill five hundred feet high and with a slope of forty-five degrees, at the most headlong speed, apparently with all the rapidity they could have used on level ground."

Again, the long-range rifle-muskets, the howitzers, and alternate charges of horse and foot soldiers did deadly work. All day long the running fight continued, with the column advancing until it reached the banks of the Spokane River, where it camped for the night.

"We had marched during the day twenty miles," Kip wrote, "the last fourteen fighting all the way. No water could be procured for the whole distance, and the men by the time they reached the river were entirely exhausted. Nothing kept them up but the excitement of the contest."

Incredibly, considering the number of hostiles involved and the length of the engagement, only one soldier was slightly wounded. Estimating that some five hundred Indians had been in the battle, Kip made no attempt to guess at their casualties.

After camping near Spokane Falls the evening of September 7, Colonel Wright soon began to see signs that the will of the Indians to resist further had been broken. Chief Garry expressed a wish to have a talk with the colonel. When it was granted, he said that he always had been opposed to fighting, but that the young men and many of the chiefs were against him, and he could not control them. Now all he wanted was peace.

"I have met you in two battles," Colonel Wright said coldly. "You have been badly whipped. You have had several chiefs and many warriors killed or wounded. I have not lost a man or animal. I did not come into this country to ask you to make peace. I came here to fight. Now, when you are tired of war and ask for peace, I will tell you what you must do.

"You must come to me with your arms, with your women and children, and everything you have, and lay them at my feet. You must put your faith in me and trust to my mercy. If you do this, I shall then tell you the terms upon which I will give you peace. If you do not do this, war will be made on you this year and the next, until your nations shall be exterminated."

While Chief Garry spread Colonel Wright's stark ultimatum among the Spokane and Yakima leaders, the command marched east toward the land of the Coeur d'Alenes. After advancing ten miles, the Nez Perce scouts rode in to say they had discovered a band of Indians on the right. Halting the packtrain and placing it under a strong guard, the dragoons under Major Grier moved on at a trot, with the foot soldiers trailing behind.

"We found it difficult to advance as fast as we wished, there being a very steep hill to climb," Kip wrote. "The dragoons and Nez Perces, therefore, outstripped us, and we soon saw them passing over the hills. They had discovered that the Indians were driving off their stock to the mountains, which they had nearly reached. Our horsemen were obliged to dismount on account of the nature of the ground, and, after a sharp skirmish, succeeded in capturing the whole band, consisting of nine hundred horses."

If the Indians of the interior country had formerly feared volunteer soldiers because of their brutality, while holding regulars in contempt, they now got a lesson in how regular army troops could behave when commanded by a cold-blooded martinet. Receiving a report from the Nez Perces that they had found a herd of Indian cattle and a number of lodges filled with wheat, Colonel Wright dispatched two companies of artillery and one of dragoons, with orders to burn the lodges and grain and drive in the cattle. Too wild to be rounded up, the cattle took to the hills. But the lodges and the grain were burned.

That evening, Kip reported, "the case of our Palouse prisoner was investigated, and it having been proved beyond doubt that he was engaged in the murder of the miners in May last, he was hung."

Next morning, December 9: "At nine o'clock, Colonel Wright convened a board of officers to determine what should be done with the captured horses. They decided that one hundred and thirty should be selected for our use, and the rest shot. It was a disagreeable necessity, but one which could not be avoided. Nothing can more effectually cripple the Indians than to deprive them of their animals."

While the brutal, sickening, daylong process of shooting the mature horses and clubbing the suckling colts to death was carried out by the enlisted men detailed to that bloody chore, Lieutenant Kip, like many of the other horse-loving officers and all of the Nez Perces, put a mile of distance and a low ridge between himself and the scene. Toward dusk, when the ordeal at last ended, Kip found himself with Swift Bird, whose bronze, handsome, intelligent face seemed frozen into stone. Fierce and fearless though the Nez Perces had been in battle, they had taken no scalps, refused to watch the Palouse prisoner hung, and would not go near the valley where the horses were butchered.

"Tell me, Swift Bird," Kip said quietly, "why is it that none of the Nez Perces in your group here took scalps, when those with Chief Looking Glass who came to the Stevens Council made such a show of the scalps they had taken in the buffalo country?"

"Because in the buffalo country we fought and killed the Blackfeet, who are enemies. Here we fought and killed Yakimas, Spokanes, and Coeur d'Alenes, who are brothers."

"If they are brothers, why do you fight them?"

"Because we want peace, as the *Suyapo* do. Because we signed a treaty and promised the white man we would be his friend."

"If your people won a battle against another tribe and captured many horses, what would you do with them?"

"Take the ones we wanted and let the rest go."

"You would not kill them?"

"No. We kill only to eat. Since we do not eat horses, we would have no reason to kill them." He peered at Kip with a puzzled frown. "Why do you kill them?"

"There's a Spanish word that describes it best," Kip answered bleakly. *"Reducido."*

"This is a word I have not heard before. What does it mean?"

"In the Southwest, as the Spaniards learned two hundred years ago, a man set afoot is no man at all."

"It is the same in our country."

"At the missions, the priests forbade local Indians to ride horses. When one did, his first ride was away from the mission toward freedom. When he was caught and brought back, his horse was taken away from him and he was reduced to the state of being afoot again. A *reducido.*"

"When I went to mission school, it was the same." Swift Bird said. "Father Spalding said horses were made by the devil to tempt Indian boys into playing hooky. The streets of hell, he said, were filled with heathen Indian boys on fast horses."

Nothing that Colonel Wright's command had done, Lieutenant Kip observed, so much prostrated the Indians as this destruction of their horses. With their will to resist broken, their stores and shelters destroyed, and their means of transportation eliminated, all that remained to be done now was to meet with the humbled chiefs and proclaim the surrender terms.

"You shall have peace on the following conditions," Colonel Wright told first the Coeur d'Alenes and then the Spokanes. "You must deliver to me, to take to the general, the men who struck the first blow in the affair with Colonel Steptoe. You must deliver to me, to take to Fort Walla Walla, one chief and four warriors with their families. You must deliver to me all property taken in the affair with Colonel Steptoe. You must allow all troops and other white men to pass unmolested through your country. You must not allow any hostile Indians to come into your country, and not engage in any hostilities against any white man. I also require that the hatchet shall be buried between you and our friends, the Nez Perces."

Though word was sent to *Kamiakin* that he would not be harmed if he surrendered, he refused to trust the white man's promises. Another Yakima chief, *Ow-hi,* did come in, and the rude treatment he received fully justified *Kamiakin*'s suspicion. Convinced of the truth of the stories that *Ow-hi*'s son, *Qualchen,* had murdered at least nine white men, Colonel Wright told the older Indian that if his son did not surrender within four days, he, *Ow-hi,* would be hanged.

Though this message was sent, it did not reach the young brave. For some reason *Qualchen* rode into camp a few days later, not knowing that his father was a prisoner and that he had been condemned without a trial. In a report dated September 24, Colonel Wright stated laconically:

"*Qualchen* came to me at 9 o'clock, and at 9:15 A.M. he was hung."

On the homeward-bound trip a detachment under Major Grier was sent to the Steptoe battleground to recover the buried howitzers and the remains of the dead, returning to the main camp September 25. Many Palouse Indians came in that same evening, seeking peace. They got it on Colonel Wright's terms when he arrested fifteen of them, hanged six on the spot, and took the others along in irons. En route, the Yakima prisoner, *Ow-hi,* was shot and killed "while trying to escape."

Four days later, camp was made on the Palouse River, where a chief named *Slowiarchy,* who had taken no part in the war, tried to help his people get favorable surrender terms. Colonel Wright was not in a forgiving mood. He would not be doing wrong, he told the Palouses, if he should hang them all.

He refused to make a written treaty with them on any terms, and threatened death to all who should cross the Snake. He then demanded the surrender of the two Palouses who had murdered miners. After a short conference among the Indians, one of the murderers came forward. The other could not be found. Wright then called for six men who had stolen the army cattle when the expedition was starting from Fort Walla Walla. They were promptly surrendered. When the council proceeded, the murderer and three of the thieves, who were recognized as notorious marauders, were hanged by the guard from a tree several yards distant. The usual quota of hostages was taken from the Palouse tribe—one chief and four men, with their families.

Since the newly built Fort Taylor would not be needed now, Colonel Wright abandoned it, turning it over to Chief *Slowiarchy* for whatever use he might wish to make of it. Reaching Fort Walla Walla October 5, the command buried the remains of the soldiers killed in the Steptoe fight, with full military honors.

The Walla Wallas, Cayuses, and Umatillas were called into council on October 9. Wright delivered his customary indictment and asked all who had taken part in recent battles to stand up. Thirty-five rose. Wright selected for execution four whose reputations were "preeminently evil."

"Thus was the last general uprising quelled," wrote a correspondent for a Willamette Valley newspaper. "Colonel Wright's methods may be regarded as harsh by some, but they were regarded as just by the Indians."

Reading that smug comment, John Crane raised a cynical eyebrow. Perhaps the surviving Indians did regard the methods as just. But the doomed Indians had not been quoted.

Tall Bird wrote that his son stopped by on his way home after the Nez Perce contingent of scouts had been discharged.

"For whatever it may be worth, Colonel Wright commended him for his energetic, courageous conduct during the campaign. But he did not talk much about his experiences. All he would say was that the white man's way of fighting a war is different from the Indian way. It is without honor or glory."

Thus, the peace Governor Stevens thought he had secured by treaty was finally brought to the region by force. In September 1858, General William S. Harney was appointed to command a new military district embracing the area. Following his arrival at Fort Vancouver, his first act was to revoke General Wool's order excluding Americans from lands east of the Cascades, throwing the interior open to settlement. On March 8, 1859, the United States Senator confirmed the treaties made with the Nez Perces, Umatillas, Walla Wallas, Cayuses, and Yakimas, and appropriated funds for their implementation.

At about the same time, the motley collection of grogshops, stores, and "parlors of entertainment" that had sprung up a mile east of the military reserve recently established on Garrison Creek, in the Walla Walla Valley, showed signs of growing into a permanent settlement. If the town were ever going to amount to anything, the saloonkeepers, merchants, and proprietors said, it would need a distinctive name.

For a brief while, in honor of the commander of the new post, the settlement had called itself Steptoeville. For obvious reasons the name did not stick. Someone then suggested that the metropolis adopt as its name the Cayuse Indian word meaning "Place of the Rye Grass," which the ill-fated Whitman Mission had used for the eleven years of its existence. Since no one could agree on the pronunciation of the word, let alone whether it should be spelled *Waiilatpu, Wyeletpo,* or *Wyelatpu,* that name was dropped, too.

Why not call the town Walla Walla?

Why not indeed.

So it was on the very site where the brush arbor had stood when the Nez Perce Treaty had been signed that the town of Walla Walla was built. Because of the lands ceded by the Nez Perces, the former council ground now lay 120 miles west of the heart of the Nez Perce Reservation—upon which, it had been promised the Indians, no white man could trespass without permission.

But it was from this distant settlement that the first white trespassers came—drawn by the magnet of gold . . .

PART FOUR

Gold and the Steal Treaty 1860-1868

1

Though he was absolutely sure he would hit a bonanza someday, Elias Davidson Pierce had been prospecting for ten years without striking it rich. Twice he had come close in Northern California, when he'd been just down the creek or across the ridge from really big finds. A third time, in the Rogue River country of southwestern Oregon, he'd actually struck a vein of what proved to be a mother lode. Trouble was, though all his years of experience and mining savvy told him that the vein should shallow and turn left, it had deepened and turned right, much to his own sorrow and the delight of a neighboring prospector who by dumb luck had filed his claim in the right place.

But like all his kind, Elias Pierce remained optimistic. One of these fine days, he told himself, he was going to cross a ridge, find a virgin stream that no prospector had ever seen before, fill a pan with gravel, swish it around, and in its final dregs find the golden nuggets of his dreams.

"What I'm of a mind to do is try the Clearwater country," he told the men drinking with him in the Blue Mountain Saloon in Walla Walla on a late September day in 1860. "If ever I seen country where gold ought to be, that's it."

"Ain't that Injun reservation land now?" Frank Bassett asked.

"What if it is? The Nez Perces are friendly—and they ain't interested in gold."

"How do you know that?" Will Parker queried skeptically.

"Three years ago, after I'd tried the Colville country and decided it wasn't worth working, I picked up several pack loads of trinkets I knew Indians liked, came down to where the Clearwater joins the Snake, and set myself up in business. Got acquainted with Chief Timothy and his band. Matter of fact, I got real well acquainted with his daughter Jane, who was just fifteen and quite a looker."

"She taken you under her blanket, did she?" leered Jim Fancher.

"Never mind where she took me. Her father and me became friends. He's a Christian, Timothy is, with a liking for white men. When I told him I was a prospector and wanted to go poking around up the Clearwater, he said with the war on and hostiles apt to be wandering around that part of the country, I'd best not go there alone. But he and some of his band were going on a camas-gathering trip, he said, to Weippe Prairie on the North Fork of the Clearwater. 'Case you don't know history, that was where the Lewis and Clark party met the Nez Perces back in 1805."

"Tell us more about Jane," Fancher said, "and what you gathered with her."

"That's the same kind of rock formations like where they found gold down in Northern California and southwestern Oregon," Pierce went on. "But on account of hostiles being around, I stuck close to the camas-gathering camp and didn't do much prospecting. Oh, I did wash a few pans from the banks of a small creek. Found some colors but didn't follow up. Mostly, what I did was ask the Nez Perces about the diamond."

"What diamond?" Frank Bassett asked curiously.

Pouring himself another drink out of the quart bottle of whiskey on the table, Pierce took a sip, made a wry face, then leaned back and smiled.

"Didn't I ever tell you about the diamond, Frank?"

"No. Not ever."

"Well, five or six years ago when I was working a claim down American River way, an Indian showed up in camp on a horse-selling trip. After he'd made his deal, he hung around, curious-like. We got to be friends. Said he was a Nez Perce from the *Koos-koos-kee* country up north. *Koos-koos-kee*, I made out, was Nez Perce for Clearwater. He said his country was a lot like that along the American River. I asked him if there was any gold in his country. That was when he told me about the diamond."

"All right, you've got our attention," Will Parker grunted. "Tell *us* about the diamond."

"This Nez Perce buck told me him and two of his buddies camped one night in a canyon along the North Fork of the Clearwater. All of a sudden, when the moon came up, a light like the brightest star they'd ever seen burst forth from the cliff wall directly across the river from their camp. They thought it was the Great Spirit's eye staring at them, he said. They were scared to go near it in the dark. But come daylight, they crossed the river and found this thing that had sparkled at them. It was a shiny, glittery rock, he said, the size of a saucer. It was embedded so deep in the cliff wall that they couldn't pry it loose. Anyway, they didn't try too long or too hard, he said, because they figured it was big medicine and best left alone. So they rode away and never went back."

"You believed him?"

"I made him swear to it three times."

"Couldn't he lie three times?"

"You don't know much about Indians, Frank, else you wouldn't say that," Elias Pierce said scornfully. "According to their code, a Indian can lie twice—but the third time he has to tell the truth, or he'll go straight to hell when he dies. What you say to him is 'Do you lay it on the ground three times?' If he says yes, what he's told you is true."

Reaching for the bottle, Jim Fancher poured himself a drink, took a swallow, belched, then said in an awestruck voice, "Godamighty! A diamond that size would be twice as big as that Koh-i-noor they found over in India a few years ago! It was worth millions!"

"What makes you so sure what this Injun seen was a diamond?" Will Parker asked skeptically. "S'posin' it was just a piece of glass?"

"It was hard, he said. So hard he couldn't even knock off a chip with his tomahawk, which he could of done if it'd been glass."

"Maybe it was a big crystal of quartz. Quartz is hard, too."

"So is your head, Will," Frank Bassett said. His face grew thoughtful. "Diamond, glass, quartz, or whatever that shiny rock your Injun seen was, you've been in that part of the country, Elias. You say its rock formations look right for gold. You say you panned colors—"

"That's right. I did. Good flakes of colors."

"You say the Nez Perces are friendly—"

"Mighty friendly. Why, a bunch of 'em even fought on the side of the whites during the war. And the only time they go up to Weippe Prairie is to gather camas. They ain't interested in gold."

"Then why don't the four of us take a little jaunt up thataway, you lookin' for the diamond, us lookin' for gold. Whatever we find, we'll split four ways."

Intrigued by the stories Elias Pierce had told, as well as by the fact that they would be the first white men to prospect the area, the four men left Walla Walla next day with a horse apiece, two pack mules, mining tools, and a month's supply of food staples. The weather was mild over the rolling, grass-covered hills which lay at low altitude between Walla Walla and the juncture of the Clearwater with the Snake. Because this was the domain of Timothy's band, Jim Fancher wanted to pay the friendly old Christian chief a visit, in hopes of getting acquainted with his pretty daughter Jane. But the other three men in the party vetoed that idea.

"We're prospecting for gold, not girls," Will Parker said. "And time's awasting."

"Thing for us to do is pretend we're just passing through the country," Elias Pierce said. "If we do that, the Indian agent, Andy Cain, won't bother us."

Despite their pretensions, Agent Andrew J. Cain, who weighed three hundred pounds and was reputed to be as conscientious as he was heavy, spotted the small party of white men shortly after the prospectors crossed the Snake and headed east up the Clearwater. He demanded to know where they were going. When they told him they were just wandering around to see what the country looked like, he politely but firmly informed them that they were trespassing on land reserved to the Nez Perces by the recently signed treaty.

"But the Nez Perces aren't using near all of it," Elias Pierce said plaintively. "What's the harm in doing a little prospecting?"

"By law, trespassing for any reason is forbidden. You must leave immediately. If you return, you will be arrested."

Since Agent Cain was accompanied by half a dozen husky Nez Perce policemen, who appeared to be quite willing to back him up, Pierce and his three friends turned their horses around and rode back down the Clearwater. Reaching Chief Timothy's village near the mouth of Alpowa Creek, Pierce had a brief talk with the soft-spoken old chief, then a longer, even friendlier talk with Jane, who, though eighteen and married now, was still very fond of the white man's trinkets, which she had learned her white friend Elias Pierce could supply in exchange for special favors.

"Made a deal with her," Pierce told his fellow prospectors that evening. "She knows a special way in."

"Well, I'll just bet she does!" Jim Fancher exclaimed with a lecherous smirk. "But you ain't gonna be greedy, are you, and keep her special way in all to yourself? Least you could do is share her with us."

"A special way into Weippe Prairie, you horny damn fool! Instead of going east up the main Clearwater, like we did, she'll guide us in by a back way. First we'll go north, like we're heading up to the Spokane country, then we'll circle around and go east and south. It's rough country, she says, and we'll have to do a lot of axwork to cut through the timber. But if we go in that way, Andy Cain and the Indian police won't even know we're there."

Jane kept her word. Just a week later, Frank Bassett knelt on the bank of a small meadow stream that meandered across the ages-old camas ground called Weippe Prairie, washed his first pan of dirt, and recovered flakes of gold he estimated to be valued at about three cents. Encouraged by that show of color, his three companions began digging, panning, and washing, too. As the pans proved to be increasingly fruitful, pan and shovel work was abandoned, a rough sluice was built from cedar bark, and the recovery of gold began on a larger scale. Even though the flakes were so light and thin that the find was christened *oro fino*—"fine gold"—eighty dollars' worth had been recovered by the end of the second day, assuring the four men that they had made an important strike.

Forgetting about the saucer-sized diamond that had inspired the venture, Elias Pierce rubbed his hands together gleefully and chortled, "Boys, we've hit it! Here's what we'll do. We'll set up a mining district with rules like they've got down in California. While you three fellas keep working here, I'll go back to Walla Walla the way we came in and spread the word among a few of my friends—"

"What about our friends?" Will Parker demanded. "Can't you tell them, too?"

"Sure, Will. Why don't each of you write down the names of two or three friends back in Walla Walla. We'll file claims in our names and theirs. That'll make fifteen or so of us, all told. By the time I get back here with enough grub and supplies to carry us through the winter, it'll be well into November, with snow due to close the trails. We'll build cabins and work through the winter. By the time the snow melts and the trails to the low country open up, we'll all have our fortunes made . . ."

Returning to Walla Walla, Elias Perce, whom his companions were respectfully calling "Captain" now, quietly spread word of the discovery to a few trusted friends, reoutfitted, and, with a party of fifteen men, returned to the area and dug in for the winter. It was now mid-November and this was high country where the snow came early and stayed late. Agent Cain and his contingent of military police learned that the white trespassers were there and set out from Lapwai to remove them. But the weather turned stormy, snow closed the trails, and the only thing the authorities could do was go back to Lapwai—and hope that the miners would freeze or starve to death.

Unfortunately for the Indians, the trespassers survived. Building a cluster of log cabins, which they named Pierce City, they continued to dig for gold despite deepening snow. By January, they were so sure they had struck a bonanza that they sent two men to the settlements on snowshoes for more supplies. In March, another member of the party followed, carrying eight hundred dollars in dust to pay off debts to the merchants. Sent downriver to Portland, the gold and news of the strike set off a blaze of excitement. Within weeks, men by the thousands were moving toward the interior.

This was in the spring of 1861. A continent's breadth away, Fort Sumter was under siege; President Lincoln was about to issue a call for 75,000 troops; and the country soon would be rent asunder by the Civil War. But in the Pacific Northwest there was bigger news.

Gold . . .

To John Crane, a letter just received from his son was of more interest than the discovery of gold in the Nez Perce country. Two months in transit from the East Coast, which was fairly rapid delivery these days, it contained several interesting bits of information:

I am pleased to tell you, Father, that my promotion to the rank of Captain has come through. At long last, my tour of duty at Fort Gibson has been completed and the dreary business of supervising the building of quarters whose purpose is to watch over this motley assembly of Indians called the "Five Civilized Tribes" is finished.

Effective next week, I will be assigned work more to my liking—the design and modification of military installations along the Atlantic Coast. Though most officers trained at West Point are positive that the talk of rebellion now circulating among the rabid element will come to nothing following President Lincoln's inauguration, the army is planning to strengthen its key posts in the South. My first assignment will be to Fort Sumter, which is on the coast of South Carolina . . .

2

As the gold rush developed during the next three years, hordes of eager prospectors poured into the region, violating reservation boundaries with a total disregard for Indian rights. Considering the large number of white trespassers, surprisingly little friction arose between them and the Nez Perces. Observing the tolerance of the *Nimipu* for the white invaders of their country, Tall Bird understood the reasons for his people's passiveness.

The first was that the stream beds where gold was found lay in high country, which the *Nimipu* used only for hunting, summer pasture for their horses, and the digging of roots.

A second reason for choosing peace rather than conflict was that many of the Nez Perces had become "settled" Indians, as the white missionaries had taught them to be. Not only had they built up their farms and herds so that they could feed themselves, they now had a surplus to sell for cash. One day he heard Chief Reuben, a settled Indian who lived on the lower Clearwater, urging a group of his people to let the white men go wherever they wished without molestation.

"Do you like to tire your backs digging in the ground? Of course not! But you like gold because of what it will buy. Then let the *Suyapo* dig wherever he chooses. When he has found gold, he will give it to you for your horses, cattle, corn, and vegetables. Is this not better than fighting him?"

Still a third—and probably the most important—reason for the *Nimipu* to keep the peace was that long years of association with the whites had taught them caution. Since the time of Lewis and Clark they had seen plenty of pushy, greedy white men, and had learned to put up with them. They had also observed how dangerous, ruthless, and deadly white men could be when given the least excuse, so they had learned to be careful.

Following the original strike in the Orofino district of the North Fork of the Clearwater, other strikes were made at Orogrande on the South Fork of the Clearwater, and at Florence, in the Salmon River country. In each case, prospectors by the thousands stampeded to the new fields, ignoring all efforts of the agent or the Nez Perces to stop them.

Since this was the domain of the Kooskia band, Young Looking Glass—

who had become its chief upon the death of his seventy-eight-year-old father in January 1863—did his best to keep the white men from overrunning their country. In his mid-thirties and habitually wearing a small mirror strung around his neck, as his father had done, *Ip-pak-ness Way-hay-ken*—"Looking Glass Around the Neck"—was no coward. On several occasions, he had proved his bravery in battles with the Blackfeet. He had ridden with the *Nimipu* escort that had protected Governor Stevens. He had not served in the campaign with Colonel Wright, for at that time his father was feuding with Lawyer. But he liked and respected the whites and felt that in return they should like and respect him.

Swift Bird was with him one day when a confrontation of a hundred *Nimipu* warriors with twenty-five white prospectors determined to go to the lower Salmon River country nearly erupted in bloodshed. When Looking Glass told the leader of the party, a brash young Irishman named Johnny Healey, that they were risking their lives invading Nez Perce land, Healey threw back his head and laughed.

"Look here," he said, "don't you know that for every white man you kill, a thousand will take his place? So why not let us go where we want to go?"

"Because this is our reservation. Because we signed a treaty saying no white man may trespass on it without our permission."

"I signed no treaty."

"Your Great White Father did. You must do as he says."

"The hell I must! He's a Republican and I'm a Democrat. Under mining law, I got a right to dig for gold anyplace I can find it. Now I'll be obliged if you'll stand aside and let us ride to the Salmon River."

Whooping and yelling, the members of the party spurred their horses forward, waving their rifles threateningly at the Nez Perces grouped behind Looking Glass. His black eyes glittering with anger, Looking Glass raised his right hand above his head. If he brought it sharply downward, that would be the signal for the warriors to aim and fire, Swift Bird knew. Fine hunters that they were, they would wreak deadly havoc among the whites—which would mean war. But the hand did not fall. Instead, Looking Glass turned on his horse, the palm of his upraised hand facing toward the warriors in a gesture of restraint. Beside him, Swift Bird spoke softly.

"You are wise, brother."

"No. They are stupid—so stupid they do not know the risks they are taking. Let the madmen dig where they like."

During the early summer of 1861, the stern-wheeler *Colonel Wright* ascended the Snake and Clearwater to Slaterville, below the spot at which Lewis and Clark had built and launched their dugout canoes. As the river fell, it became apparent that the forty-mile stretch upstream from the juncture of the Clearwater with the Snake would be too shallow for navigation by a steamboat most of the year. From then on, that juncture became the unloading point for upriver traffic.

Admitting the need for a dock and storage sheds, even though it was within the boundaries of the reservation, the Nez Perces permitted these facilities to be built. No formal permission was given to pitch tents, convert them to cabins, build log and then frame houses, construct stores, lay out streets, and implant in a matter of only a few months a population of twelve hundred people in a town called Lewiston. No matter. The town was created anyway.

In an attempt to impose some kind of order upon chaos, Agent Charles Hutchins wrote General B. Alvord from Lapwai, July 12, 1862:

"It is required, in order to maintain the laws of the United States on this Indian reservation, to protect the Nez Perce Indians from iniquitous outrages on their persons and property by vicious white men, that mounted U. S. troops to the number of at least one company be immediately sent here, and that such be permanently stationed."

Back East a war was on, and almost all regular army troops stationed in the West had departed for the greater conflict. Volunteers now manned posts in the Pacific Northwest, the nearest at Fort Walla Walla, 120 miles to the west. In response to Agent Hutchin's request, Major J. B. Rinearson and Company F, Oregon Volunteers, were sent up, arriving at Lapwai early in August.

At first, Hutchins was pleased. However, he quickly learned that Major Rinearson had no intention of removing the whiskey peddlers.

"The major's response was that he had no authority to interfere with whites who sold liquor only to other whites, whether or not the sale took place on the reservation."

This piece of bureaucratic evasion resulted in a decision by General Alvord to establish a permanent post and double the garrison by the addition of a company of infantry made up of Washington Territory Volunteers. Personally accompanying this force, General Alvord spoke to an assembly of Nez Perces October 24, 1862:

"I have come to see you in order to assure you that the government desires to do all in its power to protect you. You will never have a worse enemy than the whiskey sellers and the bad whites who intrude upon you and commit outrages upon you and your families."

Six months later, the Nez Perces learned that an enemy worse than the whiskey sellers and the bad whites was the government itself. In May

1863, the scattered bands of the tribe were asked to meet in a major council with the white commissioners to negotiate a new treaty that would recognize the realities of white settlements on Indian lands, as well as sharply reduce the holdings of the Lower Nez Perces, and the Salmon River and Wallowa bands.

According to the treaty ratified just four years before, the lands included within the reservation boundaries were to belong to the Nez Perces forever. Now the Indians were wondering: *In the white man's world, why is forever such a short time?*

3

Riding from the winter village on the lower Grande Ronde to the council ground at Lapwai, *Tu-eka-kas,* Old Joseph, passed on wisdom gained in his lifetime to *Hin-mah-too-yah-lat-kekt,* Young Joseph.

"When you go into council with the white man, always remember your country. Do not give it away. The white man will cheat you out of your home. I have taken no pay from the United States. I have never sold our land."

Although the council was originally scheduled at Lapwai in November 1862, a delay in the appropriation of the fifty thousand dollars needed by the commissioners to feed and care for the thousands of Indians expected to attend caused it to be postponed until May 1863. Informed by Tall Bird and urged to come, John Crane replied that he would be there.

"Matter of fact, my old sidekick Doc Newell has been appointed a commissioner by the federal government," he wrote. "I'll be coming up with him."

Taking an increasingly active role in the leadership of the Wallowa band was Young Joseph, who was Tall Bird's second cousin. Now twenty-three years old, standing six foot two inches tall in his moccasined feet, and weighing a muscular two hundred pounds, he was a strikingly handsome young man who had inherited his father's quiet dignity and commanding presence.

Acting as commissioners for the United States were Superintendent Calvin Hale, Agents Charles Hutchins and S. D. Howe, and ex–mountain man Robert Newell. A substantial number of the Lawyer faction insisted they would accept no interpreter but Perrin Whitman. This delayed the opening of the council for two weeks while word requesting his presence was sent to his home in the Willamette Valley and he made the 380-mile trip inland. Having come to the Oregon country at the age of twelve with his uncle, Dr. Marcus Whitman, in 1843, he had grown up with the Nez Perces, knew their language, and was trusted by them.

The two-week delay gave John Crane an opportunity to exchange visits and bits of news with his Nez Perce relatives and his white friends.

"When I heard my son, Luke, had been captured by the Rebels at Fort Sumter, I went back to Independence in the fall of '61," he told Tall Bird, "hoping he could get paroled on his promise to sit out the war or take an assignment to a post in the West. But by the time I got there, the South had agreed to an exchange of prisoners with the North on a no-restrictions basis. Last I heard from Luke, he'd been promoted to colonel and had been in three battles. Though he's trained as an engineer, he's destroying as many bridges and forts as he's building, he says, usually under fire."

"Why do your people fight?" Tall Bird asked. "What do they hope to gain?"

"God knows. From this distance, it's a senseless damn war. The South lives on cotton, which means they want low tariffs and slaves. The North depends on manufacturing, which means they want high tariffs and cheap white labor imported from Europe. Far as I can see, there ain't much to choose from between the two systems."

With the eastern part of the country in turmoil and Luke on active duty, John had realized there was no chance to see his son. So in April 1862, he'd picked up a job guiding a wagon train west.

"Kind of surprised me so many people from the border states would be pulling up roots. My train was a mixed bag of people from Missouri and Iowa, wanting to get away from the war. Lot of young single men avoiding the draft. When we got to Walla Walla, most of 'em headed for the gold fields of the Nez Perce country."

"Yes, my son Swift Bird has seen them. They have no respect for our treaty rights. But so long as we let them dig where they wish, there is no bloodshed."

"How are things in the Wallowa country?"

"Peaceful, as always. Since no gold has been found there, few white men come to our summer home. When the council is over, our band will be going there. We would be pleased if you would come with us."

"No reason why not. How's my favorite niece, Singing Bird?"

"She is married now, with a daughter two years old and another baby due in three or four moons. She still is a happy woman, who often speaks of you. How is your family?"

"Same as ever," John answered shortly, a cloud passing over his face. "Felicia has more grandchildren than I can keep track of. Being gone so much, I'm kind of a stranger to them. But I'm treated well enough when I'm home."

"Is your son married?"

"Oh, yeah, he got married six years ago while he was stationed at Fort Gibson. He and his wife have a two-year-old daughter and a four-year-old son. Right now she and the kids are living in St. Louis."

"Did you see them when you went east?"

"Matter of fact, I didn't," John said, shaking his head. "She don't think much of me. You see, I never married Luke's mother—"

"Why should that matter? Our father never married mine."

"I know! I know! In your world, there's no such thing as an illegitimate child. But in the white world, it's different—particularly when money is involved. My father—"

"Our father."

"All right, *our* father was a rich man when he died. Since I'd left St. Louis and didn't appear to give a damn about my child or the woman who bore it, he married her and willed everything he owned to the mother and child when he died. Luke was not told this until he came into his full inheritance at the age of twenty-one. By then we had met, established a good relationship, and carried on a correspondence for several years. He was shocked when he found out the truth, but he was mature enough to accept it."

"When he married, his wife did not?"

"That's about the size of it, brother. Even if she could have accepted the fact that her husband had been born out of wedlock, she gagged on the news that Luke's grandfather had married his mother, just to make sure I didn't get my grubby hands on Luke's money. Far as she's concerned, I don't exist."

"In the world of the *Nimipu,* all men are brothers," Tall Bird said quietly. "You are part of our family. When the council is over, I will take you to the Wallowa country and show you the cabin I built on my claim."

Before the council began, John rode up the valley and paid a visit to his old friend, William Craig. Past sixty now and not in the best of health, Craig said that while he might sit in on the council for a day or two, just to see what was going on, he would take no active part. Following the conclusion of Colonel Wright's campaign and the ratification of the treaty, he'd been passed over as Indian Agent for the Nez Perces; instead he'd been offered the position of Postmaster in the booming city of Walla Walla.

"But a year of sorting letters was enough for me," he said. "Reading and writing never was my long suit. So I came back here, where I intend to live out my days. Whatever comes of the new treaty talks, my Nez Perce friends say they'll let me keep my claim."

"Where do you think the boundary of the reservation will be drawn?"

"Wherever the commissioners and the settled Nez Perces want it drawn. It ain't a reservation they've got in mind, John. It's a pen. Not to keep the whites out but to keep the free-roaming Indians in."

"Will the Nez Perces stand for that?"

"Some will. Some won't. Ever since we went back to Walla Walla in '56 for a second round of talks, there's been a split growing within the tribe. Now it's coming to a head. I don't like what's happening, John. But I can't do a thing to stop it. Not a damn thing . . ."

4

Soon after the council opened, the commissioners made it clear that the changes they desired in reservation boundaries were drastic. As now laid out, the reservation covered approximately ten thousand square miles of northeastern Oregon, southeastern Washington, and north-central Idaho Territory. Originally the reason for calling the council had been to give non-Indians the right to mine the streams of the high country, travel where they chose in search of new strikes, and live in established towns. Persuading the Nez Perces to cede the few hundred square miles taken up by mining claims and towns would have been no problem. But that was not what the commissioners suggested. Instead, they made an astounding proposal.

"Good God, Doc, do you know what you're asking?" John Crane exploded to Robert Newell the evening of the council's opening day. "You're asking them to give up practically all of their lands!"

"Oh, not all," Newell answered uncomfortably. "They'll still have quite a bit left."

"The hell they will! As I read the maps you've drawn up, you're asking them to cede all their land except five or six hundred square miles along the Clearwater. Instead of selling that much land to the whites—which is all the whites need—you're asking them to turn over the entire ten thousand square miles of reservation granted them in the 1855 Treaty, with them to be penned up in a reservation one-twentieth that size."

"Well, the terms ain't carved in stone, John. They can be modified."

"They'd better be. Otherwise, you'll start a war."

After the Nez Perces had bluntly rejected the first proposal made by the commissioners, a second proposition was offered. The amount of land granted to the Indians would be doubled, $50,000 in agricultural implements would be supplied, $10,000 would be spent on mills, $10,000 on schools, $6,000 on teachers the first year, and half that amount for the next fourteen years. In addition, all the moneys promised in the 1855 Treaty would be paid, plus $4,000 or $5,000 for the horses furnished Governor Stevens and the Volunteers during the 1855–56 war. Indians living outside the new reservation would be permitted to sell any houses, barns, or improvements they had made on their property to private individuals or to the federal government, providing they did so within a year's time following the ratifications of the new treaty by the Senate.

Big Thunder, Three Feathers, Eagle-from-the-Light, and Old Joseph flatly declared, "We will never sell our land."

Lawyer at first agreed with them, then slyly suggested, "If a sufficient consideration were made, we might consent to letting the miners and settlements stay on our land until the gold is gone."

Some of the other chiefs questioned the authority of the commissioners to make a new treaty.

"Did the Great White Father send you here to steal the lands he has given us?" Looking Glass demanded angrily. "Has he gone back on his word?"

This so affronted the dignity of Superintendent Hale that he abruptly terminated the council for the day, saying, "I have nothing further to offer."

Typically, Chief Lawyer tried to pour oil on troubled waters by saying that in a few days he would offer a proposition of his own. In a few days he did. Meeting with the commissioners on the evening of June 3, he offered to give up the land upon which the town of Lewiston was built, with twelve miles around it, including the Lapwai Agency and the military post. Since his own domain was in Kamiah, sixty-five miles upriver, while the Lapwai area belonged to Big Thunder, this act of generosity on Lawyer's part was promptly rejected by the local chiefs.

After Old Joseph and several other chiefs who had accepted nothing from the government said they would not be bound by the terms of either the old or the new treaty, Commissioner Hutchins scolded them like errant children.

"Even though you persist in refusing your annuities, that action will not release you from the obligation of the treaty you signed in 1855. You are still bound by its terms."

"If this is so," Tall Bird murmured to John Crane, "why is not the government bound to what it signed?"

"A good question. Guess the answer is release from treaty obligations works for whites only."

Locked into an insoluble conflict between the commissioners and the pro–new treaty and anti–new treaty bands, all the Nez Perce chiefs present convened that evening in what Tall Bird told John Crane might prove to be the most important council the tribe had held since the time of Lewis and Clark. As it continued far into the night, the commissioners became alarmed that a decision might be made by the Nez Perces to end the talks by murdering all the whites. They became so concerned that they dispatched an urgent message to Fort Lapwai, saying they were apprehensive for their safety.

In response, Captain George Currey, with a small detachment of cavalry, rode to the Indian camp at one o'clock in the morning to see what was going on. No bloodthirsty deeds were being plotted against the whites, he discovered; instead, the fifty-three chiefs meeting in the big tent furnished by the army were engaged in a serious discussion of the future of the Nez Perce nation.

"We invited him and a comrade into the tent and gave them places by the council fire," Tall Bird told John Crane, who had felt he should not be there. "They listened to the discussion for several hours. The chiefs were debating the terms of the proposed treaty in an effort to reach some compromise. Finally convinced that there was no hope of agreement, they decided that the proper action was to disband the tribe, each chief becoming an independent leader of his own village."

Outsider though he was, Captain Currey recognized the importance of the scene.

"I withdrew my detachment," he told John, "having accomplished nothing but that of witnessing the extinguishment of the last council fires of the most powerful Indian nation on the sunset side of the Rocky Mountains."

Following the all-night council, the Nez Perce leaders opposed to making a new treaty either left the Lapwai campground or attended the talks as mere observers. With the dissenting Indians silent, the commissioners had no difficulty reaching agreement with Lawyer and his supporters, all of whose lands were to be included within the boundaries of the new reservation—one-eighth the size of the one created by the 1855 Treaty.

At the close of the Walla Walla Council in 1855, Governor Stevens had recognized fifty-eight Nez Perce leaders as chiefs, had affixed their names to the treaty, and had had each one touch the writing stick as X (his mark) was made. Now at Lapwai as the 1863 Treaty was signed, the commissioners found fifty-three "chiefs" to sign the new treaty. Though many of their names were not on the earlier agreement, in number, at least, it appeared that the tribe as a whole assented to the new document.

"Actually, every chief except one who signed the new treaty lives within the boundaries of the new reservation," Tall Bird pointed out to John Crane. "The exception is Timothy, whose village lies west of the Snake on Alpowa Creek."

"Easy enough to see why he would sign. He's been taken care of by a grant of land and the promise of a six-hundred-dollar house."

"Every nonsigning chief except one lives outside the boundaries of the new reservation. That exception is Big Thunder, who refused to sign because he dislikes Lawyer. He refused even though his band is included within the new reserve and will receive some of the benefits in the way of schools, mills, goods, and annuities."

Among the Indians, John knew, there was no question that the tribe as a whole had been dissolved and that each signing chief spoke only for his own band. But that was not the impression the commissioners gave the federal government in their report. Recognizing a piece of rank chicanery when he saw one, Captain Currey put his disapproval on record.

"Although the treaty goes out to the world as the concurrent agreement of the tribe, it is in reality nothing more than the agreement of Lawyer and his band, numbering in the aggregate not a third part of the Nez Perce tribe."

So one third of the tribe signed away seven eighths of the reservation as its boundaries had been laid out in 1855. Traditionally roaming over a region comprising 27,000 square miles, the Nez Perces had seen their homeland cut down first to 10,000 square miles, and now to a mere 1,250.

From that day on, the dispossessed Nez Perces would call the Treaty of 1863 the "Steal" or "Thief" Treaty. Young Joseph would describe it eloquently:

"Suppose a white man should come to me and say, 'Joseph, I like your horses, and I want to buy them.' I say to him, 'No, my horses suit me, I will not sell them.' Then he goes to my neighbor and says to him, 'Joseph has some good horses. I want to buy them, but he refuses to sell.' My neighbor answers, 'Pay me the money, and I will sell you Joseph's horses.' The white man returns to me, and says, 'Joseph, I have bought your horses and you must let me have them.' If we sold our lands to the government, this is the way they were bought."

Going back to the Wallowa country with Tall Bird, his family, and the rest of the band, John Crane spent a long, pleasant summer living the kind of life he loved best. As symbols of his rejection of the new treaty, the dissolution of the Nez Perce tribe, and the white man's religion—which he felt had betrayed him—Old Joseph destroyed his copy of the 1855 Treaty and the Bible given to him following his baptism by the Reverend Spalding. Though he made no threats against the whites, he marked the western boundary of his territory by setting poles ten inches thick and ten feet long in cairns of rock along the summit of Minam Grade, showing where his line was to the Wallowa country. Known as "Old Joseph's Deadline" to the few white men who saw the markers, the boundary was not an act of hostility, for Old Joseph made it clear he did not object to whites who came into the Wallowa country to hunt, trap, or fish in common with the Nez Perces. The markers simply showed that traditionally this country was used by the Wallowa *Nimipu.*

"There is plenty of room in it for both Indians and whites," Tall Bird said. "But Old Joseph says the white men must not build cabins, barns, or fences. Plows must never cut up the land."

As Old Joseph's eyesight and strength began to fail, it became customary for a young Nez Perce boy to ride with him on a horse, acting as his eyes and guide. One day, after a long tour of the valley during late summer when the lake, mountains, and sparkling blue sky shimmered with beauty, he grasped Young Joseph's hand and spoke earnestly.

"When I am gone, think of your country. You are the chief of these people. They look to you to guide them. Always remember your father never sold his country. You must stop your ears whenever you are asked to sign a treaty selling your home. A few years more, and white men will be all around you. They have their eyes on this land. My son, never forget my words. This country will hold your father's body after I die, as it now holds the body of your mother. Never sell the bones of your father and mother . . ."

In 1867, the treaty reducing the size of the reservation and placing it totally within the borders of Idaho Territory was ratified by the Senate and signed by President Andrew Johnson. Shortly thereafter, John Crane heard, Robert Newell received his long-sought appointment as Special Agent for the Nez Perces. In late January 1868, he came to see John in his Willamette Valley cabin, brimming over with news regarding what was "special" about his duties.

"A delegation of chiefs has been invited to Washington City," he said, "for a conference with the Indian Bureau and the President of the United States. James O'Neill, Perrin Whitman, me, and one other white man friendly to the Nez Perces will be paid to go along as escorts and interpreters."

"Seems a lot of expense and bother, with the treaty already signed. Or is the government adding a few more clauses?"

"Matter of fact, they are," Newell said. "Nothing big, you understand, just three amendments having to do with the allotment of lands not needed by the military post or the agency, the protection of timber on the reservation, and the payment of funds to the schools. The chiefs already have agreed."

"Which chiefs are going?"

"Lawyer, Timothy, Jason, and *Ut-sin-mali-kin,* who's a strong supporter of Lawyer. We'll get first-class treatment all the way."

"Sounds great, Doc. When do you leave?"

"Early March, likely." A grin spread over Newell's face. "Does that suit you?"

"Why should it matter what suits me?"

"Because we've agreed that you should be the other white man, you damn fool! Will you go with us?"

"Lordy!" John breathed softly. "All the way to Washington City!"

"Right. With expenses paid, first-class accommodations, and a salary to boot. What do you say?"

"My son, Luke, is stationed there, assigned to Corps of Engineers headquarters in the War Department. Sure would be nice to see him."

"Did he get through the war in good shape?"

"For an officer in the Corps of Engineers, he saw a hell of a lot of action. Wounded twice, got a couple of medals, and for awhile held the brevet rank of Brigadier General when the top brass in his regiment were incapacitated or killed. When the war ended, he was reduced to the permanent rank of Major. Now he's stuck behind a desk putting together an inventory of the forts, military roads, and bridges needed in the West to hold the Indians in line. He keeps applying for an assignment to a Western post where he can get some real action, but so far he's had no luck."

"Well, at least you'll get to see him, if you go with us. Will you?"

"You bet I will! How will you travel?"

"By riverboat to Portland, then by ocean steamer to San Francisco and Panama, across the Isthmus, and on to New York by ship. The army people have made all the arrangements."

"Why the army? Isn't the Indian Bureau in charge?"

"The best I can tell, John, the Indian Bureau isn't going to be running the reservations much longer. Since Senator Nesmith raised such a stink with his investigation, Congress has pretty much decided to put the military in charge of all Indian reservations in the West. Probably nothing will happen until this impeachment of President Johnson squabble is settled. But however that comes out, the chances are good that management of the reservations will be turned over to the military."

"With you getting a permanent appointment as Agent for the Nez Perces?"

"God knows. But at least I am getting this trip. I want you to take it with us. It's a trip we should both enjoy."

5

Understandably, the meeting with President Andrew Johnson was brief, for he had far more important things on his mind these days than greeting a delegation of Far Western Indians that had come to the nation's capital to sign papers containing minor amendments to a treaty already approved by the government. To properly dignify the occasion, Lawyer, Timothy, and Jason wore their most ornately decorated costumes, while James O'Neill managed to dip into agency funds deeply enough to outfit himself, Robert Newell, Perrin Whitman, and John Crane in black broadcloth suits and new boots, making them presentable for the occasion and for the photographic session afterward in the studio of A. Zeno Shindler, who made a specialty of recording such visits in visual form.

Ut-sin-mali-kin, Lawyer's staunch supporter and friend, was dead by then. Aboard ship a few days after crossing the Isthmus, he had come down with a high fever and sharp abdominal pains. Still unwell when the party reached New York City, May 14, he had managed to make the journey on the train next day to Washington, where the doctor summoned by James O'Neill diagnosed his illness as typhoid fever. Languishing in a hotel room while the rest of the party met with General Grant, who appeared to be a shoo-in as a presidential candidate in the fall election, and with President Johnson, who had just escaped conviction on impeachment charges by a single vote, the elderly Nez Perce chief grew steadily worse despite the best medical treatment that could be given him.

On May 25, Robert Newell wrote sadly that *"Utes-sin-mali-kin* died today of Tyfoid fever."* A day later he recorded in his dairy:

"Utes-sin-mali-kin buried at the Congressional Ground. Four carriages attended by friends."

While the three surviving chiefs and the other white members of the delegation did their sight-seeing and politicking, John Crane went to Corps of Engineers headquarters in the War Department offices and saw his son for the first time in twenty-one years. Because Luke had been very proud of his brief stint as a brigadier general during the final months of the Civil War, he had posed in dress uniform for a Brady photograph, a print of which he had sent his father two years ago, so the maturity in his face and the assurance in his manner as they shook hands came as no surprise to John. What did surprise him—so much that a lump formed in his throat, making it difficult to speak for a few moments—was how remarkably Luke resembled his mother. The smooth, clear skin; the large, soft eyes, changing color with the light from green to blue; and, most striking of all, the lustrous, curly red hair, which he wore long in an almost feminine style, floting military custom, if not defying regulations outright.

"Father, you're looking well," Luke said. "How was the trip east?"

"Say I survived and let it go at that. I'm not a good sailor." Shaking his head in wonderment, John exclaimed, "It's hard to believe, Luke, that it's been twenty-one years since we've seen each other."

"I know. A lot of country and a lot of events have kept us apart. Not by my choice, certainly. As I've written you many times, I keep asking for duty in the West. But they say they need me here."

"How is your family?"

"Healthy and happy. Yours?"

"Fine. Felicia had three daughters when we married, you know. They all have husbands now and more children than I can keep track of. Of course, I'm gone a lot, so I don't see much of them."

"You're here with a delegation of Indians, according to what I read in the papers. Something about amending a treaty?"

"Just a matter of cleaning up a few minor details."

"Must be important details, else you wouldn't have met with President Johnson and General Grant—which I hear you did."

"Lordy, news does get around here!"

"It certainly does. This is the most gossipy place in the country." Luke eyed him shrewdly. "Will you be seeing General Grant again?"

"He's invited me to have lunch with him next week. He seems to be very interested in what's going on in the Pacific Northwest and along the Oregon Trail. I'll tell him what I know."

"If you can bring up the subject without being too obvious, inform General Grant that you have a Corps of Engineers son who would love an assignment in the West. Particularly with my classmate and friend, Colonel George Custer, in western Kansas."

"Hell, son, General Grant strikes me as the kind of man I can be honest with. Hasn't your job since the war been to list the needs for military posts and roads to protect emigrants and settlers?"

"It has."

"Then who would be better qualified than you to supervise the building of these facilities?"

"Assignment in today's Army is not necessarily based on how well qualified an officer is for a specific post," Luke said with an impatient shrug.

"It's partly a matter of luck, partly a matter of who you know. If you get on well with General Grant, drop my name and Colonel Custer's. I'd give my eyeteeth to campaign with George again."

During that first visit, Luke said nothing about inviting his father to his home to meet his wife, Constance, and their two children, Abigal and Peter. But a week later, after John had talked to General Grant and gotten a favorable response to his casual statement that he had a son in the Corps of Engineers who was eager to serve in the West, Luke dropped by the hotel and told his father that his wife wanted him to dine with them in their home two evenings later.

"Let me be honest with you, Father. When I learned that you had not married my mother, and that Grandfather had done so in order to make sure I received my inheritance, I was shocked. But by the time I married Constance, I had seen enough of the world to understand how such things could happen and to forgive you for them. Constance, however, with her strict Presbyterian upbringing, could neither understand nor forgive. In spite of all I could do, she has consistently said that she would never let you into our home."

"I understand. Much as I would like to meet her and see my grandchildren, I won't go where I'm not welcome."

"Lately, she's mellowed, Father. She'll accept you as my father and as the grandfather of our children. In return, she asks that you never reveal the darker aspects of your and Grandfather's relationship to our children."

Good God! John mused sardonically. *If the details of my own running away from responsibility had shocked Constance deeply, how would she react if informed that her children's great-grandfather had sired a child by a Nez Perce woman sixty-two years ago, a child whose numerous descendants knew who their white ancestor had been, a child with whom John himself was now on friendly terms? For that matter, what would Luke's reaction be if he were told about the Indian branch of his family?*

"Son," John said quietly, "it's been the deepest regret of my life that your mother died before I could go back to St. Louis and marry her, which I fully intended to do. All that matters to me now is meeting your wife and getting acquainted with my grandchildren. Believe me, I will do nothing to hurt them."

Though that first dinner and evening with Luke, Constance, Abigal, and Peter in their comfortable Georgetown home was a stiff ordeal for John Crane, he managed to carry it off with the same formal politeness and quiet dignity that had served him so well when he had visited the family attorney, Samuel Wellington, and thirteen-year-old Luke at the Wellington estate a few miles outside St. Louis twenty-one years ago.

At the age of eleven, Peter Crane was blond and blue-eyed, and gave promise of growing up to be tall, as his grandfather and great-grandfather had been. Abigal, at nine, had brown hair and eyes, like her mother, carried herself with her mother's reserved dignity and grace, and seemed to regard her grandfather as a curious creature paying her family a visit from another world.

Constance herself was a beautiful woman, the model of what a career officer's wife should be. Impeccably and richly furnished, the home was well staffed with colored servants, whom the mistress of the household pointed out had been given their freedom long before President Lincoln had thought of emancipating them. Though she treated them well, it was clear from their manner that they were ruled by hands of steel encased in velvet gloves.

"The house has more room than we need," she told John. "But it was such a good buy, Major Crane and I couldn't resist it. It was built ten years ago by a Southern senator who never dreamed that the North would go to war over the slavery issue. We bought it from his estate, after he died of apoplexy."

"Luke tells me he acquired the Samuel Wellington home near St. Louis, a few years ago."

"Oh, yes! We own all kinds of property in and around St. Louis. If and when Major Crane is transferred to a post out West, we plan to sell this place at a handsome profit. The children and I will move to the Wellington estate and live there while the major does his tour of duty."

"You wouldn't plan on living at a Western post?"

"Heavens, no! What would the children do about school? At Fort Gibson, where I did live for a while, there were not enough officers' children to support a school. Which meant tutors must be hired or the children must go to school with the children of enlisted men and Indians. Certainly I believe that the Indian children should be educated. But they're so smelly and dirty."

Reminded that several officers' wives at Fort Lapwai had expressed similar reactions after visiting the Nez Perce encampment there, John made no reply, though he was sorely tempted to tell Constance that several Indians had complained to him about the smell of the white ladies, who all too often substituted pungent perfume and potent cologne for the daily bath most *Nimipu* took winter, spring, summer, and fall when a stream, a lake, or a sweat lodge was available.

Though Luke and Constance did their best to conceal it, John sensed that a rift existed between them over Luke's career as an army officer opposed to his prospects for gain in the world of finance. Having inherited substantial properties and business holdings from both his grandfather's and grandmother's estates, Luke was a wealthy man in his own right, John knew, while Constance herself possessed sizable assets handed down to her by her family. If Luke so desired, he could resign his commission, go back to St. Louis, and spend his life in comfort managing the family's business affairs. But in conversations with his father during the two months John stayed in Washington while the delegation did its politicking with government officials, Luke made it clear that he had no intention of leaving the Corps of Engineers until he had achieved two goals.

"First, I want to be part of the leadership that creates a modern army in every sense of the word—organization, ordnance, fortifications, roads, and communication. Second, I want the permanent rank of General by the time I reach retirement age. In the peacetime army, with the officer list swollen by Civil War veterans, advancement won't be easy, I know. That's why I want to join Colonel Custer, who knows how such things are done."

"From what I've read about Custer," said John, "his scraps with the Sioux and Cheyennes have been little more than isolated skirmishes. Of course, that's the way Indians fight. They don't like a decisive battle."

"Custer will force them to it. Mark my word, he'll bring them to bay sooner or later."

Intrigued as Lawyer, Timothy, and Jason had been with the sights of the nation's capital and the attention paid them by its political leaders, after two months in Washington during the growing heat and humidity of summer they found that the city's charms began to pall. Lawyer complained of homesickness to Robert Newell, who administered a remedy of which he was known to be fond.

"Lawyer, Timothy, and Jason got tight late at night," he recorded in his journal August 11.

Next day, the three Indian chiefs continued their work with the Indian Bureau, at last signing the amendments to the treaty.

Cheered by the news that the trip home would be made not by sea but overland by rail, John Crane spent his last evening, August 21, with his son and his family. Enjoying after-dinner cigars and brandy with Luke in the relative coolness of the screened-in veranda, John discussed his future plans.

"Lawyer, Timothy, and Jason petitioned the President to appoint Doc Newell as Agent, which he did. Doc says he'll give me a job at the Agency, if I want it."

"Do you?"

"I've got a lot of friends in the upriver country, Luke. So far as climate goes, the Nez Perce country suits me a lot better than the Willamette Valley, where it rains most of the year. Of course, the Willamette is home to Felicia and her children. She would never leave."

"You have property there?"

"All I need."

"We've never discussed money, Father, but from what you've left unsaid, I gather you haven't accumulated much during your lifetime. In your declining years, how will you live?"

"As I always have, I suppose. As an emigrant guide, an Indian Agency interpreter, or a handler of horses. There's still a lot of wild country and unsettled land in the Pacific Northwest where a man who's a good hunter and trapper can live without money. Over the years, I've made a lot of Nez Perce friends who regard me as a sort of relative. If need be, I could go live with them."

A look of distaste came over Luke's face. "Surely you're joking, Father. You wouldn't want to become a squaw man, would you?"

"No, I wouldn't, son," John said lightly, "though there are worse ways to live, believe me. I was just repeating what's been said a lot about Doc Newell, Perrin Whitman, and me in Washington these past two months—that we've lived so long with the Indians and are so sympathetic to them that we're more red than white under the skin."

"Would you consider living in St. Louis?"

"With you and your family, you mean?"

"Not exactly *with* us, Father. That might not work out. But I have all kinds of business interests in St. Louis where there might be a place for you, if and when you should need it." A disturbed look came to his face as he rephrased his thoughts. "What I'm trying to say is that if the time should come when you need care and a place to live, I would be willing to provide for you—up to a point."

"That point being where your wife would object?"

"Surely you can understand why she feels as she does."

Surely John did understand. In all likelihood, the question of a son's duty to a father who had deserted him before he was born and now was reentering his life in hopes of sharing the son's substantial inheritance had been discussed by Luke and Constance many times during John's stay in Washington. What Luke offered now was no doubt the final compromise accepted by Constance: *Take care of the old coot, if you feel you must; but I won't let him live in our home.*

"I'm obliged for the offer, son," John said gently. "But the way things look now, I'll live out my days in the Pacific Northwest." Stubbing out his cigar and waving away the proffered refill of brandy, he got to his feet. "By the way, the last time I talked to General Grant, he said his first priority, so far as containing Indian hostiles is concerned, will be building a string of forts in the Sioux country. He'll keep you in mind . . ."

6

Leaving Washington, D.C., August 22, 1868, the delegation went by train to New York City, Chicago, Omaha, and the end of track on the still-building Union Pacific near Fort Bridger, Wyoming. From there, a company of cavalry—with two army ambulances, half a dozen covered supply wagons, and enough spare horses to let the Indians and the white men ride if they chose to—escorted the party on west to Fort Walla Walla, Lewiston, and Lapwai.

With Central Pacific rails laid across the Sierras now, and Union Pacific steel pushed into the Wasatch Mountains toward Utah, it seemed likely that the lines would meet to the north of the Great Salt Lake next summer. When trains began the transcontinental run, John Crane was told, a man could travel from Omaha to San Francisco in the incredibly short time of four days.

Lord, how the years fly! he mused. Viewing long-familiar landmarks such as the Bear River Mountains, the Tetons, Shoshone Falls, Snake River Plain, the Owyhee, Blue, and Wallowa mountains, he recalled that when his father had passed through the Nez Perce country with the Lewis and Clark party in 1805, it was unknown to white men, though the *Nimipu* had lived in it for ten thousand years without putting an iron horseshoe print or a wheel mark on the land.

Times changed. He accepted that. But, by God, it had been no small feat that he and a few men like him had accomplished in their time. They ought to be given some credit for that. And they ought to be listened to when questions like how to deal fairly with the Indians came up, for if anybody knew the answers, they did. But the arrogant politicians and military men he had met in Washington held such a rigid, simplistic attitude toward Western Indians that it would be bound to cause bad trouble if it were not modified. His own son, Luke, typified their thinking.

"The day of the wild, roving, Indian is done," he had told his father firmly. "If the Indians won't settle down and start living like white men of their own volition, we'll have to whip them, put them onto reservations, and force them to accept civilized ways. My tour of duty at Fort Gibson convinced me there is no alternative."

The most Doc Newell could offer him for the subagent job on the Nez

Perce Reservation was fifty dollars a month, subsistence, and quarters. John still had not made up his mind whether to accept or reject the position when the delegation reached Fort Walla Walla on a hot, dry, dusty afternoon in late September. Awaiting him there was a letter written a month before by his oldest stepdaughter, Faith, who of the three sisters had always been the most friendly to him:

I am deeply saddened to tell you that Mother passed away last week, after being seriously ill with a bronchial ailment since last spring. When pneumonia developed, there was no hope. It was typical of her that she would not let me write you about her illness, for fear it would worry you. We did get the doctor to come see her and he gave her the best treatment he could, but she got worse and worse and finally just went to sleep and did not wake up.

Not knowing exactly where you are at this time, I am sending this letter both to Washington, D.C., and to Fort Walla Walla, which you wrote Mother you would pass through on your way home. She was very fond of you, as I know you were of her. Sincerely, Faith.

Fond.

Sincerely.

Faith.

All warm, solid words typifying the kind of woman Felicia had been, the kind of children she had raised, and the kind of home she had made for him. In some ways, he had more feeling for her and her daughters than he did for his son's wife and her children, whose world was as alien to him as his was to them. But Luke, Abigal, and Peter were blood kin, which Felicia's daughters and their children were not. At his age, blood ties were precious, for they were all the family he had.

No. Not all. Tall Bird and his children were family, too. Given the choice of spending his declining years as a recipient of the limited charity of his son, of becoming a barely tolerated outsider living with Felicia's children, or of moving into the world of his Nez Perce relatives, he had no problem deciding what he would do.

"Doc, I'll take that subagent job," he told Robert Newell. "Just give me a couple of weeks to go home and settle my affairs."

About the Author

For many years a regular contributor to *Liberty, The Saturday Evening Post, Esquire,* and *Collier's,* Bill Gulick has published sixteen novels, several of which have been turned into movies, such as *Bend of the River, Road to Denver,* and *Hallelujah Trail.* His first nonfiction book, *Snake River Country* in 1971, was given the Pacific Northwest Booksellers Award as the best nonfiction book of the year.

He has written and produced three historical outdoor dramas: *The Magic Musket* in 1953; *Pe-wa-oo-yit: the First Treaty Council* in 1955; and *Trails West* in 1976 and 1977, which was selected by the United States Department of Commerce as one of America's top ten family spectaculars for 1976.

Making his home in Walla Walla for the past thirty years, he has worked with the Nez Perces, Umatillas, Walla Wallas, Cayuses, and Yakimas on a number of projects to bring about a better understanding of Indian rights. In 1976 he was project director for a $24,000 Washington State Humanities Commission Grant given *Trails West,* in conjunction with Whitman College and the Whitman Mission National Historic Site, to pay Indian advisers and actors performing in the production and to hold eleven public forums in which Indian and white experts discussed Indian treaty rights.

His wife Jeanne, who assists in research, secretarial, and editing work, has just retired from her position as a research librarian at Penrose Library, Whitman College, where most of the material Gulick has gathered over the years now is deposited. He is past president of the Western Writers of America, Inc. Two of his *Saturday Evening Post* stories have won that organization's prestigious Spur Award as best Western short story of the year.

In 1983 he was given the Levi Strauss Saddleman Award by the Western Writers of America "for an impressive career writing fiction, nonfiction, and drama of the West."